PRAISE FOR KANA WU

"Solidly recommended for fans of women's friendship and single mother stories." — Midwest Book Review, on *She Calls Her Mom*.

"Highly recommended for readers who are tired of the typical chick lit romance, and are ready for something light as air and just as refreshing." — K.C. Finn for Readers' Favorite, on *No Romance Allowed*.

"The main characters are loveable and endearing, and Wu's handling of past regrets and secrets withheld endow the couple with a blithe honesty and vulnerability that is sure to warm the hearts of readers of this engaging series." — Self-Publishing Review, 4 stars, on *No Secrets Allowed*.

"I finished it at 4am, I couldn't put it down, it's really good." — Goodreads Reviewer, 5 stars, on *No Romance Allowed*.

"Beautiful short story! I fell in love with everything about the story. Wonderful characters, great plot and storyline, and very eloquent writing." — Goodreads Reviewer, 5 stars, on *She Calls Her Mom*.

"The plot of this book surprised me and kept me interested." — Goodreads Reviewer, 5 stars, on *A Warm Rainy Day In Tokyo*.

"This is a gripping women's fiction suspense novella...I enjoyed reading this book and will definitely recommend it." — Goodreads Reviewer, 5 stars, on *She Calls Her Mom*.

"Nothing is better than sitting with a book that pulls you out of the real world." — Goodreads Reviewer, 5 stars, on *No Secrets Allowed*.

"This book has a very positive vibe to it." — Goodreads Reviewer, 4 stars, on *A Warm Rainy Day In Tokyo*.

"There wasn't any toxic character trying to take the other down. It was pure love and we all need that nowadays." — Goodreads Reviewer, 4 stars, on *A Warm Rainy Day In Tokyo*.

"Short and sweet - but it packs a punch." — Goodreads Reviewer, 4 stars, on *She Calls Her Mom*.

"Such a sweet and meaningful novella. I smiled, I laughed, I teared up! Quick and easy read." — Goodreads Reviewer, 4 stars, on *She Calls Her Mom*.

"*A Warm Rainy Day In Tokyo* not only offers a Hallmark style love story, but also an intriguing peek into life in Japan through the eyes of a foreigner. Kana Wu's characters are lovable and easy to root for, and she builds a masterful and immersive setting for them as well." — Goodreads Reviewer, 4 stars, on *A Warm Rainy Day In Tokyo*.

"Verdict: Loved it!" — Goodreads Reviewer, 4 stars, on *No Secrets Allowed*.

"An agreeably warm story that bounces along effortlessly on the genuine chemistry of its lead characters…Wu takes the much-loved tropes of the genre and makes them her own." — The BookViral Review, on *No Romance Allowed*.

"Readers who enjoy romance novels with a touch of suspense will appreciate this book." — OnlineBookClub.org, 4 stars, on *No Romance Allowed*.

OTHER NOVELS BY KANA WU

No Secrets Allowed

A Warm Rainy Day In Tokyo

She Calls Her Mom

NO Romance ALLOWED

SURVIVING ON RAMEN
— or —
BREAKING HER PROMISE

book one

KANA WU

For my mom and my dad.
Thanks for always believing in me.

CHAPTER 1

The wind had been picking up since noon. Trees and bushes twirled, bent, and swayed wildly. Fallen leaves and broken twigs marred the beautifully manicured gardens, stone paths, driveways, and resident patios in the Pacific Hills Apartments complex.

Sitting on the bench by my bedroom window, I watched the disarray worsen each time the wind howled and occasionally felt the window glass tremor. The weather had been crazy like this for two days since the red flag, and a high-winds warning was announced in Southern California. Yesterday, a eucalyptus tree fell in Tustin, a next-door city to Irvine, injuring two pedestrians.

Though it was February, California winters were usually mild, somewhere around forty-five degrees Fahrenheit. However, because of thunderstorms the day before, the temperature had dropped by ten degrees, according to the weather report on my laptop screen.

While typing a password to login into my bank's website, something outside my window caught my eye. The wind snatched a baseball cap off a boy walking across the green belt, and each time he tried to grab it, the wind kicked it just out of his reach again.

Chuckling, I shifted my focus back to the screen. The smile on my face faded, and my stomach churned to see the total balance: $246.75.

Not much left!

Biting my lower lip, I calculated quickly. With the paychecks I would get the next two Fridays, there would be enough to pay only this month's rent and barely buy food. Sighing, I stared at the screen.

Since Lizzy Walter, my ex-roommate, moved to Seattle three months ago, I had been struggling to pay the rent on my own. I'd had to cut back on all my expenses and learned to make do with oatmeal, eggs, instant noodles, and the occasional banana. My salary as an accountant was not enough to support my $2,500-a-month rent payment for the two-bedroom apartment. If I'd had a roommate, half would have been manageable.

Or I could move to a cheaper apartment?

That was out of the question because I did not have enough money for a deposit.

I wasn't proud of myself. Whenever people learned I was an accountant, they always assumed I was good at managing my money, but I wasn't. I wasn't a shopaholic, but I *loved* shopping. I had brand-name bags, shoes, and clothes sitting in my closet, waiting for me to wear them. In my money-tight situation, I had begun to realize those expensive things didn't bring me any happiness at all.

Move to a different company with a higher salary?

That wasn't the best solution either. I hadn't built much of a resume yet since I'd graduated from college less than a year ago.

I'd already put ads for "renting a room" on Craigslist and received some responses. Too bad no one acceptable had inquired yet. Most of the applicants were job hoppers, college students, jobless, single parents with a kid, or someone who only needed a temporary place. Some males had responded to the ads, although my criteria were clear: a female with a steady job, not a smoker (because I had asthma), and willing to rent for at least two years.

A disadvantage of putting out the ads was that I got a lot of spam and telemarketer calls.

A few weeks ago, I had taken flyers to work and given them to my three closest coworkers, Sylvia, Lena, and Yoo-Shi. We all worked in the accounting department at Myriad Food and Beverage, a distributor for frozen food and beverages ranging from soft drinks to wine and spirits. Sylvia Santos and Kim Yoo-Shi were part of the alcohol division, while Lena Hunter and I were in the nonalcohol division.

"No male roommate?" Lena had commented as we ate lunch together in the office lunchroom.

"Nope. That wouldn't be appropriate," I'd answered.

Sylvia nodded. "It's not good for a single young woman to live with a man," she'd said in her Philippine accent. "I think living with a male roommate would lead you to have a 'romance relationship,' and that would be messy!"

Yoo-Shi put the flyer on the table. "I had a male roommate for two years in Seoul. We were both single and didn't fall for each other. In fact, we helped each other. One day, my roommate fell in love with a girl and asked for my opinion. It was fun, like having a brother or a cousin." With a pout, she continued, "I wish I had a male roommate now because it is fun and less drama. Not like living with the bitchy roommate I have now."

We'd all looked at her in sympathy. Her current roommate was a single, large-frame woman in her early forties with a long nose and long, ash-blonde hair. Her voice was deep and throaty. I'd met her once when picking up Yoo-Shi, and when she talked, she looked down her long nose at me as if I were her humble subject. Initially, Yoo-Shi had said the lady was nice, then her opinion changed as her roommate showed her true colors. But for some odd reason, Yoo-Shi couldn't kick her out.

"I agree with her," Lena had said, tossing her golden-blonde hair over her shoulder. "When I lived in Chicago for my first job, I had a male roommate two different times. I already had a boyfriend, but he lived in New Jersey. My roommates also had girlfriends, but they lived in a different state too. We were fine—barely had an argument. They kept the apartment clean and helped me with computer issues. We've kept in touch."

"Really?" I widened my eyes. "Wasn't your boyfriend jealous? I don't think I could do that to my boyfriend."

"Well, I'd told him about my intention upfront and asked his permission. He appreciated my openness and was fine," Lena had said. "If they disagree, well, better you don't do it. I'm lucky my boyfriend was so open-minded, which is why I married him. It's up to you, Rory, and don't do it if you aren't comfortable."

Yoo-Shi had nudged me. "I don't understand why you can't live with a guy. You're single, and it's socially acceptable for opposite genders to live together."

"I know, but…it's complicated because I already made a promise.…Sorry, I can't give details." I'd lowered my gaze.

Yoo-Shi had seemed unsatisfied but didn't say more.

"Don't worry, Rory. We'll try to help you," Sylvia had said, pulling her long black hair up into a bun.

Later on, I'd gotten a few referrals from my coworkers, but those fell through because the prospects either found a cheaper room, moved in with family, or stayed where they were.

I felt queasy thinking about my current condition. Maybe I should work weekends. There was a dance academy near my apartment that constantly put out an ad for a receptionist. Or I could cashier in a little grocery store a few blocks away. Its employees always looked happy. But the thought of a part-time job made me cringe because I'd lose so much of my free time.

On the other hand, it might be better than living on instant noodles.

My phone rang, its melodic tone interrupting my miserable thoughts. I glanced at Lizzy's name flashing on the screen.

"Hi, Rory! How are you?" greeted Lizzy, talking above her noisy background.

"Marvelous! But hey, I can't hear you. Where are you?" I asked.

"Terry and I are in a cinema for the new Marvel movie. So crowded today. Hold on. Let me find a quiet spot." From her breathing, I could tell she was walking fast. "Have you seen the movie yet?"

"Not yet. I—" I didn't want to admit to her that I didn't have money for such leisure. "Maybe sometime next week."

"Okay. Make sure you watch it. You are a Marvel movie girl." Lizzy chuckled. "Oh, yeah, the reason I called you: I need a favor."

"Sure, what's up?"

She drew in a breath. "An hour ago, my boss texted me about an IT emergency in a client's office, close to your apartment in Irvine. I should be there next Monday, but I don't want to stay in a hotel. Can I crash on your couch for a night?"

"Sure. I'd love to see you again," I said. "Besides, I don't have a roommate yet, so please come."

"I'm sorry about that. Don't get discouraged. You'll find someone great," she said.

I let out a sigh because I already felt hopeless. "Thanks. I'm working on it," I said.

"Terry said he gave your ad to any female coworkers he knows who might be looking for a place. Hope one of them will contact you soon," Lizzy assured me.

"Aw, he's so sweet," I said. "Please thank him for me."

Terry, her boyfriend, had just moved to Seattle a week ago. I believed wedding bells would ring for those two soon.

"Will do. Hey, don't be shy when you need help, okay? I always think of you as my sister."

"Okay."

"By the way, does Mrs. Ishida know you're looking for a new roommate?" Lizzy asked.

I grunted at the heavy weight that landed on my chest when Lizzy brought up my aunt's name. I loved Aunt Amy but was scared of her at the same time, mostly because I didn't want to burden her anymore. I owed her for taking care of me after my mom, her younger sister, passed away, and I wasn't a docile kid back then. At fifteen, I'd successfully turned her beautiful black hair gray. So, for once, I wanted her to enjoy her single life in Boston without having to worry about me.

"Hey girl, are you there?"

Lizzy's voice brought me back to reality. "Um…yes, I'm here. No, I haven't told her yet," I mumbled. I pictured her rolling her hazel eyes.

"It's been three months since I moved out, so you'd better tell her soon," she said after a long pause. "I can't imagine how mad she will be if she finds out you kept her in the dark."

I winced at the reminder.

"Well, I can't force you to tell Auntie Amy, anyway. But if you need help, Terry and I are here for you," said Lizzy.

I nodded as if she could see me.

"Hey, I've got to go. Terry will get worried if I'm not back. See you Monday."

"Okay. See you, and a big hug to Terry," I said.

"Sure thing."

We hung up. I sighed and dropped my phone on the bed, then headed toward the kitchen. A bowl of colorful M&M's sitting on the counter looked tempting, so I sat in one of the high chairs, lifted its glass lid, took a few, and plopped them into my mouth.

Since Lizzy had brought up my aunt, my thoughts flew back to a moment a year and half ago. It was during the last six months of my bachelor's degree studies when she'd told me about her job offer in Boston. I remembered vividly the joy I felt for her as she would return to the city she loved.

I'd wanted to stay in our apartment, but Aunt Amy thought it was a bad idea for me.

"Move to a studio or one-bedroom, Rory," my aunt had said. "I know you have a part-time job now, but your wage won't cover the rent."

"But this location is close to campus and my job," I'd said stubbornly. "Doesn't this apartment complex have a one-bedroom, too?"

My aunt had pursed her lips. "There are many other apartments near your campus. Besides, I've already asked the office manager, and she said there are no studio or one-bedroom units available at the moment."

I had avoided my aunt's eyes while going over all my reasons for not wanting to move. It was challenging to juggle my time between my job, classes, and schoolwork. My weekends were already dull and boring, mostly full of writing papers. I didn't think I had enough time to sell or donate stuff in preparation for moving. My head had pounded each time I thought about it, and living in a student apartment was a no-no. Most of those students loved partying more than studying. If I wanted to graduate on time, I had to avoid living there.

Besides, I loved Pacific Hills. It was situated uphill with gorgeous surroundings, and the neighbors were great too. I had built good relationships with the staff and already knew who was reliable and who was not. The monthly program was superb, with free classes like yoga or tennis twice a month. I doubted I would find all that anywhere else.

My aunt had narrowed her eyes while listening to me.

"Please let me stay until I graduate and get a permanent job, then I'll move to a one-bedroom," I had begged my aunt. "I'll find a roommate too."

"Well," she'd said, looking straight at me, "after listening to your *reasons*, I assume you've also thought about the *consequences* of staying here, because I don't want to hear you complain about the cost later. Just so you know, I won't help you pay the rent, but I'll help you choose a good roommate to share your expenses with her. Think of it as my last duty as your guardian."

I'd wished she could help pay the rent until I graduated, but I wouldn't take back my words. Overly confident, I'd agreed.

Before she left for Boston, Aunt Amy had found Lizzy, the daughter of a church friend, to be my roommate. Everything went smoothly until Lizzy got promoted and had to move to Seattle.

I laid my head on the countertop, thinking. My aunt had sacrificed a lot for me, including moving to California when I was accepted as a student at the University of California, Irvine. It was unfair to ask for her help if I was the one who insisted on living in this apartment. I decided to keep trying to find a roommate on my own and, if I didn't find one in one more month, I would call her.

CHAPTER 2

On Sunday morning, the wind died down. The apartment complex grounds were a mess of leaves and broken twigs strewn over wet ground. On my way back from jogging, I saw a huge tree had fallen and blocked the sidewalk around the manmade lake near my apartment. No victims, but one car that was parked on the curb had been smashed.

I was about to go around the fallen tree when I heard my phone buzz. I took it out from my running belt. On the screen, I saw a new email notification from Rowena White, my accounting manager.

I groaned. *Not again!*

Last month, she had requested that Lena and I reroute our office emails to our personal emails so we could help in our off-hours with a project for Samuel Hamilton III, the owner of Myriad. Desiree Lang, the general manager, had told us about the possibility that Mr. Hamilton would establish a partnership with a company somewhere in Europe.

It was a "hush-hush" project, and only people in the accounting department knew because we were the group that worked on and processed the financial data. The rest of the departments would be informed later to prevent any negative issues. The project hadn't even begun, but Rowena was already taking advantage of our personal time. Since then, almost every Sunday, she emailed us to finish our reconciliation reports so she could review them at nine o'clock Monday morning. It was crazy, but what Rowena wanted, Rowena got.

I scoffed at her email, inserted my phone back into my running belt, and continued jogging. Luckily, I had already done most of my tasks and had only three more left. Still, they would take half of my precious Sunday to complete. *Ugh!*

Around noon, I finally finished the reconciliation reports and submitted them to Rowena's folder before sending a text to Lena.

Are you done with your report?

My phone vibrated two seconds later. Tapping on the screen to open the text, I chuckled at the lightning emoji she sent. I wasn't in the mood for teasing her and responded by sending a thumbs-up emoji.

I inserted the office notebook into the computer bag with a sigh. In the last two months, I hadn't felt any excitement about working at Myriad. I still liked my coworkers and enjoyed wine tastings or free lunch events, but my manager was unbelievable.

I remembered the day I had interviewed with Rowena ten months ago. I'd been impressed by her easygoing manner and was excited to work for her. The first few days in the office were perfect, but the new-job bubble deflated on the fourth day. The honeymoon period had ended, and Rowena showed her real personality. She wasn't easygoing anymore; the promise of "we'll train you until you've become an expert" had been forgotten.

"I'll only explain this once, so you'd better remember and not make me repeat it," she'd said in a bossy tone, pointing her forefinger in my face.

Since then, I'd felt uncomfortable around her as if she were releasing an unpleasant aura. Rowena was very moody and impatient. My stomach clenched each time she passed my cubicle. I hadn't understood, and still didn't, why she always furrowed her eyebrows at me whenever I asked her for advice. She'd quickly stopped answering my questions and told me to check the history of each report. She 'd even suggested that I wait until Lena came back from Chicago and ask her.

Lena had gone to the Windy City for a family emergency before my first day and wouldn't be back for a couple weeks. I was pretty much at the mercy of Rowena because there was no one to help me. I'd quickly become friends with Sylvia and Yoo-Shi, but they couldn't help because they were from a different division.

To make matters worse, I'd been making tons of mistakes. Cold beads of sweat ran down my spine each time Rowena emailed me back with WRONG ACCOUNT written in capital letters in the subject line.

When Lena had returned to work, I liked her right away. She was super-patient. Her golden-blonde hair bounced as she nodded in sympathy while reading all the notes from Rowena on my reports. Slowly, she'd taught me to understand Myriad's accounting process, and after only a couple of hours training with her, I'd been able to do my job better.

Lena was well-liked around the office. Upon her return, coworkers would stop by her desk and ask about her family. Rowena had said nothing. However, from my peripheral vision, I'd been able to see her staring at Lena while she was having a conversation with a lady from the tax department.

Later that day, Rowena had called Lena to her office. Through the window, I had been able to see that Rowena's face was twisted, and her lips were puckered as if she were eating something sour. I'd been surprised how Lena had come out of her office calmly, with a smile. I'd been intrigued to learn from her about how to deal with Rowena.

I was too naïve to read the situation because, one day, as I went to the ladies' room on the third floor, I found Lena wiping her tears as I entered. She startled, and her teary eyes had widened, then she glared at me.

"Why are you here?" she'd asked, pushing a lock of her long hair out of her face. "Are you spying on me?"

"Of course not," I'd said, shaking my head. "I like coming up here whenever I need to be alone. Besides, this is the cleanest restroom because nobody uses it."

She'd stomped her foot. "Don't you dare tell anyone about this."

I'd moved aside as she left the room abruptly, her footsteps echoing in the empty hall.

When I'd returned to my cubicle, which was next to Lena's, her face was as calm as the ocean's surface with a small smile on her lips as usual, but she avoided me. Two days later, she'd approached me and asked if I'd like to go out to dinner with her. I'd been curious about her behavior and agreed right away. We'd gone to an open-air mall about twenty minutes from our office and ordered dinner from one of restaurants nearby. While we'd waited for our food, Lena poured her heart out about how Rowena treated her staff and how Desiree knew but didn't do anything.

"That's awful. Why does Desiree let this happen?"

"You don't get it, do you?" she'd asked with a bitter smile. "Desiree is Rowena's friend. They used to work together."

I'd blinked, speechless. No wonder they seemed to get along well.

"I'll tell you another story." Lena had shifted in her seat. "Have you been in our documents storage at the next-door building?"

I'd shaken my head.

"Well, that storage is dirty and messy, which is why we call it 'the dungeon.'" Lena made air quotes with her fingers. "A month ago, Desiree decided we would use one of our Fridays to clean the storage as a team. On the day, everybody helped but Rowena."

"Why?"

"I overheard her telling Desiree that she had a ton of reports to get done and asked permission to stay in the office." Lena had curled her lips. "Don't get me wrong—I don't care if she comes with us or not, but I didn't like her remark. She said, 'So long, suckers.' I was the only one who heard it because I was the last one left and happened to pass her office when she said it. She's a jerk, I tell you."

"Maybe she was joking?" I'd tried to give Rowena the benefit of the doubt.

Lena scoffed. "Rowena? Joking? You haven't known her too long, have you?" Her eyebrows had lowered and pinched tighter. "Soon you'll see how cunning she is."

"Did anyone else, like Christina or Sylvia, notice that Rowena got out of cleaning day?" I'd asked.

Lena had shrugged. "Christina looked annoyed when Desiree said Rowena wasn't joining us. If I'm not wrong, Christina had asked permission to leave early for her son's award ceremony that day, and Desiree had told her no. Sylvia and Yoo-Shi…well, they are neutral with Rowena. I know Sylvia has a beef with Desiree because she was promised to be our division accounting manager, but it didn't come true once Rowena joined the company."

Lena had taken a deep breath and looked at me. "I'm sorry to tell you all these things. You must think I'm a bad person—talking ill behind someone's back. Well, you're an adult and can tell the difference. As your senior, I want you to be careful in the office. No matter how badly Rowena treats you, don't go to Desiree, not even to HR. No one wants to work with a crybaby. Just bite your tongue and do your job. Once you feel you can't stand it here anymore, find another job."

My stomach had steadily tightened as I wondered how long I could survive in this such a toxic environment. Obviously, there was no such thing as a perfect place to work.

"After all you've been through, why are you still working here?" I'd asked carefully.

Lena had been taken aback and didn't respond right away. "Well, this office is near my house," she'd said, lifting her gaze to me, "and I'm working toward getting my CPA license, so I think it's wise to stay until I get it." She'd studied my face. "Please keep what I've said just between us, okay?"

"Yes, of course," I'd nodded.

After that, we'd become close friends who provided comfort and support to each other whenever Rowena was harsh to one of us.

CHAPTER 3

Another week passed without a potential roommate. Lizzy's short stay had been like a breath of fresh air. We'd chatted and laughed like the old days. But once she'd left, reality pulled me back, especially at the sight of my bank account balance dwindling after a credit card payment.

Suddenly, instant noodles, oatmeal, and eggs were dancing in front of my eyes and chanting at me, *"We love you, Rory! We love you, Rory!"*

The chanting stopped as my phone chirped for an incoming message. I flicked the screen open and read an email from Amazon Marketplace.

> ***Congratulations, someone is interested in buying your Tory Burch Fleming tote and the Coach cross-body bag. Please follow Amazon Marketplace's rules on sending your merchandise...***

I liked the tote and the bag, but I needed to buy some real food. Maybe it was time to forget my pride and ask for my aunt's help.

The next morning, before going to work, I was putting the shipping boxes in my car when I heard Rick Perkins, my seventy-two-year-old neighbor, call my name.

"Rory, my good neighbor! Good morning, young lady!" He grinned, creating deep wrinkles at the corners of his eyes. His cheeks were pinkish, and the sweat pooling around the front of his shirt indicated he must be coming back from his morning jog.

"Good morning, Rick," I answered, closing the car door. "Five miles as usual?"

Nodding, Rick took off his baseball cap and used his fingers to smooth down the white hair underneath. "I'm not young anymore, so five miles is good for me."

"You aren't old," I replied. I wasn't lying. For his age, his body was slim and sturdy.

He chuckled, pushing up the long-sleeved T-shirt that had been hiding tattoos he'd gotten while in the Marine Corps. "Thank you, but my body can't lie. So, young lady, are you ready to conquer the world?"

"Absolutely!" I grinned, pumping my fists in the air.

Rick smiled his approval. "So, how's Amy doing? Is it still cold up there?"

"She is doing fine. Just busy with her volunteer work. Last week, she sent me a few pictures of the blizzard. It was unusual even for February. Um, let me show you... ." I dug in my purse for the cell phone, then scrolled through the picture gallery folder and showed them to him.

Aunt Amy and I had met Rick and his wife, Maggie, about three years ago when their cat, Tubby, ran away during the Fourth of July fireworks. That chubby cat had snuck into my half-open window and hidden under my bed. I hadn't been aware of his presence. My aunt, who was allergic to cats, had found him the next day unintentionally. Poor Aunt Amy! With teary eyes and a red face from sneezing nonstop, she'd found me in the kitchen and asked between sneezes if I'd hidden a cat in my bedroom.

"Of course not!" I'd cried, running to my room. "I like dogs, not cats!"

Under my bed, I'd seen Tubby's eyes glowing back at me. He'd hissed fiercely when I tried luring him out. How Tubby had jumped down from Maggie and Rick's apartment on the third floor was a mystery. Maybe someone had forgotten to close a door, and the cat had taken a leisurely walk in the neighborhood and run to the closest place to hide when the fireworks started.

Once my aunt moved to Boston, my relationship with Rick and Maggie became closer. Maggie loved cooking and used me as an excuse to bake and cook because she had no one to spoil, considering all her grown-up kids lived outside California.

"Have you found a new roommate yet?" Rick asked after looking at the pictures.

"Not yet," I answered, putting my phone back into my purse. "It's not as easy as I thought."

Rick gave a nod of understanding. "But you've sent out the ads and flyers, right?"

I nodded.

Rick squinted down at me. "Let me guess—Amy doesn't know about this, does she?"

I lowered my gaze. "If Maggie happens to talk to my aunt, please don't tell her," I begged, looking up at him.

"Don't worry about that," he assured me. "Listen, let me help you. When you have time, stop by my place and bring the flyer. With my luck and connections, maybe I could find someone for you quickly," Rick said without hiding the pride in his tone.

I gave a little smile. That was what I liked about Rick: always helpful.

"Okay. Tomorrow after work, I'll stop by," I said.

"Good." Rick smiled, watching something behind me. "Now, here comes Leo, my partner in crime." He pointed his finger at Leo, my next-door neighbor on the same floor, walking toward us with a basketball in his hands. Leo was about the same age as Rick but still liked to play basketball.

I grinned, waved to Leo, and got in my car.

Rowena's office light was off when I put my bag in my cubicle. Usually, our arrival times in the office were almost the same, which bothered me somehow.

"It's hard to believe you arrived before her," commented Sylvia, popping her head over our cubicle's divider as I turned on my notebook.

"Maybe she overslept after brewing up an evil potion last night," Lena scorned.

My lips twisted at the comment while Sylvia snorted, holding her laughter.

"Trust me," Lena added, "if you searched her office, you might find a witch's hat and a broomstick."

"I dare you!" Sylvia said, laughing.

"Psst…she is coming!" warned Yoo-Shi from her cubicle near the entrance.

Immediately, we all looked down at our computers as the door swung widely. Rowena's heavy footsteps filled the quiet room. Without greeting us, she went straight to her office, and a split second later, I heard the heavy thud as she slammed her Longchamp bag onto her desk.

What a bitch!

Lena said to me in a Skype message.
I smirked and replied.

She woke up on the wrong side of the bed, I bet.

Lena replied.

Almost every day? Rory, please. She always does when she feels like we were talking behind her back. She's simply a bitch.

Rowena tended to be passive-aggressive whenever she felt unhappy toward someone. Unlike Desiree, she would give that person the cold shoulder all day and accumulated his or her mistakes before badmouthing them in front of Desiree, who didn't seem interested in finding out why Rowena always came to her and bitched about her subordinates. She was too busy polishing her department's public image as a fun place to work, full of smart, young people and good teamwork.

My respect toward my manager had steadily been decreasing along the way, but I had to give her credit for always hitting deadlines and not wasting time with senseless chatting. It was unfortunate that her hardworking attitude wasn't accompanied by compassionate, open-minded, and appreciative behavior towards her staff. Her condescending personality was a terrible fit for a manager. If Desiree had cared about healthy relationships between management and the team, she would have been the best person to control Rowena's negative tendencies.

At two o'clock, there was a quick meeting for the finance and accounting departments. The conference room was already packed when Yoo-Shi and I arrived, so we squeezed into the back corner behind a few other employees. In the meantime, Valerie Tanaka, our executive vice president, stood at the head of the conference room with her hands clasped in front of her, her angular eyes scanning the room as she waited for the chatter to die down.

"Thank you for coming," she said in a clear voice as the room became quiet. "I'm going to give you an update on our partnership project. Mr. Hamilton has announced the name of our future partner: White Water, Inc." Val paused for effect. "White Water is a British wine company. Their finance team will fly to the States in three weeks, but they will be in New York first before coming here. Please keep in mind that this partnership is vital to us because White Water is highly reputable in the wine industry. They distribute branded wines to high society, royalty, and the wealthiest families in the world. So, please welcome them while they are here."

"How long will the process take?" someone asked.

"I'm not sure. Maybe two or three months; maybe longer. I bet White Water teams will have tons of questions once they look at our profit-and-loss statements and financial audit reports. Next week, all general managers will give me names of people who are their subject-matter experts, and they will work with White Water teams. So… ," Val scanned the room, "any questions or concerns?"

"Are we going to get free lunches when the Brits are here?" someone cried.

Chuckles filled the room, and all heads whipped around to find who was daring enough to throw a joke at the always-serious Val.

"Maybe only for those who are working with their team," she answered. "Okay, if there are no more questions, thank you for coming today, and we'll see you again when the White Water teams are in town."

At once, the noise of chairs being pushed across the floor was heard as people rose from their seats. The meeting room doors were opened wide as employees poured out. Before going back to work, Sylvia and I went down to grab some fresh coffee in the lunchroom.

"I overheard that the founder of White Water is a great-grandnephew of one of the dukes in England," she said, filling a coffee cup, "and the current president is his son."

I whistled my surprise. "A company with royal blood."

"Yup." Sylvia nodded and moved over so I could get some coffee too. "I'm happy with the partnership, but to be honest, I worry too."

"Why?" I asked.

Sylvia looked down at her cup for a moment before replying. "Myriad is the third company I've worked for. Usually, talks of a partnership project, or whatever term management used, ended with the company being acquired by the other. But maybe I'm wrong. Maybe Myriad is different and won't sell. So…just ignore me."

"Our gross profit is strong this year, up twelve percent compared to last year," I said, referencing a financial report I'd read. "I don't think Mr. Hamilton would sell."

Sylvia shrugged. "Remember the big fire we had last year in Northern California? It burned up most of our wine suppliers' warehouses, and millions of dollars were lost. Without their wine and other products, there isn't anything for us to distribute. If that's still the case, there is no more alcohol division. Wine is Myriad's most profitable product line."

"Last night, I googled about White Water and found that"—Sylvia lowered her voice—"it also owns forty-eight percent of Red Wine, Inc. Red Wine is our main competitor in the US. So, if our partnership is successful, it means White Water will have two companies in the same business line. Do you think they wouldn't merge us into one company?"

Her words made sense. All of sudden, I felt my stomach churn.

Sylvia nudged me. "Hey, don't be scared. Maybe I'm wrong," she said in a cheerful tone.

Looking at her, I bit the inside of my cheek. "Myriad is my first job. If we were let go, unlike you who has more years of experience, I'll have a hard time finding a new job. Besides, I don't think it will be easy for me to get a reference from you-know-who."

Sylvia gave me a sympathetic nod. "Stop overthinking. Christine would be happy to vouch for you. So would I."

"Thanks, I appreciate it," I said.

"My pleasure. Let's get back to work before you-know-who turns you into a frog." She made a frog sound.

I laughed until my sides ached.

Late in the afternoon, after work, I stopped at a grocery store for a rotisserie chicken, salad, and fruit. On the way back home, my phone buzzed, and Rick's name showed on the screen. Hoping for something good, I answered the call.

"Hi, Rick!" I greeted him through the speakerphone. "How are you?"

"Hey, Rory. Listen, I have good news. Are you home now?"

My heart pumped hard. *Good news!* "Not yet, but I will be in ten minutes."

"Okay, I'll wait for you," said Rick.

"See you soon." I hung up.

Rick was talking to Jose, one of the security guards, as I parked my car in front of my apartment. I'd always been amused by Rick's friendly manner because he could talk to anyone about anything, from the weather to sports to culture to food.

Still chatting away with Jose, Rick waved to me as I got out of my car. The two men parted, and Rick headed in my direction.

"For you." He thrust a plastic bag out to me.

"What's that?" I asked, accepting the bag from his hand. It was heavy.

"From my beautiful wife," he winked. "She made a blueberry cheesecake this morning and gave you a quarter of it. Some oranges from her sister's garden. And your favorite food, a tray of meatloaf."

"Aw. She is so sweet." My heart filled with warmth. "Now I feel rich!" I held up my bags from the grocery store.

Rick chuckled, giving me a thumbs-up. Together, we walked toward my apartment.

"So, you said you have good news for me?" I asked as we arrived in my kitchen.

Rick nodded and sat on a tall chair at the kitchen bar while I took the food out of the bags and laid it out on the countertop. The smells of meatloaf and rotisserie chicken made me hungry.

"A woman named Jane Ryder called and said that she's interested in the room. But…," Rick stopped and gazed at me, "only for nine months or less."

"Oh." I lowered my head to hide my disappointment.

"Yeah. She's here for a short-term project and will go home when it's done," Rick said. "But I think you should consider, because she's willing to pay for six months' rent upfront."

My eyes widened as my brain made a quick calculation: *$1,250 multiplied by six is…*"What? $7,500 in advance? That's a lot of money! No, nobody is willing to pay that much. It sounds too good to be true."

"Yup, that's what I thought." He gave me a piece of paper.

I nibbled my lower lip while reading the phone number written on it. "Do you think she is a liar?"

Rick half shrugged. "If she hasn't called me in two days, you'll know the answer," he said as he rose from his seat and walked to the front door.

"Thanks for your help, Rick. I appreciate it," I said as he turned the knob and walked through the doorway. "And thank Maggie for the food."

"Our pleasure. Good night, kiddo," he said, and closed the door behind him.

I sighed and looked at the phone number. No one was willing to pay that much. Shaking my head, I crumpled the paper and tossed it into the trash can, then headed to my room for a quick shower before dinner.

My dinner was lavish with a piece of meatloaf, rotisserie chicken, and steamed rice. Then, I had the cheesecake for dessert. A blissful sigh escaped my lips as I tapped my stomach gently. If only if I *were* rich, I would have a skillful chef like Maggie.

Later, at eight, Lizzy video-called me.

"We *adopted* a puppy!" she shrieked, turning her camera to Terry holding a mixed golden cocker spaniel in his arms. "Her name is Kiki."

"Oh my God, what a cute puppy! Hi, Kiki!" I squealed, waving my hand in front of the camera. "Aww, she is so adorable. And the eyes…My heart is melting!"

The puppy's coat was long and curly and the same color as Terry's hair. When he planted a kiss on the puppy's head, for a second, it looked like he had hair extensions.

"How could her owner have had the heart to put her in the shelter? She's so sweet!" My eyes fixed on the puppy.

"We don't know, but she has a new home now," said Terry, lifting the puppy's paw and waving it to me. "Hi, Auntie Rory."

I chuckled and waved back to the camera.

The puppy seemed content in Terry's arms, pressing her head to his chest when Lizzy put the phone closer to her face.

"I'm so jealous because I think Kiki prefers Terry to me," said Lizzy, turning the phone back to herself.

"Don't be silly," I laughed. "Soon, she will know that you are a good mom for her."

Lizzy grinned widely, her eyes sparkling with pride. "So, any news about a roommate?" she asked.

"Rick got a call today, but I don't think it's a serious offer," I said, and told her about Jane Ryder and her promise to pay six months' rent in advance.

"Sounds too good to be true," said Lizzy. "No one is willing to pay upfront like that."

"That's exactly what Rick and I thought. Oh well. Not my luck yet." I rubbed my temple.

"Don't give up, okay?" Lizzy comforted me. "You'll find someone great. I believe God will help you."

"Thanks, Lizzy."

"Hey, why did you guys suddenly decide to get a dog?" I asked, diverting the topic. I knew she would ask me if I was fine financially, but at that moment, I wanted to forget about it.

Beaming, slightly pinkish, Lizzy explained that they wanted to have a baby soon after the wedding but were scared, so Kiki could be the best way to "practice" their parenting skills before having a real child. Terry's eyes sparkled when he chimed in, with Kiki sleeping peacefully in his arms.

Terry and Lizzy were meant for each other. I was happy for them but also jealous of Lizzy, who had gotten a good man in Terry. I shouldn't have been worried about that, given that my monetary issues needed to be resolved before I could even think about a serious relationship.

CHAPTER 4

Sleep eluded me that night. My mind constantly spun about Jane's offer. She met my roommate criteria, except for the rental term. But anything that sounded too good usually ended up bad.

My computer's office clock read 9:00 a.m., but I already had a hard time keeping my eyes open.

I should go for coffee.

Lena's cubicle was still empty because she had a doctor's appointment and would be in shortly. Rowena wasn't in her office because she, Desiree, and Christine had a weekly meeting with Valerie to review our division's performance.

Standing up, I looked over at Yoo-Shi, whose cubicle was behind mine. She was looking seriously at her screen with her reading glasses sitting on the middle of her nose. At twenty-nine years old, she was too young for reading glasses. She lifted her head at the sound of my fingers, tapping on the edge of her cubicle.

"Wanna go down for some coffee or tea?" I asked in a half whisper.

Pushing her eyeglasses up, she shook her head. "I have to pass this time. Christine wants me to redo this journal entry after finding an error on the sales tax report. Sorry."

"No worries," I said, turning to Sylvia, whose cubicle was next to Yoo-Shi. "Sylvia, how about you?"

"Sorry, I have a conference call with our operation team in New Jersey in ten minutes." She pointed to the papers she'd been organizing.

What a bummer!

"Okay, I'll go down by myself. See you later."

I left my computer on, just in case Rowena returned from the meeting before me and tried to tell Desiree I had snuck out of the office early.

My three-inch heels clacked on the hard floor as I reached the corridor to the lunchroom. The room was empty as I entered through the swinging door and took a paper cup from the stack on top of the water cooler. I filled the cup with water, and the cold liquid instantly woke me up a bit. Feeling refreshed, I went for a refill.

"Are you planning to drink it all?" a familiar voice asked from behind me.

Whirling around, I came face-to-face with a sandy-haired guy in an orange-checkered shirt. Jason Grant was from the purchasing department, whom I'd met during my new employee orientation. He was kind and helpful and one of the most handsome guys in the office. Lena called him Prince Charming because of his angelic face. Yoo-Shi, the smallest among the four of us, liked him because of his tall, athletic build. "It would counteract my short gene if I married a tall guy like him," she'd said.

I used to crush on him and had always tried to synchronize my lunch or break times with him. When someone had told me he was in a serious relationship, I'd stepped back just to be friends with him.

"Hey, Jason. Sorry, I didn't know you were waiting," I said, moving aside.

Adjusting his glasses on his nose, Jason smiled. "Just kidding, Rory. I'm sure there's enough for both of us."

"No worries. I'm done," I said, waving my hand to the dispenser. "Now, I need to grab some coffee." I spun and headed toward the Keurig machine.

"If I'd known I'd meet you in here, I'd have brought your favorite tea," Jason said, helping himself to some water. "So, how are you?"

"Good. Just busy with the reconciliation reports. How about yourself?" I asked, choosing hazelnut flavor from the many boxes of K-cups and plopping it into the machine.

Tightening the cap of his water bottle, Jason turned to face me and leaned against the water cooler. Under the dim lunchroom light, I detected a flash of sadness across his face and a gloomy expression in his beautiful green eyes.

"I broke up with Cindy." Taking a deep breath, he ran his fingers over his hair.

"Ooooh. Sorry about that," I said. In a split second, I felt empathy for Jason's breakup, yet I was secretly thrilled to find out that he was available. "When did that happen?"

He adjusted his glasses and gazed at the floor. "We broke up two months ago," he said. "Our lifestyles were too different. I like watching movies, and she doesn't. She preferred to stay home and cook or bake rather than going out. I like cycling, and she doesn't. She always dressed so plainly, even for parties. I tried to encourage her to dress more fashionably, but she would get upset with me. I gave up after being patient for two years. Now it's over, and I moved on." He shrugged. "It is what it is."

His face lit up as he lifted his eyes to me. "Hey, I remember you mentioned you were looking for a roommate. Found one yet?"

"No luck yet," I shook my head.

"I see." Jason nodded. "If the room is still vacant, I'm interested. Would you mind having a male roommate?"

"Why are you looking for an apartment? I thought you already had one," I said nervously.

"It was Cindy's apartment. I've been living with my brother since we broke up, but now he and his wife just had a baby. So, what do you say I move in? We can carpool to the office. Wouldn't it be great?"

My heart almost jumped out of my chest. *Oh my God. Did I hear him correctly? Jason wants to live with me!*

"Um, actually, I'm looking for a female roommate," I said, rubbing my ear.

A thin cloud seemed to wash over his face.

"Sorry." I lowered my eyes to avoid his.

Jason chuckled half-heartedly. "Don't worry about it. Never hurts to ask. And if you change your mind, the offer still stands. I don't mind paying a bit more than your previous roommate paid," he added with his angelic smile.

"I'll let you know," I said, controlling my hammering heart as we walked toward the door together.

Jason pushed the door open and held it for me. I could smell his fresh scent as we walked down the hallway toward the foyer. He flashed me a smile before turning to his office.

For the rest of the day, that conversation bugged me. I couldn't take my mind off his request to be my roommate. With just one small criterion change, my financial problem would be solved, and Jason was an excellent candidate. He had a permanent job and would likely stay longer (hopefully), and I already knew and liked him.

But how would I tell my aunt? Maybe her reaction wouldn't be as bad as I'd been assuming, especially if I told her I'd been subsisting on the top ramen diet for more than three months. Even though worrying about my aunt's reaction still made my palms clammy, I was determined to tell her that night.

CHAPTER 5

My aunt *wasn't* my mom, but she was *like* a mom to me.

I was nine years old when I moved in with her after my mom passed away. However, after ten years together, I couldn't shake the feeling that she'd taken me in from a sense of obligation and hadn't had the heart to see me enter the adoption system. She could have given me to my first cousins, but none of them would help me, as I was considered the daughter of a black sheep.

I didn't have a feeling of love for Aunt Amy, like between a daughter and her mom, but mostly respect and a sense of gratitude for her raising me. As a result, I'd developed a habit of trying to make my aunt happy and needing her approval. I wanted her to see me as a smart, capable, and trustworthy person. I didn't necessarily agree with all her opinions, but in many areas, including this roommate issue, I felt obligated to follow her rules. I couldn't break the rule, but I couldn't ask for her help, either, because she would rescue me while giving me that look of disappointment she reserved for my moments of incompetence.

Sitting on the couch after work that evening, I rehearsed the conversation I intended to have with my aunt about my taking a male roommate. Regardless of how many times I practiced the words, I was sure I'd be letting her down.

Sighing, I took a photo of my mom from the small side table and gazed at it. It was the last picture taken of her before she passed away. My mom and my aunt were posing in front of their childhood home. My mom's hazel eyes squinted in the bright light, and the wind tossed her light-brown hair about her face. In her lavender dress, her cool-toned skin looked radiant. Standing side by side with my aunt, who had dark-brown eyes and hair, no one could tell they were siblings. My mom was more like Grandma Audrey, who was German-Australian, and my aunt was more like Grandpa Kenji, who was Japanese.

I didn't know what my dad looked like. My mom had been upset each time I'd asked, so I stopped asking. My skin was fair, with light freckles on my nose like my mom's, but my angular eyes and hair color were like my aunt's.

"It would be different if you were alive, Mom, but you'd probably be on Auntie's side anyway—after the pain you experienced," I mumbled, putting the picture back on the table.

Clenching my jaw, I reached for my phone and almost dropped it as it rang unexpectedly. The screen showed it was Rick calling. Dropping a hand over my chest, I brought the phone closer to my ear.

"Hey, Rick! How are—"

"Rory, I'm glad you answered. Are you home?"

"Yes," I said.

"Are you home or not?" Rick asked again.

"Yes!" I yelled into the phone, having forgotten about his hearing. For a seventy-two-year-old man, he looked healthy and still ran five miles every morning, but he could not hear without his hearing aids.

"Okay, don't scream. I can hear you," he said. "I have good news. Remember Jane Ryder? She seems serious about her offer because she called again this morning. Can I stop by your place to give you the details?"

"Sure. Please come."

"Can I come or not?" said Rick.

"Yes!" I repeated loudly.

"Okay, okay, I hear you. Don't scream like that. Young people love screaming lately. Okay. I'll see you soon." He hung up.

Twenty minutes later, Rick was sitting at the kitchen table with me, thankfully wearing his hearing aids.

"So, this Jane Ryder is serious about being my roommate?" I looked up at Rick, tapping my finger on the paper.

Rick nodded solemnly.

"And she offers an upfront payment of $7,500?"

Rick nodded again. "What do you think? Will you accept her offer?"

I read Rick's scribbles of her information on the paper. *Jane Ryder. Richmond, London.*

"I can tell you are uncertain about accepting something this short-term." He gazed at me. "Maybe you need to be flexible. If you insist about only accepting a roommate who can stay for two years, how long will you last on the ramen diet?"

My mouth fell open. *How did he know?*

Rick chuckled at my expression. "I'm a father of three daughters." He tapped his chest. "One of them has a personality like yours, so I know what you've been through, preferring to suffer alone. Also, on the weekends, you barely go out with your friends. Am I correct?"

I grimaced at his sharp observation.

Rick chuckled, placing his hand on top of mine and squeezing it gently. "Take that offer," he said firmly.

"Yeah, maybe I should," I said, clearing my throat.

"You should." He clasped his wrinkled hands. "Now, text her and make an appointment to talk to her through…what is that…*tsk*—" Rick flicked his finger while thinking, then his face beamed, "ah, video call!—so you can see her face, get to know her, and let her know you. If you feel good, just go for it. My gut says she is a good lady. Oh, by the way, you still have her phone number, right?"

Damn. I already threw it in the trash.

Somehow, Rick read my mind. "You didn't lose it, did you?" he said, squinting at me.

My cheeks warmed. Avoiding his gaze, I walked over to check the trash can. "Uh, I didn't think she would call," I mumbled, peering into its contents.

"Young people never have enough patience to wait, to have faith." He shook his head.

I grinned in embarrassment as I searched the trash. Snatching up the small piece of blue paper, I waved it in the air and said, "Got it!" I grabbed a notepad and pen and wrote down the number, then tossed the old one because it was smeared with cooking oil and ketchup.

"Great. Before you contact her, maybe you need to check social media to make sure she isn't a criminal. Nowadays, it's easy to search for information about people. Gosh, my grandkids are only teens, and they already have Facebook accounts." He cackled.

"Do you have one?" I asked.

Rick's cackling got louder. "Nah, I'm old school. Don't even have online banking. I like going to the bank—talk to the teller, meet new people."

I smiled at his comment. "Speaking of the bank, should I ask for her proof of employment to make sure she can pay me?" I asked.

"That's a legit thing to do," he said. "She lives in Richmond, meaning she has money, but it doesn't hurt to be sure."

Around a quarter to eight, Rick left my house after helping me jot down the important things I needed to find out about Jane. I was glad to have his help. He was the closest thing to a father figure I'd ever had.

CHAPTER 6

Two days later, I had a video call with Jane after dinner. She was in her early thirties, the same age as Lizzy. Her layered brown hair was perfect for her pale skin and sterling-gray eyes. She was in her office during our call, so I checked off my list about confirming her employment.

"Rick told me you were looking for someone more long-term. Will you be all right if I only stay for six to eight months?" asked Jane in a thick British accent.

"Yes, it'll be fine," I answered. Getting six months of rent upfront was unheard of, and it would allow me to start looking for a new roommate with a lot more lead time. As Rick said, I would be stupid to refused. As for Jason… well, I had to put that idea aside, because Jane's offer was the better one.

Jane beamed, and she eagerly promised to send a check for the full rent. She informed me that her flight would land at the Los Angeles Airport at 11:00 a.m. on Saturday, and she expected to arrive at my apartment sometime around 1:00 or 2:00 p.m., depending on the traffic that day.

My heart leaped as I glanced at the calendar on my kitchen counter. In three more weeks, I would have a new roommate, which meant I should clean my apartment soon, because I had to admit that I'd been a bit lazy since Lizzy left.

Unfortunately, my plan to clean didn't go well. After my conversation with Jane, work kept me unusually busy. Almost every day, I arrived home around eight in the evening and had to work on the weekends too. My skin became dry, and dark circles were obvious underneath my eyes from lack of sleep.

A week before Jane's arrival, I woke up extra early. My body screamed for sleep, but I had to clean the apartment. Dragging my feet to the bathroom, I leaned over the sink and splashed some water on my face to wake me up. I shrieked from the cold and quickly grabbed a towel to prevent the water from trickling down my back. It had already made it down to my waist, but that was enough to kick the sleepiness out of my system. Forty-five minutes later, after two cups of coffee and two soft-boiled eggs, I was ready to begin.

"Which room am I going to clean first?" Pressing my lips tight, I surveyed the room, not feeling proud of myself. There was a pile of empty instant noodle bowls next to the sink and books and magazines scattered over the carpet in the living room. The only area I didn't have to clean was the second bedroom, where Lizzy used to stay, because she had left it and the bathroom spotless. My ex-roommate had been a clean freak.

"Well, you are the dirtiest one." I pointed to the kitchen. "Let's clean you up."

I put in my earbuds and turned on some electronic dance music for inspiration. Equipped with a bottle of Windex Multi-Surface, trash bags, and a lot of rags, I sprayed Windex generously on the kitchen countertop and wiped it down with the rag. The upbeat tones of "Hey Brother" by Avicii powered me through the painful cleaning time.

The fridge and cabinets weren't missed. I cleaned the shelves and threw away some expired products. Slowly, a pile of dirty rags and full trash bags were piling up on the kitchen floor. I only took a short break before continuing to clean the living room and my bedroom as well. It wouldn't hurt to show Jane the entire apartment.

After almost five hours of nonstop cleaning, I was exhausted. Looking around, a sense of pride crept over me. The kitchen and living room were spotless, with books and magazines arranged neatly on the coffee and end tables.

"Finally!" I lay down on the carpet in a starfish position.

I had almost dozed off when my phone rang, but I ignored it. In the last couple days, a private number had been calling. I had picked up twice, and no one answered except some weird, staticky voices on the other end. I figured it was just a prank or a robocall from a telemarketing company.

CHAPTER 7

Jane's arrival day had finally come. I glanced at my watch and knew her plane must've landed at LAX by now. Feeling giddy with anticipation, I hugged myself, knowing I could end my frugal lifestyle and my dependence on instant noodles. It would be nice to have a friend in this apartment again. The only thing I hoped for was that Jane's personality wouldn't change like Yoo-Shi's bitchy roommate had.

Around two o'clock, the doorbell rang. I scanned the living room one last time, then headed for the door. Clearing my throat, I pulled up the corners of my lips as my hand turned the doorknob.

As the door swung open, I said, "Hey, welc—"

I felt the corners of my lips drop when I found the person who rang my doorbell wasn't Jane Ryder but a tall man with a full beard and dark aviator sunglasses. He was wearing a gray long-sleeved T-shirt, old jeans, and a gray baseball hat with brown hair sticking out from under it. He shifted a navy-colored backpack from slipping off his shoulder as he removed the sunglasses. His wrinkled forehead smoothed as he fixed his light-brown eyes on me calmly.

Intimidated by his beard, my instinct was to shut the door, but I refrained. Instead, I looked at him and asked, "Can I help you?"

"Yes, maybe you can," the man said in a thick British accent. "Is this 211 Maple Street, number 77? Rory Arrington's apartment?"

I nodded. "Yes, that's correct. What can I help you with?"

The crinkle on his forehead appeared again. "You are…Rory?" he asked carefully, trying to hide his surprise.

"Yes," I answered, "and who are you?"

He scratched his chin and mumbled, "I thought Rory was a man's name."

"Sometimes, but I'm a *female* Rory," I answered calmly. "Since you're looking for a *male* Rory, maybe you need to go to the leasing office for help. Have a good day!" I stepped back to close the door.

But the man was audacious. He placed his foot in the doorway to prevent me from closing it.

"Hey, what do you think you're doing? Get away from my door, or I'll call the police!" I cried, kicking his foot while taking out my phone from my jeans pocket.

"No! Please don't call the police!" Looking panicked, he swiftly withdrew his foot.

I seized the opportunity and slammed the door. As I was about to lock it, he said, "Jane Ryder sent me here."

I was stunned. I cracked open the door to peek out. "What do you mean, Jane Ryder sent you here? Where's she now?" I asked through the opening.

"I'm Peter, her brother. Jane can't come because she had surgery last week and has been prohibited from flying."

His answer left me speechless. I slammed the door again and locked it this time. The sound of my heart pounding filled my ears as I called Rick for assistance.

Rick dashed over in record time and brought Lou, the apartment complex security guard. With two ex-marines present, I didn't have to worry about Peter trying anything stupid while hearing him out in my kitchen.

Lou stood at the kitchen counter while Peter sat on the sofa with Rick. I grabbed a seat on the ottoman across from the men as Rick asked for Peter's ID. Peter calmly removed it from his wallet and handed it over while offering a polite smile to Lou, who was squinting at him.

I had a hard time seeing any resemblance to Jane in Peter. Jane looked professional. Her brother looked like a hobo with his bushy beard hiding most of his face. His clothes were scruffy and worn, and his brown hair hung unkempt about two inches past his ears. Good thing he didn't smell—at least he'd taken a shower.

"My sister tried to call you, but no one answered." Peter looked at me as he took a long white envelope from his tattered backpack and extended it to me. "This is a letter from her to you."

"When did she call me? I didn't see a missed call from her," I said, taking the envelope. "She could have emailed me, too."

Peter shrugged, leaning back on the sofa.

I recognized Jane's handwriting from the check she'd sent. The letter explained that she'd experienced excruciating abdominal pain and had been rushed to a hospital five days before her scheduled flight to California. A CT scan revealed that her intestine had been perforated, and infection was flowing through the tear and into her body. If she hadn't had emergency surgery right then, she would have died. Before the surgery, she assigned someone from the office to contact me, but they hadn't been able to reach me via email or phone. Sending her brother to my apartment was the only solution she could think of, considering he'd been assigned to help her in California anyway. At the end of her letter, Jane asked me to call her so she could explain herself.

Dumbstruck, I stared at the letter until a soft tap on my shoulder brought me back to reality.

"He suggested we call Jane," Rick said, glancing at Peter. "I think that's a good idea."

"Yeah, Jane suggested the same thing." I waved the letter and turned to Peter. "Is it okay to call her at this hour?"

"Yes. She's waiting for your call," Peter said.

Swallowing, I took my phone from the coffee table in front of me, dialed Jane's number, and put it on speakerphone at Peter's suggestion. I sighed inwardly. *I can't believe this is happening to me!*

After the third ring, someone picked up, asking me to wait so she could connect me with Jane. I glanced at Peter.

He shrugged as if to say, "I told you she sent me."

Jane said, "Hello?" then switched our call to video.

"Oh, Jane!" My heart sank to see how pale she was. Her hand was attached to an IV dangling above her head. She winced while shifting slightly on the hospital bed. Her cheeks were sunken with black circles under her eyes. I cleared my throat to push down the sudden sadness rushing over me; her appearance reminded me of my mom after the accident that had killed her in the end.

"My brother must have arrived?" she said.

"Yes, he is here," I replied, glancing at Peter, who was now looking down at the hat he was twirling with his fingers. "He mentioned that you'd tried to call, but I didn't see your missed calls."

"Someone in my family had tried to call you, but he had a hard time with the connection because of the blizzard," said Jane, after pausing for a moment. "And I made a mistake on writing your email address without a dash between your first and last name, which is why my email didn't go through."

When she mentioned the blizzard, something struck me. "Wait, I remember! There were a few calls from a private number. I thought it was a prank or tele-marketer because, each time I picked up, I couldn't hear anything but a choppy, staticky voice. Afterward, I stopped answering the calls," I explained. "Sorry."

"Please don't. It was my fault for forgetting to remove the private setting on our phones," Jane said apologetically. "I'm glad Peter found you so we could finally connect."

"So…when will you come to California?" I asked.

Jane shook her head. "I can't. I need another surgery next month," she said. Her voice sounded tired. "Sorry, I have to cancel my rental agreement."

My stomach felt heavy. "I understand. No worries. I'll return your check to your brother." I nodded, diverting my eyes from the screen. *Goodbye, money. Welcome back, instant noodles.* "Well, thanks, and get well soon, Jane. It was nice to…hey!"

I hadn't seen Peter lean closer to snatch the phone from my hand.

Ignoring my glare, he sat back and aimed the camera toward himself. "Hi, sis!" he greeted her, waving his hand.

Jane shrieked. "Oh my God, Peter! What happened to your face? When was the last time you shaved?"

"I don't remember," he grinned widely, rubbing the bridge of his nose with his finger. He glanced sideways at me, and I fixed him with an annoyed glare.

"And you went to Rory's apartment like that? Didn't even try to change your…scruffy clothes? How embarrassing!" Jane sounded genuinely disgusted.

"Don't worry, I took a shower this morning." He sniffed his clothes. "Besides, you have to blame Marcus. From the way he explained it, I thought Rory was a man."

"You moron! Why would you think I arranged to stay with a man?" Jane snapped. "It's not Marcus's job to give you a detailed explanation. You aren't a child! Even if Rory were a man, do you think it is polite to show up at some-one's house looking like that?"

"Obviously, yes." Peter smirked mischievously. "I thought Rory was one of your ex-boyfriends."

"Shut up, Peter. If I weren't sick, I would strangle you for saying that. Now, give the phone back to Rory," Jane said sharply. "Don't forget to cut your hair and shave. For heaven's sake, don't you dare show up at our client's office with that beard!"

Grinning, Peter returned the phone to me before his sister finished her last sentence.

"I'm so sorry, Rory. My brother is…," Jane took a deep breath, her eyes closing for a brief moment, "a pain in the neck."

I glanced at Peter briefly before shifting my eyes back to Jane. "Get well soon, Jane."

She nodded and thanked me, and we hung up.

Clenching my phone, I looked at Rick, who was giving me a sympathetic expression. If I hadn't remembered whom I was with, I would have wanted to bawl. I stood up and retrieved Jane's check from my bedroom, which I was glad I hadn't cashed yet.

"This is your sister's check." I held it out to him.

Peter replied, "You don't need to return it. Since I'm here to replace her, I'll need a room. Do you think you can take me as your roommate?"

"What?" My jaw dropped.

Peter looked at me solemnly, cocking his head slightly as if trying to look endearing.

From the corner of my eye, I noticed Rick's eyes widen and then heard him chuckle.

"Just a second." I raised my index finger and signaled Rick to accompany me to the patio.

"Since everything is okay, I'll get going," Lou commented, pointing toward the door.

"Thanks, Lou."

Lou nodded and slipped out, while I closed the sliding door that separated the patio and the living room, leaving Peter alone inside.

"His offer caught me off guard. What do you think?" I said as we stood outside.

Rick glanced through the doors at Peter hunched over his cell phone. "I'm sorry this happened to you, but I can't make the decision for you," he said carefully. "If you want to decline his offer, that's okay. If you want to accept him, well, we know that he is Jane's brother... ."

"But I don't know Jane any more than I know him."

"That's true. But you did check her background, she was coming here for work, and you saw with your own eyes that had to change. She's been honest with you, and she is his sister." Rick jerked his head toward the living room, where Peter was still busy with his phone. "This chap is not a total stranger."

"But look at him! Do you think I want to live with anyone who looks like a hobo?"

"Jane told him he couldn't meet clients that way," Rick assured me. "I think he'll clean himself up."

I rubbed a hand on the back of my head. "I don't know, Rick. I'm confused."

A buzz from my phone interrupted us. I took it out and found a text from Jane:

> *Rory, my brother said he would like to fulfill my rental agreement. I'll take full responsibility for his behaviour. Forgive his appearance, but he is a good person...only occasionally a handful. Please let me know if you are comfortable with the arrangement. If not, I'll understand.*

I showed the text to Rick, who nodded. "I think, since you need the money quickly and Jane is vouching for him, you'd better accept the offer," he said.

Biting my lower lip, I looked inside at Peter. "Um, I'll have to tell my aunt," I said after a long pause.

"Yes, you should." He nodded again. "Just keep in mind that Amy is strict, but she is also a considerate person. Remember, no parent would give stones if the children asked for bread. Sometimes we parents are put into awkward positions too. We tend to want to protect our kids from any harm, but we also have to let them stumble so they can learn to stand on their feet. Just be honest to your aunt about your situation. I bet she won't make any fuss."

Weighing his comments, I gazed skyward at the beautiful orange streaks as the sun leaned toward the western horizon. Thin layers of clouds looked like pink cotton candy floating gently in the sky. Birds squawked loudly as they flew over the patio to the trees near the lake. For a moment, I felt envy for their freedom, not having to worry about the world or people's opinions.

Jamming my hands into my jacket pockets, I turned to Rick. "Okay. I'll take him in and tell Auntie Amy later."

Rick's eyes brightened, and he gave a nod of approval.

As we returned inside, I shared my decision with Peter. His face lit up with joy as I extended my hand for a handshake.

"You'd better take him to Lynette for some paperwork now before she leaves…unless you want to deal with Tania or Reta tomorrow, if you know what I mean." Rick glanced at the clock on the microwave.

Lynette was the leasing manager and always took Sundays off. Tania and Reta, her assistants, were often bitchy and sloppy. Between them, Tania was better at her job and the nicer of the two, so people preferred to deal with her more than with Reta. She also had better fashion sense to complement her dark skin and slightly chubby body shape.

I agreed with him and turned to Peter. "Let's go to the leasing office."

"Sure, but can I use the lavatory to clean up first?" he asked.

"He has a good conscience," I thought inwardly, and showed him where the bathroom was.

After several minutes, Peter came out just as I was getting my house key from the kitchen drawer. He had combed his hair and tied it up with a rubber band. His face was clean and his beard brushed. He grinned widely at Rick and I, who looked at him in surprise.

"Look at you! You look different once you've cleaned up." Rick smiled. "Okay, kids, you should get going. See you around, Rory, and …" He looked at Jane's brother.

"Peter, sir," Peter replied.

"Ah, yeah. Peter. Saint Peter." Rick chuckled and waved his hand in dismissal of his poor memory, then headed toward the door.

Peter followed him, and I locked the door after us. We walked along the brick path leading to the office. In the intersection near the rose bushes, we split; Rick turned to the left, and Peter and I continued on toward the right, down a tree-lined path.

Along the way, Peter admired the apartment complex. "It's cozy but modern." He looked around. "I like your apartment too. It feels warm…like a home."

My nostrils flared happily at his compliment. It was the first I'd ever received about my decorating taste. My aunt used to criticize the way I arranged or picked my stuff. Lizzy never criticized me, but she'd bought a few things to make the apartment look more elegant.

On the way to the leasing office, I shared my knowledge about Pacific Hills with Peter. The apartment complex had six three-story buildings and was built on a massive piece of land overlooking the side of Playa de Troya, a human-made lake. The building's architecture was a fusion between modern and Tuscan styles, with soft and muted green foliage and yellow sunflowers as its accents.

Due to its advantageous location by the lake, residents who lived in rooms facing the water could enjoy breathtaking sunsets from their patios. Unfortunately, I didn't have such a privilege because my apartment was on the first floor, which also meant my rent was cheaper.

"Let's go through the back door," I said as we turned to the narrow path that led us to the beige door with a card reader next to it.

I swiped the key through the reader, and the door swung open, revealing a narrow corridor with another door at the end. As we walked down the corridor, we passed an adjacent room that was used as the fitness center. I stopped to show it to Peter, and he seemed interested in the well-maintained gym.

I pushed through the connecting door, and the scent of chocolate chip cookies tickled my taste buds. Inhaling deeply, I stepped into a spacious, elegant living room with Mediterranean vibe. Artworks and tapestries accentuate the ambiance, while the substantial stone fireplace emitted a warm, homey feeling.

We reached a white marble round table in the center of the room, surrounded by dark-brown armchairs and an olive-colored sofa with plush pillows and a red cover. On the table were a couple of ceramic squares with different types of cookies.

"The cookies are for everyone. Management always bakes a few batches a day. You can come here every morning for fresh coffee and scones. Cool, huh?" I stopped at the table for two chocolate chip cookies and offered one to Peter, who refused it.

"I don't like chocolate chip cookies," he said, walking over to the French doors that led to a junior-Olympic-size swimming pool.

Munching my cookie, I followed him.

"Wow, that's an awesome pool!" he said with his hands on his hips.

"It's heated too."

"Could we have a party here?" he asked as his gaze came to rest on the poolside gazebo equipped with a bar and firepit.

"Of course, you'd need to schedule it with the office because this place is always in high demand," I explained.

"I see." Peter nodded.

"Hey, let's go back to the leasing office before it closes." I turned back to the living room.

Lynnette was talking to Tania as we stood in front of her office. She signaled us to take a seat inside. After introducing Peter to them, I stepped out to wait in the living room with my favorite cookies, while Lynette went through lease paperwork with Peter.

Sitting on the big sofa, I could see Peter through the office window. I was glad he'd tidied up before meeting with Lynette. I couldn't imagine what she would have thought if she'd seen him earlier.

The sofa was cozy, and the tranquil music playing in the background relaxed my tense muscles. My eyelids grew heavier, and I decided to close them briefly while waiting for Peter.

It seemed like I had just closed my eyes when a soft shake on my shoulder startled me. I jumped, looking up at Tania, and then I noticed Peter grinning widely from behind her.

"The sofa is cozy, isn't it?" Tania teased.

"Very much," I said, feeling warmth in my cheeks. "Could I borrow it?"

"We'll charge you hourly." Tania winked and turned to Peter, giving him a sweet smile. "So, Peter, again, welcome to Pacific Hills Apartments. If you need anything, feel free to contact us." Her long, sparkly-red-manicured nail pointed at the cookie trays. "By the way, since you said you like the cookies, I have something for you." Tania signaled for him to follow her as she walked to the kitchenette and retrieved a tray of cookies with different flavors from behind the counter. "Why don't you take this and let me know later which flavor you liked best. I'm always happy when people enjoy the cookies I bake from my Granny's recipes." A proud smile flashed across her lips.

My mouth was agape. *Peter likes the cookies? Didn't he say earlier that he didn't like them?*

"I shall. Thank you." Peter smiled, taking the tray from her hand, and following me toward the exit. "I like here. The ladies in the office are kind, too," he commented to me when we were outside the office.

"If they weren't, they wouldn't have any tenants." I chuckled.

Peter grinned and lifted the cookie tray. "And they gave me this for free."

"Tania must like you. She rarely gives away free cookies," I remarked. "Next time, tell her you like brownies too. They're so good, but she only bakes them a couple times a year."

Peter tilted his head, looking confused. "I don't like brownies."

"Just ask her. Since she likes you, she might be willing to bake a tray just for you," I suggested casually. "And if you get it, just don't forget about my sharing policy. It's in our contract."

He chuckled and nudged me with his elbow. "You are a sly girl!"

I laughed and playfully nudged him. "You said you don't like chocolate chip cookies. Why did you accept them when Tania gave you a tray?" I reached out and grabbed one with white chocolate chips on top.

Peter looked down at the cookies in front of him, contemplating. "Well, let's just say I have a weakness for beautiful women who try so hard to feed me. I don't have the heart to refuse them," he answered.

"Man... ." I rolled my eyes and shook my head.

By the time we were back at my apartment, the sun was already setting. The lights on the garden paving and in the courtyards were beaming their soft yellow light across the landscape. Peter put the tray on the kitchen counter while I took off my jacket and hung it on the standing coat rack near the front door.

"Since everything is done, I think it's time for me to go back to my hotel," Peter said, looking at me as he slung his backpack over his shoulder. "See you tomorrow."

"Hey, what about the cookies?" I stopped him as he walked through the door. "Take some with you."

"I don't like cookies, remember?" he said.

"B—but...that's a lot of cookies," I stuttered.

"Consider them a gift for allowing me to stay here. So, Roomie," his hand tapped my shoulder, "enjoy the cookies, and see you tomorrow!" He winked and then walked out and closed the door behind himself, leaving me speechless.

That night, I called Lizzy to inform her about my new roommate.

"Congrats!" she said. "Jane is from London, right?"

"Her name is Peter now," I replied, and told her everything that had happened.

"Wow!" Lizzy remarked after listening to my story. "That's the most bizarre thing I have ever heard. The sister can't come, and the brother replaces her. Double wow!"

"I know, right?" I sighed, leaning back against the bed and staring at the ceiling. "I have no choice but to accept him. Oh, God," I covered my eyes with a hand, "now I have to tell my aunt about him."

"Yeah, tough for you," said Lizzy. "But don't overthink it. I believe Auntie Amy will understand. Living in California is expensive. You were lucky to have a good aunt who could afford to live in such a nice area, but with your salary you need a person to share the rent, and you've been struggling to find a reliable roommate until now."

I puffed out my cheeks like a puffer fish and considered her argument. Maybe she was right—I was overthinking it. But my stomach quivered as I anticipated the conversation with my aunt.

"Maybe you'd like to explain to her that we live in the twenty-first century and that two adults of opposite genders living together is socially acceptable?" I asked casually.

"Oh no. No, *I* won't," she laughed. "But I understand her fear. Remember what happened with my mom? She was afraid that the gleaming life in Los Angeles would change me, her little girl who grew up in a small town in Minnesota, but I proved to her that I could focus on my career, and now, I've found a good man in Terry. I think sometimes we only need to prove to our parents that we aren't children anymore."

I let out a deep breath.

Lizzy chuckled. "You'll be fine."

"Do me a favor?" I said.

"Yes?"

"If I'm too chicken to tell her, would you claim Peter as your long-lost cousin?"

Lizzy burst out laughing. "Are you crazy? She knows my mom, and I bet you a hundred dollars that Auntie Amy would ask her about it."

"Of course, you're right. It was just a thought."

CHAPTER 8

On Sunday morning, I called my aunt to make my confession. Pulling my legs close to my chest, I waited for her to pick up the phone and glanced at my watch to double-check if I had called too early, when she might be volunteering at her church's bookstore.

"Hello, Rory. How are you, dear?" Aunt Amy answered.

In the background, incoherent voices and laughter made me wonder if she was still at the church.

"I'm good. How was the sermon?" I asked, hoping she wouldn't ask if I had attended church that morning.

"It was good…about the prodigal son—nothing new—but Pastor Owen always delivers the story in such an interesting way." Aunt Amy chuckled. "You should listen to the recording online."

"Yeah, sure. I'll listen to it when I have some free time. By the way, Auntie, I have something to tell you. Is this a good time to talk?" I asked.

"Uh, sorry, dear. Not now. I'm at Gail's house—my friend who had the accident three months ago, remember?"

"Uh-huh," I mumbled, trying to recall the story.

"So, call me later, then. Actually, tomorrow would be better. Sorry, dear, I'm needed. Bye now," she said.

But I need you too.

"Okay. Bye, Auntie," I said, but she'd already hung up. I dropped my phone and pulled my hair down with both hands. My confession would have to wait.

Around noon, Peter texted that he would be arriving in about ten minutes. I fussed about, straightening up the common areas, then went out on the front stoop to wait for him. The sun was hiding behind the clouds, which was my kind of weather—bright enough but not too hot. I gazed out at the parking lot.

A few cars passed by, but after twenty minutes there was still no sign of Peter. It would be impossible not to notice a tall guy with a bushy beard, right?

Then Peter's voice called out to me.

I looked around for where the voice had come from and noticed a hand beckoning from behind the open trunk of an Acura TLX. I couldn't figure out how I'd missed seeing him pull up.

"You're here!" I approached his car. "How come I didn't see you?"

My feet halted as I realized the guy behind the trunk lid wasn't Peter. This guy had a clean face, no beard at all. His eyebrows were thick but perfect above deep-set brown eyes. His brown hair was styled in a crew cut with added volume toward the front hairline. He was the same height and had the same hair color as Peter, and he flashed a smile at me before diving back into the trunk.

He took out a medium-sized box and gave it to me. "This one isn't heavy," he said in Peter's voice.

Dumbstruck, I accepted the box while staring at him.

"Would you quit staring at me like that?" he chuckled, taking a square backpack from the trunk and slinging it on his shoulder.

I couldn't believe the transformation. "Are you really…Peter?" I asked carefully.

He blinked. His eyebrows tugged together, giving me bewildered look. "Since the last time I checked in the mirror, yes," he said.

I almost dropped the box. *What?*

"Something wrong?" he asked, still knitting his brows.

I shook my head. "No. Of course not. You look…normal…and totally different without your beard and your long hair."

"Ha! Thanks! I accept that as a compliment," he said. "You didn't recognize me, huh?"

I shook my head again. "No, you look so different."

Delight flashed across his face for a second, then he picked up a large, heavy box with both hands. His sweater sleeves were rolled up to his elbows, revealing his muscular arms. They looked strong and sexy.

Tires squealed as a car turned too sharply nearby and startled me. Shifting my gaze away from him, I felt ashamed to catch myself staring at his muscles. Thankfully, their owner was busy adjusting the box in his grip.

"Yeah, I decided to clean myself up," he said. "It wasn't easy to shave, either. Do you know how long I've been letting it grow?"

I shook my head.

"A year."

"Really? I didn't know it took that long to grow a beard. Why did you shave it off?"

Peter looked annoyed as if he wanted to say, *"I know what you thought of me yesterday."* Finally, he glanced at me and replied. "I had to. Jane would kill me if I showed up with that beard in our client's office. If only she knew how many girls had fallen in love with me because of that beard."

I chortled but stopped quickly as my eyes caught Peter's sharp glance at me. "Yes, of course. I believe you," I replied, nodding exaggeratingly. "Follow me. I'll show you your room."

Peter nodded and caught up with my pace. "Some girls say I look mature with the beard," he continued.

I sucked on my lower lip, then gave a half shrug. "Maybe," I said in an encouraging tone, trying not to laugh, "but everyone's different. I didn't like it, and when I met you yesterday, I thought you looked like an old man."

To my surprise, Peter tilted his head back and howled. "You are an honest person, Rory. I like it."

I forced a smile and, with my free hand, unlocked the door and pushed it ajar with my foot.

Peter stepped inside as I held the door with my back. "Yes, come to think of it, maybe I look older in the bushy beard."

"Sorry. I didn't mean to offend you," I apologized.

"I'm not old enough to be offended," he said. "I'm twenty-three."

"Got it." I laughed, relieved that he didn't seem upset. "Your room is on the left, by the way."

He nodded and turned to the left, heading toward the door I'd left open.

"You didn't bring much stuff," I commented, putting the box on the floor near the bed.

"Not yet. Some of it just shipped from London today. Most of this is Jane's office files," he explained. "Originally, I just came to assist her with the project and then was planning to return to London next week. But then, as you heard," his expression changed and sadness flashed on his face, "she needs another surgery, so I have to be here longer than I'd planned."

"I'm sorry about your sister…and I hope you enjoy your stay here," I responded.

A small smile appeared on his lips as he nodded. "I'm sure I will."

In a very short time, I helped Peter move the boxes and luggage from his car to the bedroom. Then we decided to go out for a late lunch. It was almost one-fifteen by the time we left the apartment.

To welcome him, I drove him to my favorite barbeque place called Rib Joint. Peter was eager to try American food. When we arrived, the parking lot was crowded. Luckily, I found a narrow spot in the corner that my Ford C-Max would fit in.

I liked the food in this little place because of its Memphis-style barbecue ribs. Their spicy dry rub made the ribs juicy, and the meat practically fell off the bones and melted in your mouth. Their homemade cornbread and butter were out of this world; I always asked for seconds.

As we entered, Peter raised his eyebrows at the bar that was already packed with early afternoon drinkers. He didn't say anything, and we found a seat in the back corner of the busy dining area.

"You've been here a lot, haven't you?" he asked after the server took our orders. "That guy"—he pointed toward the kitchen— "knows your regular order, and the barman asked about your aunt."

"Yeah," I said with a smile. "I come here often. The guy at the bar is Max— he's the owner. His wife, Lindy, is my aunt's friend from yoga class. Although my aunt doesn't come here with me anymore, Max still considers me his loyal customer."

Peter nodded. Soon after, the server brought us our drinks and a basket of warm, sweet cornbread.

"So, what brings you to California?" I asked Peter, taking a piece of breads The aroma made my mouth water. Tearing off small pieces, I chewed slowly, savoring the flavor.

Peter covered his bread with the homemade butter and replied between bites. "Well, I can't tell you in detail. It has to do with a business partnership process."

"I see. So, if you can replace Jane like that, it means you work for your family company, right?" I asked.

Peter shrugged. "Something like that."

"In that case, why did she look for a room? Wouldn't it be better to stay in a hotel?" I asked.

Peter shrugged again, bringing the glass of water to his lips. "My sister has peculiar preferences. I didn't understand that either," he said before taking a sip.

"And how about you? Why did you agree to replace her and stay in my apartment? I would have thought you would prefer to stay in a hotel, with housekeeping and amenities and stuff," I said.

Peter gazed at me, his eyes sparkling. For a moment, he looked like a kid thinking of doing something naughty. "Well," he said, setting his glass down on the table, "I could stay in the hotel like other employees, but let's say I'm doing Jane a favor by not breaking the contract with you. How about that?"

"Hmm, you sound so—"

"Mysterious?" Peter interjected.

I chuckled. "No, not mysterious. So—"

My words were cut off as the server arrived with our orders and placed them in front of us.

"Yay! Let's dig in," said Peter joyfully. "That's what Americans say, right?"

I nodded. Once my teeth sank into the tender, juicy meat, I forgot what I'd wanted to say. Peter didn't pursue it either. His excitement reminded me of Alfred, my childhood best friend whom I'd lost contact with for a decade. Now I wondered where he was. Maybe he was still in Colorado.

"Here are the roommate house rules," I said, handing a piece of paper to Peter over the kitchen counter. It had been hours since lunch, after which I had taken my new roommate for a city tour. "Take a look and let me know what you think."

There was only one rule when I lived with Lizzy: *clean up your own messes*. We also had a routine of cleaning the apartment together on Saturday mornings. Lizzy was a clean freak, but I didn't mind because my aunt had also been one, and my ears became accustomed to the constant reminders: "Use a coaster each time you put your glass on the coffee table," "Put the book back on the shelf," "Don't forget to turn off the light when leaving a room."

I was glad to find Lizzy wasn't as strict as my aunt, and she understood that living with a roommate meant we had to be considerate of each other. We cleaned up after ourselves and cohabited respectfully with each other, so we never had any problems.

Since I had accepted Jane as my new roommate without knowing about her illness—and later her brother replacing her—I thought it best to establish a set of solid house rules so that we could live peaceably. Those were the rules I now gave to Peter.

He looked comfortable in his blue sweatpants and T-shirt. Although he was sitting across from me, I could smell the scent of shampoo on his wet hair. Taking the list, he began to read. His eyes squinted, causing a deep crease on his forehead as he read aloud:

"'Rule number one: Clean up your own mess. Rule number two: Label your food unless you want to share it. Rule number three: Take turns taking out the trash, vacuuming the living room, and cleaning the kitchen.'" Peter glanced up at me. "Will we have a schedule for these chores? I'm not the only one doing chores, right?"

I knew he would throw me that question. It was fair. Shaking my head, I pointed at a piece of blue paper on the fridge. "Don't worry. We'll take a turn once a week. This is my week of cleaning, and you can relax until next Monday."

Peter nodded. "'Rule number four: Do your own laundry.' Is there a laundry service around here?" He looked up at me.

My eyebrows rose. "Why? Are you planning to send your clothes to the cleaners? It will be expensive," I said, studying his face.

Peter shrugged and continued reading. "'Rule number five: If you break something, replace it.'" As he read, his face had twisted into a funny expression.

I grinned.

"'Rule six: Turn off the lights and any electronics when done using them. Rule seven: Lock the front door each time you leave. Number eight: No overnight guests.'" Peter raised one eyebrow. "Really?"

Our eyes met as he lifted his face. I shrugged. "Yeah. I'm not comfortable with you bringing dates home. They can come hang out—just let me know so I can give you some privacy—but no overnights."

Peter gave a half shrug and continued. "'Nine: No roommate romance.'" A deep crease appeared between his eyebrows. "Have you experienced this before?" he asked.

I shook my head. "Have you?"

Peter tilted his head, pondering the answer. "I've heard it can be messy," he said shortly, swatting something away from his face.

"I've heard that too. So, no roommate romance," I said.

Smiling, Peter gave me a thumbs-up.

Looking at him, something clicked in my mind, and my hand flew up to cover my mouth.

Peter's eyebrows knitted together. He said, "Are you okay?" as he waved his hand in front of my face.

"I forgot to ask you something," I said almost in a whisper, biting my thumbnail.

"What?" he asked, looking tense.

"Do you have a girlfriend?"

Peter's eyes widened. "What?"

I waved my hands in front of me. "No, no. Please don't misunderstand. I asked because, if you have a girlfriend in London or elsewhere, and she doesn't agree with your living here with me, I'd have to let you go to avoid any trouble in the future."

A smile slowly appeared on his face. "I don't have a girlfriend." He shook his head. "How about you? Does your boyfriend know you have a male roommate?"

"No boyfriend. Broke up a year ago," I answered.

"So, we are good, then?" Peter asked, gazing at me. "No jealousy from our significant others and no romance between us." He grinned at the last words.

"Thanks, and sorry for the question," I said, letting out a huge breath.

"No problem," he said, then went on reading. "'Rule number ten: We will add more rules if necessary.' Are we going to need more than nine rules?" He put down the paper on the countertop.

"Maybe." I flashed a smile.

Peter shifted in his chair and folded his arms on the counter. His eyes glittered with amusement, staring at me.

"So…," I said, nodding toward the papers with my chin, "any questions? Or maybe you have some ideas for additional rules?"

He shrugged. "I think we have enough rules."

"Great," I chuckled, beckoning Peter to follow me. "Now, let me show you where the cleaning supplies are kept."

Peter didn't comment, although I could tell he was tempted to roll his eyes when I explained the concept of using different trash bins for different purposes. Nevertheless, he behaved well.

"Since you're new here, you're welcome to text or call me with questions if you need to, okay?" I said, looking at him.

"Yes, ma'am," said Peter, saluting me.

I smirked, feeling glad he seemed to be an easygoing person who liked joking around.

"Is there a roommate curfew?" he asked, slipping the paper into his pocket.

For a beat, I thought he was joking, but he was looking at me solemnly. "No, no. No curfew," I said with a shake of my head, "but I feel more secure if the door is bolted, so I think we need to inform each other if we are going to stay overnight somewhere else."

Peter gave a slight nod, seeming to ponder something. "Sounds good," he said, then stood from his chair.

I gazed up at his tall figure. Peter must have been six feet tall. Standing next to him, the top of my head only came up his chin.

"I still need to unpack before bed. Have a good night, Rory, and thanks for everything today," he smiled.

"My pleasure. Good night, Peter," I said as he headed toward his room.

Sitting comfortably on the sofa, I stretched to pick up the framed picture of my mom. Lately, my longing for her presence had grown stronger whenever I felt lonely. Over the past six months or so, I'd been struggling to recall my few sweet memories with her. It seemed like her memory was fading away from my mind, and each time I looked at my childhood photo albums, I felt as if I was looking at someone else's photos. Lizzy had tried to comfort me by saying maybe it was because I was so young when she'd passed away.

I pulled the picture closer to my chest and hugged it as the familiar pain stung my heart again.

Closing my misty eyes, I mumbled, "I hope you don't mind my having a male roommate. Auntie will be upset, but I promise you I won't argue with her, because it's only for a short term. I also promise to save more money so I can move to a one-bedroom apartment soon." Sniffing, I put the picture back and forced a smile at my mom as my finger caressed her face. "Good night, Mom." I stood up and headed to my room.

CHAPTER 9

The next morning, I hit the snooze button on my alarm five times. It was late for me because I usually woke up around five, but I'd been busy journaling until one o'clock in the morning so I could sleep in peace.

Dragging my feet, I went to the bathroom, turned on the faucet, and splashed my face with water. The cold pricked my skin and woke me up a little.

"Now, I need a *strong* coffee," I mumbled.

Yawning, I opened my bedroom door and walked to the kitchen. Standing in front of the coffee maker, I put a cup underneath the spout and pressed the start button. The machine hummed for a couple seconds, then the aroma of freshly brewed coffee filled the air as the dark liquid flowed into the cup. Closing my eyes, I inhaled deeply. *Soooo refreshing!* The Big Bang blend from Peet's Coffee never failed me.

After only a few sips, I was startled by the front doorknob rattling as if someone was trying to break in. *Burglar?!? But Irvine is one of the safest cities in America!* I thought.

I jumped behind the counter, opened the drawer, and picked up a knife, but dropped it back in when the door opened enough to reveal Peter's face. His face and neck were shining with sweat, and his cheeks were slightly pinkish from the morning cold. I'd forgotten about him.

"Hey!" he said, panting. His hand closed the door behind him. "Good morning."

"Good morning," I greeted, and returned to my seat. "You're up early."

"I usually do wake early for a jog. Besides, I can't wait to enjoy California's weather. Gosh, I *love* the weather here!" he said, and smiled widely while taking off his shoes. "Did I surprise you coming in just now?"

"A little." I held up my forefinger and thumb to show an inch gap. "I'm just not used to having a roommate yet. Besides, my previous roommate wasn't an early bird."

"Ah, I see," said Peter, bending over to pick up his shoes. His eyes widened, then he looked embarrassed, but he continued to the shoe rack in front of his bedroom door.

When he returned to the kitchen, he was already taking off his jacket. In only a long-sleeved T-shirt and long jogging pants, the muscles of his upper body were easy to make out. I had to shift my eyes back down to my cup.

"Feel free to make some coffee. The beans are in the jar next to the machine," I said, pointing.

"Thanks," he said, opening one of the kitchen cabinets for a cup. He dispensed some hot water from the dispenser next to the cabinet, saying, "I prefer tea."

"Oh."

"But that coffee smells good." From one of the drawers, he took out a box of tea and picked one sachet that he dipped in his cup. A familiar smell began to fill the air.

"Earl Grey," I said, watching as he moved to sit on the other side of the counter.

"You know?" he asked.

"My aunt's favorite," I said.

Peter glanced at the picture of my mom and my aunt on the side table. "Is that her?" he asked, pointing with his head.

I nodded. "Yes, with my mom." I flashed a smile, wrapping my hands around the cup. "My aunt is on the left."

"Your mom is pretty," said Peter, sipping his tea. "I saw the picture clearly when you were talking to Jane."

I flashed a smile. "Thank you. If she were alive, that would make her happy to hear," I said.

Peter looked surprised, then gave a nod of sympathy. "Sorry, I didn't know," he said in an apologetic tone.

"It's okay. I was nine years old when she passed away," I said.

"It must have been hard for you," Peter said gently.

"Yes," I admitted. "It wasn't easy back then, and it's not easy even now. I miss her, especially during my birthday, Christmas, or Thanksgiving, or each time I have a problem." I stopped talking as pain jabbed my heart.

"Yeah, being alone on a birthday or Christmas is tough," Peter said, his eyebrows pulled down. He took out the tea bag from his cup and threw it into the trash can. "I'd better shower. Don't want to be late." Then he stood up from his chair, taking his cup with him.

I glanced at the clock on the kitchen wall: 6:45. "Yeah, me too." I guzzled my coffee, slipped down from my seat, and washed and rinsed my cup. As I set it to dry next to the sink, I felt Peter staring at me. Turning, I watched a mischievous smile on his face. "Why are you looking at me like that?" I asked.

Smiling, Peter pointed down at my legs. "You forgot to put your pants on."

I looked down and shrieked. I was wearing my Hello Kitty sleep shirt. Originally, it had reached down to my knees. Since I wore it often, and the hem had been getting scraggly, I had cut it eight inches above my knees to match the pastel color pajama pants I'd bought a year ago. Last night, I'd taken the pants off because it was too warm in my room and then forgotten to put them back on when I got up.

Heat rushed up to my cheeks. I ran to my room and locked the door.

Damn! Peter must think I did it on purpose. I groaned silently, covering my face with my palms. *And I was sitting and crossing my legs. How long had he noticed?*

Peter shouted through my door, "Don't worry, Rory. My eyesight is bad in the morning, so I didn't see a thing. Trust me!"

His assurance didn't make me feel relieved at all.

By the time I locked the front door, Peter had already left for work, so I didn't have to see him again right after the embarrassing moment. His mischievous smile kept flashing in my mind as my car rolled along the I-5 North freeway that, thankfully, wasn't too crowded for a Monday morning.

Thirty minutes later, I entered the gate of Myriad's parking lot. There were no more spots in the front, but I found one in the rear end of the parking area next to a big Tundra truck with a blind spot mirror as big as an iPad. Stepping out of my car, I heard someone call my name. Swirling, I saw Jason walking toward me fast. As usual, he looked adorable with his glasses sitting on the bridge of his nose. His sandy hair looked shorter and combed neatly. As he got closer, I smelled his subtle, fresh fragrance.

"Good morning, Rory," he greeted me.

"Morning, Jason." I smiled to him. "Did you cut your hair?"

"Yes, I cut it over the weekend." Jason nodded, running his fingers through it.

"Looks good."

Jason beamed. "Thanks."

Together we walked across the parking lot toward the back entrance.

"So, any updates about your roommate?" asked Jason with a raised eyebrow and a questioning gaze.

I stopped and placed a hand to my forehead. "Oh, I'm sorry. I meant to tell you I already found a roommate, but it completely slipped my mind. Are you still looking?"

Jason tilted his chin down and frowned, then turned his head toward the parking lot as if he were expecting something. "Yes, I'm still looking. But I'm happy for you," he said, smiling, but his smile didn't reach his eyes.

"I'm sorry," I said with a wince, darting a glance at him.

"That's okay," Jason said, sliding his ID card into the card reader to open the door. He held the door for me but avoided my eyes.

As I entered the hallway, I sensed a cold stare on my back. Turning, I only saw Jason smiling as he held the door for a lady from the payroll department. She threw a smile to Jason and nodded to acknowledge me.

Jason's gaze met mine as he started down the hallway. "Have a good day, Rory," he said.

I sighed and climbed up the stairs to the second floor. *Shouldn't he be happy that I finally have a new roommate?* I wondered. Then something clicked in my mind that made my heart skip. *No way! He just broke up with his girlfriend. He wouldn't be looking for a replacement this soon, right? Or would he?*

My cheeks warmed with the thought.

During lunch, I told Sylvia, Lena, and Yoo-Shi about my new roommate, only to immediately regret sharing the embarrassing moment from that morning with them.

Sylvia threw her head back, laughing. Lena leaned over, tapping our table with one hand. Yoo-Shi's eyes were getting smaller and teary. They couldn't stop laughing.

The lunchroom was full of people; at least half of them looked around for the source of the commotion. Andrew, a senior accountant from Myriad Food, stopped by and asked to be let in on the joke.

I whisper-shouted, "Stop laughing! People are looking at us." I looked down and pretended to eat my lunch.

Lena and Yoo-Shi finally calmed down, but Sylvia seemed immune to my misery and couldn't contain her laughter. At least she reduced the volume while she wiped tears from her cheeks. "I'm sorry. That was hilarious. I wish I could've seen your face. He wouldn't think you did it on purpose, would he?" Sylvia bit her lower lip to hold her laughter.

"That's what I'm afraid of." I covered my face with my hands. "I'm so stupid!"

Yoo-Shi poked my shoulder playfully. "Nah, you aren't. It was a harmless mistake."

Lena nodded in agreement. "Yup, I made a mistake too. Although not as bad as yours."

I groaned in response.

Yoo-Shi tugged my sleeve. "At least you were wearing panties, right?" she whispered. And both she and Lena burst out laughing again.

"Shut up!" I slapped her shoulder hard, feeling hot on my face. "I'm not that bad. You and your dirty thoughts!"

Sylvia chuckled and lifted her palm. "Okay, ladies. Stop embarrassing her, shall we?" she said. "So, tell us, what does Peter look like?"

"Ahem." I sat straight, placing my folded hands on the table. The three ladies leaned toward me. "He is British with a thick accent. Maybe six feet tall, well-built, and I could tell because"—I lowered my voice—"when he took off his jacket I could see his muscles."

"Ohhh!" my friends said, almost in unison.

Yoo-Shi poked my shoulder. "Can I meet him?"

"He is not a pet," I chuckled, winking at her.

"What does his face look like?" asked Lena, signaling Yoo-Shi to stop protesting.

"Hmm…He looks like …" I scratched my chin, trying to think of a person to compare him to. Then I snapped my fingers. "Now I remember who he looks like."

"Who?"

"He looks a little like Theo James from the *Divergent* movie," I said, feeling satisfied to find the answer.

Lena's eyes widened. She swallowed her sandwich quickly and whacked my arm.

"Hey!" I protested. "What's that for?"

"Is he that handsome?" she half squealed. "Oh, my Lord. I'd faint if I were you."

I rolled my eyes. "I said 'a little.' Besides, you're married! And you too," I said, pointing at Sylvia, who wrinkled her nose in protest.

"I'm single," chimed in Yoo-Shi, raising her hand.

I shook my head. "I'm not a matchmaker."

"You are so mean!" Yoo-Shi protested.

Lena tugged my sleeve. "If he is similar to Theo," she said, leaning toward me and squinting her eyes, "didn't you go weak at the knees when you saw him?"

I shrugged. "The first time we met, he looked like a hobo. But after he'd shaved off his beard, I didn't really focus on his face. The only thing on my mind was that he's the guy who's paying me six months' worth of rent."

"I can't believe that you are so materialistic," Sylvia groaned.

"If you'd been on the top ramen diet for almost four months, you'd feel my pain," I scoffed. "Okay, okay, I admit he is a good-looking guy, but he's not my type."

"So, did you add 'no romance' to the roommate rules?" she asked.

I nodded, giving her a thumbs-up. "Yup."

"Good girl," said Lena, patting my shoulder playfully.

"Now, since you are living with a guy, you have to control your behavior and the way you dress," said Sylvia.

"Why?" I asked.

Lena and Yoo-Shi gave a smile, leaning on their seats while Sylvia sat straight and folded her hands on the table, with her eyes locked on me. I recognized the familiar posture she tended to use each time she wanted to explain something in long sentences. *Here we go!*

"Everything is up to your behavior," Sylvia began. "Don't behave coquettishly or wear suggestive clothes or pants. Stop wearing your Hello Kitty nightshirt. No low-cut blouses or T-shirts. Avoid tempting the guy with that kind of clothing. Remember, if you behave properly, guys will respect you. Don't be like one of them." Sylvia pointed with her chin to the right, where three ladies sat around another table, laughing and chatting. "They wear very low-cut tops to show off their breasts and then toy with people's eyes who can't help but notice."

I glanced at the woman in the middle, remembering the day she'd shown up at the office wearing an especially revealing blouse.

"She even bad-mouthed a poor new girl for glancing at her boobs!" Sylvia's nose wrinkled. "So absurd! She blamed someone for the temptation she created. Of course, anybody with eyes would glance at her—women or men—because she's putting herself on display. If I were her boss, I'd have told her to go home and change."

I chuckled. Growing up in a strict Catholic family, Sylvia always had puritan views about appropriate attire. It bothered her if anyone dressed ostentatiously at the office. For her, the office was a place of work, not a beach. I couldn't agree more.

"So, don't disgrace yourself by showing off your body, okay?"

"Okay, Moms." I gave a playful bow, then winced as they each slapped my shoulders. I put my lunch bag in front of me to duck the smacks. They stopped once I promised not to call them moms anymore. I looked at them one by one as we were laughing together. It was rare to have good friends in the office, where we could laugh together and comfort each other.

CHAPTER 10

The following morning, I made sure to check my clothes before leaving my bedroom. As I entered the kitchen, Peter was taking a carton of eggs I'd bought to share from the refrigerator.

"Good morning," he said joyfully, closing the fridge door with his elbow.

"Morning," I said, moving to coffee maker. The machine hummed as I pressed its start button to grind the beans. "Are you going to cook something?" I asked, glancing over my shoulder.

"Soft-boiled egg," Peter answered, taking out a saucepan from the lower cabinet. He added some water and put the eggs inside the pan, then placed it on the stove. The blue flame licked the bottom of the pan as he turned on the stove dial. "Want some? We can have two each. I'll buy more eggs later if I go to a supermarket."

"Sure," I said, putting my mug under the spout of the coffee maker. "You know, you're the first roommate I've had that will cook breakfast for me."

"I thought it would be fun," Peter grinned.

In the meantime, the coffee was done brewing, and the air in the kitchen was thick with the aroma of roasted beans.

Peter lifted his nose to take in the smell. "I prefer to drink tea, but I *really* like the smell of coffee," he said, filling his teacup.

"You should try it," I suggested.

"Maybe I should." He placed a tea bag into the cup.

I smiled.

While waiting for my coffee to cool, I took a bottle of vinegar from the kitchen cabinet and walked toward the sliding door to the patio. Outside, the sky was softly blue brushed with thin, orange clouds. Cars leaving the parking lot broke the early morning quiet.

I walked to the corner of the yard and bent over, searching the grass intently. Yesterday morning, I'd found cat poop next to my bamboo plant. It must have been one of my neighbors' cats, although I was certain it wasn't Rick's because Tubby wasn't allowed to roam around since the Fourth of July accident. I'd gagged as I wrapped the poop in a plastic bag and threw it in the trash can. Then, I'd searched online about preventing cats from pooping in the same spot and found that sprinkling some vinegar around the spot should do the trick.

I sprinkled each corner of the yard, hoping the vinegar's pungent odor would keep the cats away. Satisfied, I went back inside. As I pushed the sliding door aside, my nose caught a whiff of something acrid coming from the kitchen. I turned around and saw smoke coming from the pan that Peter had used for boiling the eggs.

"Peter! The eggs!" I cried.

Peter rushed out of his room and opened the front door to air out the burnt smell while I took the pan off the stove and put it under the faucet. My other hand turned on the exhaust hood to suck up the smoke. The pan sizzled as the water touched its surface. I groaned silently to see the bottom of the pan was dark brown from burning, and the eggs were cracked and singed.

"Sorry. I forgot about the eggs," Peter said. His face turned slightly pink, and he avoided my eyes.

I debated whether to reprimand him for his carelessness, but I didn't want to say anything. He looked ashamed as he threw the eggs into the trash can, and that was enough. I was relieved the smoke alarm wasn't on because I'd removed the battery. It was super-sensitive and would go off each time I cooked. The last time I'd made stir-fry chicken, it had blared loudly and almost deafened me.

"I'm sorry." Peter gazed at me and then at the pan. "My fault. I'll buy a new one."

Rubbing my temple, I looked at him. "It's an old pan, anyway. But next time, maybe don't leave the kitchen while you're cooking something."

"I promise," he said. "I got caught up in something for work."

"Well, no eggs for our breakfast, then," I said, taking a jar of jam and the loaf of bread from the refrigerator. "Want some bread and jam?"

"I can toast the bread," Peter offered.

I shook my head. "Thanks, but no. Sorry, but I don't want any more of that awful burnt smell. Good thing the alarm didn't go off. It would have woken all the neighbors."

Peter looked bashful as he took out two plates. He walked to the refrigerator and wrote something on the rules list posted there.

Curious, I stood behind him.

He wrote, *Rule #11: Never leave the kitchen while cooking, and use a timer if necessary.*

I smiled and tapped his shoulder. "Good job, mate," I teased.

Peter smiled back and returned to his chair. Together, we enjoyed our first breakfast as roommates.

CHAPTER 11

As usual, my day at the office wouldn't be complete without a scolding by Rowena. She was in her usual bad mood that day, and when she was in that state, facing a pit bull would be preferable to her. Since she'd arrived, Lena and I had been trying so hard to be quiet and not ask any questions or make any mistakes, but she found something to bitch me out about anyway.

I was upset, but I was more curious about her attitude. One time, I'd asked Sylvia why Rowena was always in a bad mood, and she said that Rowena's husband was always out of town for work, leaving her to take care of their two little boys like a single mom. It wasn't our fault that her husband was never home. Why did she take her anger out on us?

Once I finished reconciling five bank reconciliation reports, I checked my emails and found several from Rowena. I winced at the words in capital letters and highlighted in red. She always did that to make her point.

> *Fix the prepaid entry. The detailed content was wrong. You DID last month, and why don't you remember?*

> *Fix the purpose on your journal entry 031219AA, because that's WRONG. I already told you to fix it, so WHY didn't you?*

Fix the account number for Accounts Payable expense. That's WRONG!

Groaning silently, I checked the journal entries I'd created but didn't see anything wrong besides the date, which I hadn't changed on the prepopulated entry. I typed a message to Lena through Skype.

Lena, could you look at my journal entries and help me figure out why Rowena said they are wrong?

Okay, share your screen with me,

Lena replied.

I clicked on the computer icon at the top of the Skype screen to share my computer with Lena. Once she'd accepted my invitation, she could see my screen on her computer. After several minutes, I got her response.

It looks fine to me. She has pigeonholed you lately, huh?

I sent her a nodding emoji.

Welcome to my world,

Lena replied.

Chewing on my lower lip, I turned off screen sharing and went back to my work.

The door swung open, and Christine entered our office, smiling at me as I looked up to see who had come in.

"Hey, guys, why is it so quiet in here?" Christine asked in her happy voice as she walked to her office across from Rowena's. "I went to the Target shopping mall and happened to see this new bakery store and bought cookies for everyone. I put them in the snack room, so feel free to have some, okay?"

The snack room was not a room but an empty shelf between Yoo-Shi's and Juan's cubicles. We used half of it to keep our shared snacks.

"Thanks, Christine," said Yoo-Shi and Sylvia in unison.

I thanked her, too, but my voice sounded timid like a mouse's. Lena would probably send her a thank you through Skype.

Rowena's office door opened roughly, and she called me with a sharp tone. "Rory, come to my office!"

I took a deep breath before standing.

Rowena scowled as I entered and impatiently beckoned for me to look at her monitor while I stood next to her desk. "What did I tell you on the first day you here?" she asked in her deep, throaty voice.

"To be a detail-oriented person," I said weakly.

"So, why do you keep making mistakes?"

I swallowed before answering. "I double-checked my journal entry and couldn't see what is wrong. Could you let me know where the mistake is?"

Rowena glared at me and scoffed. "The detailed content is wrong. You can't pay a maintenance fee twice a month." She tapped her finger hard on the table.

Reluctantly, I showed her the backup documents I'd brought with me. "I emailed Tammy from Santa Ana's office, and she said there was a new policy released starting last month that we would receive two invoices for building maintenance."

"But tell them that we need only one invoice each month," Rowena demanded. "I don't want to see the fee booked twice."

"Okay, if you say so," I replied.

"Not because I say so, Rory!" she said, louder than before. "As an accountant, you have to think, not do everything automatically. Maybe when you were in your part-time job you could do everything on autopilot. Not in here. Use your brain!" Then she flapped her hand to shoo me out of her office.

As I expected, Rowena would make my life miserable by pulling all my journal entries and telling me to fix every single thing, like commas or dots, and she wanted all the journal entries reposted with a completed backup the same day. In her email, she double-underlined the word *completed* in red.

Stay strong, Rory, In two more hours, we get to go home.

Lena messaged me through Skype.

Thank you,

I messaged her back.

Unfortunately, my work wasn't done when everybody else left at five o'clock.

I was the last one in Myriad's office by the time I finally finished. Rowena had left at 4:30 because her son had a swimming lesson. As soon as she was gone, Lena had come to my desk and groused.

"When my daughter had a state math competition, Rowena almost didn't let me go, saying I made up the story." Lena had rolled her eyes. "Gosh, I hate her!"

Outside the building, the parking lot was empty but for a few cars. I looked around with a little hope, but Jason's car wasn't there. Climbing into my own, I let out a breath and closed my eyes. My right shoulder hurt as if someone were pressing a blunt stick between the muscles. With my opposite hand, I massaged the area for a while before heading home.

My stomach growled as I walked along the garden path to my apartment. The I-5 South had been bumper-to-bumper from a crash that had happened three miles before my exit ramp. I usually had some chocolates or a granola bar in my car for emergencies, but not this time.

As I approached, I noticed that the light inside my apartment was already on. Peter must have been home.

I took a deep breath and lifted the corner of my lips before opening the door. I didn't want to show him my dark, brooding side yet. Pushing the door open, I dropped my jaw at the sight of the mess in front of me.

Peter was mopping the floor. When he tilted his face at the sound of the door opening, dark-red liquid dripped from his hair, down his face, and onto his shirt. Then I noticed blotches of red on the kitchen counter, the wall, and on the ceiling.

"Oh my God, you are bleeding!" I cried, throwing my bag on the floor and rushing to him. Many bad scenarios flashed in my mind, but I froze mid-step as I smelled something fruity and sweet.

Flushing, Peter grinned as I reached out to touch the red liquid on his cheek and sniff it.

"It's not blood, it's—"

"Strawberry?" I said, irritated and tense.

He nodded. "And blueberry and raspberry. I wish my blood smelled this good," he joked.

I didn't smile as I stepped past him to see the mess in the kitchen more clearly. I saw a blender with less red liquid inside the glass than outside, its lid on the floor, the cutting board with strawberry stems on the countertop, half-full blueberry and raspberry containers, and a pint of orange juice.

"I was trying to make a juice smoothie," explained Peter from behind me. "I put everything in and then forgot to press down the lid. When I turned on the blender, the lid flew off, and juice spewed out all over the place. Sorry."

I looked straight at him as heat flushed through me. I was tired and hungry and irritated from dealing with my bitchy boss all day, traffic sucked, and now the apartment was a sticky disaster. Without saying anything, I walked straight to my room.

Peter followed. "Hey, Rory…Roomie? I'm sorry. I will—"

Slam!

I froze for a second because I hadn't meant to slam the door that hard. Sighing, I went straight to the bathroom to splash cold water on my face. Peter must have thought me childish, but at that moment, I just wanted to be alone.

I looked up to see my reflection in the mirror. Two red eyes on a wet face looked back at me. Water dripped down my cheeks and onto my blouse. Good thing my makeup was waterproof.

"Calm, Rory. Calm…," I said, closing my eyes. I patted my face with a towel when a knock on my bedroom door startled me.

"Rory, are you still mad? I'm sorry for the mess," Peter said through the door.

I sighed as another knock sounded. If I didn't open the door after several moments, he would probably knock again.

Peter's eyes scanned my face and my damp hair as I opened the door and stepped out of my room. He'd already changed into a clean T-shirt.

"Wow. You really had a bad day, didn't you?" he said, pointing his finger at the tip of my nose.

I batted his finger away and shuffled to the living room, but I couldn't help glancing back at the kitchen. It was already clean, and the blender, knife, and cutting board waited in the sink, but the sweet fruit smell lingered.

"I'll wash them, don't worry," said Peter, as if he could read my mind.

I nodded weakly and sat on the sofa. I hugged a dog-shaped pillow I'd bought at the Orange County Fair in my first year in California. It wasn't made for a sofa, but the size was perfect to snuggle while watching TV.

"My boss was on a rampage today and made me fix a never-ending list of mistakes just to torment me. I left the office late and got caught in traffic because of an accident on the freeway. When I finally home, you …" My voice trailed off, and I waved my hand toward him and the kitchen. As I felt the heat behind my eyes again, I bit my lip, not wanting him to see me cry.

"I'm sorry." Peter's head was down, but his brown eyes peeked up at me. "I didn't mean to mess up our home."

His words "our home" touched my heart and brought a smile to my face.

Tension on Peter's face seemed to melt away as he gazed at me carefully. "Are we good?" he asked.

"Unless you don't wash the blender," I answered.

Peter nodded. "I will," he said, lifting his right hand. Right after, his face twisted as a loud growl came from my stomach.

My cheeks filled with warmth. "I was so upset at the office, I forgot to stop and get dinner," I said.

"I already bought eggs. Do you want some?" he asked.

I thought he was joking, but he looked serious. "No more eggs today," I said, holding both hands up to stop him.

Peter smirked and went to the closet in the entrance hall to get his jacket. "Let's grab some food," he said, putting it on.

I looked at him, surprised.

"I'm hungry too."

"You haven't eaten yet?" I asked.

He pointed his head to the kitchen. "I thought to make smoothies for dinner, but …" Giving a half shrug, Peter came to me and extended his hand in invitation. "Come, I've given you enough mess today, so it's my treat."

He gave an affirming nod as I looked at him hesitantly. With a smile, I accepted his hand. Peter pulled me to my feet, and I almost hit my forehead on his collarbone. Standing close like this, my five feet and four inches seemed very petite compared to his height. I looked up at Peter, who was looking at me gently with his light-brown eyes. A smile crept over his lips as our eyes met, and I felt something inside me quivering for a second, and that ticked me off.

Jerking my hand away, I cleared my throat and said, "I'll grab my jacket."

Peter moved aside to give me room.

I felt his eyes on me as I went to the closet.

"What do you want to eat?" he asked, playing with the car key in his hand.

"Hmm. Have you tried Vietnamese food?" I asked, adjusting my jacket collar.

Peter shook his head. "Maybe next time. I don't feel adventurous tonight."

"Salad? Burger? Chinese food?"

"Chinese food will be fine," he nodded. "Do they have fried rice?"

With a big grin on my face, I gave him a look that said, "Really?"

His eyebrows rose. "What?"

"Nothing," I shrugged. "It's Chinese food. Of course they have fried rice."

Peter made a face and held the front door for me. "Chinese it is," he said, locking the door behind him.

A warm wind blew softly across the parking lot as we headed toward Peter's car. Summer was near, and the cold weather would be gone soon. That made me sad because I loved winter season in California.

My eyes widened as we approached a Tesla Model S sitting in his space. Its silver paint sparkled under the light above the carport.

"Wow, is it new? Did you just buy it?" I asked in awe, running my finger over its smooth hood. Peter must have a good salary because the Model S would cost him more than eighty thousand dollars. "What happened to your last car?"

"That was a rental, and today I only had to work a half day, so I had time to go to the dealership," he explained. "I like this car because it has a wider boot."

"Boot?" I asked, gazing down at his feet in confusion.

"Ah, I meant trunk," he corrected, blushing. "Sorry, I'm still adjusting to American terms."

"Oh, a boot is a trunk. Got it." I smiled and got into the passenger seat. "Ouch!" I yelped as my head hit the doorframe.

"Are you okay?" Peter asked. Our hands touched as he reached to check my head.

I moved my head away from his hand, wincing. "It's just lower than I expected."

"Yes, sorry, I should have told you," he said, then closed my door and hurried around to the driver's seat.

Peter climbed in more carefully than I had and studied my face for a moment before putting the car in reverse. "Where are we going?" he asked, glancing at the rearview mirror.

I told him the address.

Peter nodded and repeated the address to the car's navigation system. Slowly, he drove toward the main entrance of the apartment complex. Traffic was light as we hit the freeway. The digital clock on the dashboard showed 7:45 PM, past my usual dinnertime.

"Hey, can I ask you a question?" Peter said, his focus on the road.

Nodding, I couldn't take my eyes off the dashboard with its seventeen-inch touchscreen display. The leather seat was luxuriously comfortable and seemed to hug me from behind. The car was amazing!

"Your name is Rory, and Rory is a male name," he said.

"That's not a question," I teased.

A smile flickered across his lips.

"My real name is Aurorette, but my grandpa called me Rory, and I like it better," I explained.

Peter tilted his head and said, "Aurorette sounds so…French."

I chuckled, nodding. "My mom loved anything French. She spoke the language too." I watched pedestrians crossing the street as we stopped at a traffic light.

"That's cool. Did she speak any other languages?"

"Japanese and German," I answered.

"Japanese? That's a difficult language." Peter cocked his head.

"My grandpa was Japanese, and my grandma was German-Australian, which is why my mom could speak both languages," I explained.

Peter nodded understandingly while turning the steering wheel to the right to exit the freeway. "Yeah, I guess I can see that," he remarked. "Do you speak Japanese?"

"Nope." I shook my head.

"What about your dad? Is he American?" asked Peter.

I looked out the window as we passed an open-air mall. Its parking lot had been expanded but still wasn't enough to accommodate patrons' vehicles. From the freeway, I saw cars driving around and around the lot, waiting for a space.

"Yeah," I answered shortly. I didn't like questions about my dad because I didn't know anything about him other than he was an American.

Peter seemed to detect my reluctance and swiftly changed the subject, asking my opinion about his getting an annual pass for Disneyland.

The dinner with Peter was fun. He didn't mind trying any dishes I ordered, although he still ordered fried rice as a backup, just in case.

From the way he held the chopsticks, it was obvious he wasn't good at it. I offered to ask the waiter for a fork and a knife, but he refused. Laughing at him would have been rude, so I hid my smile when he tried to pick up a chunk of beef, and the meat kept slipping out of the chopsticks, back onto the plate. After several attempts, he got the meat to his mouth, and I couldn't help but clap my hands for him.

Yoo-Shi's advice about having a guy for a roommate—like having a brother or a cousin, she'd said—flashed through my mind as I glanced up at Peter reading his fortune cookie. He had the crazy idea that we should add "in bed" at the end of our fortunes, and we laughed at how that made the messages funny.

On the way home, I had a weird feeling that I'd known Peter for longer than a few days. Maybe because he was easygoing and good-natured. He was polite to the server when he asked for an extra plate. Ben, my last ex-boyfriend, had always been a bit arrogant. He had gotten a little better after I complained, but he seemed to lack compassion in general.

After we arrived, Peter went straight to the sink and washed the blender, chopping board, and knife. Since there were only a few dishes, I suggested he wash them by hand instead of in the dishwasher, and he did so without complaint.

Wearing a pair of long yellow gloves, he poured the dish liquid into one sink and ran hot water in it. Foam bubbled up and covered the dishes, then headed for the sink's edges. He must have poured more soap than needed.

Peter gave a weak smile as foam dripped over the edge to the floor as he washed. When he started rinsing, water sprayed everywhere because he turned the faucet on full blast. The front of his T-shirt and pants became soaked, which made me laugh uncontrollably until my sides hurt. It had been a while I had a good laugh.

CHAPTER 12

The following morning, Peter had already gone for his jog when I entered the kitchen. Gazing around, I let out a sigh that it was still intact and mess-free. No burning smell or wet floor. For thirty blissful minutes, I enjoyed the quiet morning by myself, listening to the birds chirping on the maple trees outside and drinking coffee.

Peter returned while I was in the shower, and he was still in his room when I left for work.

In the office, Rowena seemed to be in a good mood. She threw a thin smile as I bumped into her in the hallway. It was a rare sight; normally she looked straight ahead while rushing to wherever she needed to be.

Around ten, Val Tanaka sent an email to all accounting and finance employees to announce that White Water's team would be in our office next Friday, which was more than a week away. She mentioned that the founder's son might join the team and expected us to clean our workstations to make a good impression on the British team.

I groaned. I didn't have time for cleaning. But after lunch, Desiree took us to task tidying our cubicles, especially the refund clerks with their mountains of paperwork. She ordered them to put the stacks of papers in boxes and store them underneath their desks.

Even Rowena cleaned her office. Lena nudged at my elbow when she piled her papers neatly on the credenza.

During our cleaning time, Val visited our department. Her angular eyes sparkled, thanking us for our cooperation. Desiree's face beamed at the praise. If I had been in her shoes, I would have been happy to get the recognition too. However, since the conversation with Lena about how Desiree managed our division, my eyes were open to her prioritizing her reputation in front of Val than actual performance or taking care of her staff. She put most of her effort into creating the illusion that her department was tight-knit and high-performing rather than focusing on functionally making it a better department. If she'd cared more about her staff than her image, she could have been a good leader.

Lena and I took piles of used papers to the shredding room and passed Val, who was with Lisa Chia, another general manager, coming back from downstairs. Valerie nodded and smiled at us as we passed, but Lisa didn't make eye contact with us. Many people said Lisa was a snob, but no one would dare irritate her because Valerie was her friend. In some ways, Lisa and Rowena were in the same position—their bosses were also their friends—but I'd heard Lisa treated her staff nicer.

"I heard the founder's son is still in his forties, and handsome, too," said Lena as we entered the shredding room.

"How do you know?" I asked, letting her shred her papers first.

"From Theresa," Lena said, feeding the shredder. Theresa Cortez was Val's executive assistant and Lena's neighbor.

"To my aunt, Richard Gere is hot and handsome," I chuckled.

Lena grinned. "Well, that's possible. Anyway, we'll find out this Friday," she said. "If this guy is as hot as they said, it will be worth it to see."

I laughed.

"Hey, how's your roommate?" asked Lena, brushing paper debris from her hands as she moved aside to let me use the machine.

"He is a good person. Last night was our first time having dinner together, and it was fun," I said, feeding my papers into the machine. "But he is a jinx for my kitchen."

"What do you mean?" Lena asked, leaning on the cabinet with her arms folded in front of her chest.

I told her about the smoking eggs and the blender accident.

"Oh my God. He reminds me of my sixteen-year-old nephew who doesn't know anything about cooking because my sister spoils him," Lena said. "Your roommate must be a momma's boy."

I shrugged. "Maybe."

"He should have asked you if he didn't know what he was doing. Maybe his pride forbids him. You know how guys like to act tough and seem like they know everything," Lena said.

"True," I said. "Okay, I'm done shredding. Wanna go for lunch?"

Lena nodded. "Let's go. I'm hungry from all that cleaning," she said as we headed back to our cubicles.

CHAPTER 13

It was déjà vu.

I returned from my morning jog to the sight of Peter mopping the kitchen floor, with flour scattered on the cabinets and countertop. His eyes overflowed with guilt when he looked up at me.

"What happened *this* time?" I asked.

Peter held the mop in his right hand and scratched the back of his head with the other. I noticed the flour smeared on his chin and right cheek. "Well …" He cleared his throat. "I craved pancakes and thought to make them for breakfast and share them with you. Everything was going so well. I measured the flour and the eggs perfectly. When the recipe said to whisk the batter with a fork, I tried, but it made my wrist hurt… ."

"And?" I prompted since he'd paused.

"And I found your hand mixer in the lower cabinet. But when I turned it on …" He pursed his lips.

My eyes widened, prompting him to continue.

"I turned the mixer to the highest speed before inserting it in the bowl, and, you know…the flour and the eggs ended up flying everywhere," he explained, rubbing his nose and leaning on the mop handle with both hands. He glanced around at his handiwork.

I scanned the kitchen, calming the conflicted presence of the angel and the devil on my shoulders. The devil in me wanted to kick him to the curb, while the angel reminded me that people made mistakes from time to time.

"I already cleaned most of the mess," he offered.

I looked at him, speechless. How was it possible that the man his age couldn't cook simple things like boiled eggs and pancakes? What planet was he from? He was going to singlehandedly destroy my kitchen.

"Well," I cleared my throat, "have you ever heard of ready-mix pancakes? You just add water, shake it up, then pour the batter on the pan."

His eyes widened. "There is something like that?"

"On this planet, yes," I answered.

Grimacing slightly, Peter gazed at me. "Sorry."

"Did you really want to make them to share with me?" I asked.

Peter nodded. "Yes. I have a great recipe from someone who always made them for me. Fluffy but not too thick. I thought you would like it. But yeah, I'm not good at cooking."

"I can tell."

His gentle eyes looked at me shyly, then down to his feet like a little boy who'd made a mistake. I'd never known a young man like him. He was weird, but in a sweet way. Oddly, I felt a similar warm feeling spread in my heart, just like a few days ago, and that annoyed me.

"Give me the recipe, and we can make pancakes together on the weekend," I blurted without thinking.

His eyes brightened. "Really? You don't mind?"

"Just let me help next time. It's better than you messing up my kitchen again," I said. "But for the time being, please don't cook anything else."

Peter's cheeks turned red. "One day, I promise you, I'll cook you something delicious," he said as he took the mop out to the patio to dry.

I took two bananas from the tray on the counter and tossed one in his direction as he returned. Peter caught the banana and sat next to me. "Thanks for not being mad at me, Roomie," he said, peeling the banana.

"One more time and I *will* be mad," I said, winking and swallowing the last bite of my banana. "But I think it's time to add another rule." Standing up from my seat, I went to the fridge, grabbed a pen, and added a new rule to the list.

Chewing, Peter rose from his seat and stood behind me.

I wrote, *Rule #12P...*

"What is 12P?" he asked.

I lifted my left hand to stop him and continued writing. *Don't cook anything unless you are sure you can make it or Rory is around.*

"P is for Peter," I answered, pushing the cap onto the pen. "This rule is especially for you."

Peter scoffed. "I'm not that bad," he protested.

I chuckled.

"Well, at least my intentions were good," he corrected with a smile.

"Sorry, Roomie. When you get really good at cooking, we can remove the rule," I said, tapping his shoulder and heading toward my room to take a shower.

"But my intentions are good!" he called after me.

"Don't worry, I hear you!" I said, waving my hand but unable to stop smiling.

Peter might not have a talent for cooking, or he was a jinx for my kitchen, but his room was always tidy. His door had been ajar the day before, and I'd peeked. I was surprised to see all his books neatly placed on the shelves and no clothes on the floor. It was a contrast to my childhood friend's messy room. Peter's was the first clean guy's room I'd ever seen.

Suddenly, I felt a pang of shame for not keeping my room as tidy as his. My books were on the floor, my closet was messy, and sometimes my jacket or my bag was on the floor. If I was in a hurry, I didn't make my bed. It was clear that I needed to make a change. Starting that day, I forced myself to tidy up and make my bed every morning before work.

On Saturday afternoon, a few days after the pancake disaster, I was coming back from my weekly grocery shopping when a stocky lady of about fifty came out of Peter's room. She had a green basket of cleaning supplies in her left hand and a vacuum cleaner in her right. Her gray hair was wrapped in a large polka-dot scarf with some locks of hair sticking out.

"It's almost done," she said as she passed Peter sitting on the sofa playing a car race game on TV.

"Thanks, Claudia," he replied.

"*De nada.*" She smiled and stepped outside.

I read *Go-Green Maid* printed on the back of her shirt.

"Is she who I think she is?" I asked Peter as I stood in front of the refrigerator. Keeping his eyes at his game, Peter nodded.

"Why is she here?" I blinked, genuinely confused by her presence.

The cleaning lady returned and went straight to his room again.

"Playing tennis," Peter answered, casting a brief glance back at me, then rolled his eyes. Turning his attention to his game again, he continued, "Of course she comes to clean my room. I've already arranged for her to come twice a week, on Wednesdays and Saturdays. She'll be coming again on Wednesday, so you can ask her to clean your room too," Peter added cheerfully.

My mouth dropped open. Holding a bag of white bread in my hand, I froze in the middle of the kitchen, staring at him. Now I knew why his room was always tidy. Obviously, his idea of cleanliness was different than mine. Keeping my room tidy meant I had to put my stuff away properly every day. For him, it meant hiring someone to pick up after him.

"But you can do it yourself, can't you?" I said after a long pause.

Peter shrugged. "She's better and faster."

I fell silent on his pragmatic thought. Still, cleaning services were expensive—at least $65 for one room, not including a tip for each visit. That was a week's worth of groceries for me.

"So, are you planning to hire her to do your weekly cleaning too?" I asked carefully, since I sensed that his answer would surprise me.

Peter stopped playing and scoffed, looking hurt. "Of course not. I can throw the trash into the garbage bin outside. But yes, she'll take care of the rest. I already gave her my cleaning schedule," he said, pointing his finger up and grinning with self-satisfaction.

I gave a weak laugh at his unique personality. My head whipped around to the front door as I heard a knock. I turned to see a delivery guy holding some clothes covered with clear plastic, peeking through the door the cleaning lady had left open as she continued her back-and-forth trips.

"Sunshine Cleaners for Mr. Peter Ryder," the guy called, smiling at me.

"Yes," Peter answered, standing up from his seat. From his pocket, he took a wad of bills and paid the delivery guy. He must have sensed that my eyes were following his every move, because he stopped, glancing at me.

"They can clean my clothes better than I would." Peter's voice sounded defensive, although I hadn't said anything.

"Yeah, I've heard that recently," I commented. "Look, Peter, I'm not fond of strangers coming in and out of my apartment. So, is there anyone else I should know about?" I deliberately raised my eyebrows and tilted my head.

Peter didn't seem to catch my sarcasm and nodded. "My massage therapist will be here tomorrow. If you'd like, you can get a massage after me. It's only $120 per person," he answered.

My hands dropped to my sides. Now I'd heard enough. I had to limit all these people coming into my apartment. Heading straight to the list on the fridge, I added rule #13: *No strangers come into this apartment except for the cleaning lady.*

CHAPTER 14

Peter had lived with me for more than a week, and Aunt Amy still remained unaware of his presence. I'd attempted to contact her, but she seemed especially busy, perhaps because Easter was around the corner, and she was busy preparing for the event.

After dinner, I sat down and typed a text informing her that I had a new roommate. Since Peter would be home until late, and if my aunt decided to yell at me, no one would hear but me.

> *Auntie, I know you hate texting, but I wanted to tell you that Lizzy moved to Seattle, and I have a new roommate.*

Then I pressed the send button and set my phone next to me on the sofa.

My eyes were staring at the TV, but my mind wasn't focusing on the movie. My stomach fluttered each time I glanced at the phone. Ten minutes passed before it pinged with an incoming text.

In a flash, I picked up the cell phone and flicked its screen open to read my aunt's message.

> *Good, I'm glad. Hope your new roommate is as helpful and reliable as Lizzy.*

> *So far, yes,*

I answered.

My aunt sent two thumbs-up and added that she was in a meeting with her church friends, which meant the conversation was over.

I was stunned but happy at the same time. Although uncertainty still lingered in my chest, my aunt's responses indicated that she wasn't concerned. At least she now knew I had a new roommate.

Consoling myself, I poured a glass of wine and sipped slowly. The wine relaxed my body and made me warm. A different movie was on by then, but I didn't care much. Holding the dog-shaped pillow, I leaned my head on it and tried to focus on the TV screen.

The sound of a door being slammed startled me. Not sure how long I'd dozed off, I sat up and rubbed my eyes. It was around eleven thirty.

"Ugh," I grunted as another door slammed close by. I realized that it must have been Sam, the eighteen-year-old son of my upstairs neighbor, coming back from partying with his friends as he often did when his parents were not home.

My eyelids were heavy as I staggered to my feet and walked to the kitchen to turn off the light. Then my ears caught Peter's voice coming through the kitchen window I'd left open for the breeze. When I opened the door and looked out, I didn't see any sign of Peter.

"Maybe my ears trick me." I glanced once more time. "I should go to bed."

I was about to close the door when I saw a shadow emerging from the dense bushes just to my right. It was Peter, and he wasn't alone. He was talking to someone about his own height, standing about ten feet away from me. His guest's face was also unclear, since they were standing under the shadow of a magnolia tree, but I could see the other man had ginger hair.

Peter and the ginger-haired man seemed to be having a serious conversation or perhaps an argument from the way they moved their hands. Peter grabbed the man's hand when he turned to leave. I couldn't hear the conversation clearly but picked up odd words as the breeze blew them in my direction. Peter's voice was pleading.

"You can't…You're the best…I love you…always love you…always care… Please don't go!" And Peter pulled the man into his arms.

I stepped back inside and closed the door quietly, my heart pounding. The incomplete sentences I'd just heard kept running through my mind again. I couldn't believe it, but I'd witnessed Peter confess his love to a ginger-haired man.

I sighed. Suddenly, I felt my chest being pricked by blunt needles.

My morning alarm buzzed many times as I kept pressing the snooze button. I'd been awake since three in the morning but didn't want to get out of bed. I felt a pang in my chest as I remembered last night. Rolling on my back, I stared at the ceiling and threw an arm across my forehead.

I think I know why.

"Rule number nine, Rory! You are the one who wrote that rule," I whined, slapping my forehead.

Composing my feelings and thoughts, I got up and washed my face in the bathroom sink. After drying off, I walked into the kitchen and found Peter's tea mug was already in the sink.

"He must be on his morning jog," I murmured, making a cup of coffee for myself. I pressed the button, and the machine hummed gently. Soon, my coffee was ready, and I took the cup to the patio to enjoy the fresh morning air and try to forget about last night.

Outside, the sky was partly cloudy, and the fresh breeze embraced me. With a deep breath, I put the cup on the table and sat on the patio sofa. A mockingbird perched on the magnolia tree sang a medley of songs, which to my sleepy mind sounded like a lullaby. I was tempted to close my eyes but worried I'd end up late for work.

"Maybe just five minutes," I mumbled.

Next thing I knew, someone was poking my shoulder.

"Aaahhhhhh!" I jumped from the sofa, knocking the cup off the table, and it shattered on the floor.

I stared at Peter bending over me, with his forefinger still extended towards my shoulder. He carried his running shoes in his other hand.

"Geez, what are you doing?" I said, raising my voice. "You scared me."

"I didn't mean to startle you, but you were snoring," Peter said. He also gestured toward the corner of his mouth if he wanted to say, *"You were drooling too."*

My palm was a bit wet as I wiped the corner of my mouth. *How embarrassing!* "I should clean up this mess," I said, heading inside the house.

Peter's mouth twisted into a smile as I pushed past him.

"Did I snore loudly?" I asked, opening the closet door to get a broom and a dustpan.

Peter shook his head. "You were purring like a cat," he said, pressing his smile. "I didn't know you were so cute when you slept."

"Shut it!" I hissed as my cheeks filled with warmth.

Our hands brushed unintentionally when Peter took the broom and dustpan from me. My hand tingled at the contact like static electricity. Watching him sweep the floor, I hid my hand behind my back.

"Why did you fall asleep on the patio? Didn't you sleep well last night?" he asked over his shoulder.

I bit my lower lip, wondering if he was aware I'd been awake when he came home. "Not really. When I have a lot going on at work, I don't really sleep well," I lied.

Peter nodded and brought the dustpan to the trash can to throw away the shattered coffee mug.

"Thanks," I said as he put them back inside the closet.

"No worries," he said. "Well, you are lucky I'm a good roommate. I was so tempted to take your picture while you were drooling."

"Did you?" My eyes widened.

Peter winked. "I told you, I'm a good roommate." Then he waved his hand and headed to his room. "Time to shower."

I watched him go, still feeling his skin on mine. Letting out a sigh, I returned to my room. As I brushed my teeth, I heard buzzes from my phone on the bedside table and hoped it wasn't Rowena already.

I flicked open the phone, finding the text message was from Peter. My brows wrinkled together as I read his text.

Rory, I ran out of toilet paper. Do you have extra? Can I borrow it now?

I blinked at the message. I remembered about putting five extra rolls under the bathroom sink in Peter's room right before he'd moved in.

I replied,

you can use the rolls under the sink.

A second later, another ping came.

I used them all.

Huh?

Wait—five extra rolls under the sink and one, *still new*, on the holder, meaning six rolls of toilet paper gone in such a short time. He didn't need as much toilet paper as a woman would use, right?

Alarmed, I texted him back.

You used five rolls of toilet paper already? What did you do with them?

His answer came shortly.

I've used them to wipe the sink or if the floor is wet. Sorry.

I felt my jaw drop. Unbelievable! He could have asked me if he didn't have cleaning towels. I had plenty!

"Patience, Rory…patience." I took a deep breath and exhaled slowly. I replied to him.

Sure. I'll give you one.

Another ping came.

Could you put it in front of the bathroom door? My room isn't locked. Thanks, Roomie!

I groaned. From my closet, I took one roll of toilet paper, two clean hand towels, and one cleaning rag and took them to his room. Turning the knob, I pushed the unlocked door open and entered his room. My eyes scanned his entire space for the first time. The blanket was folded on the end of his bed, and his jackets hung in a row on the wall hooks. There were books stacked neatly on the floor by his bed.

My phone vibrated with an incoming text from Peter again.

Did you bring the TP yet?

Impatient little twerp! Rolling my eyes, I put the roll and the towels on the floor next to the bathroom door.

"Peter, the toilet paper is on the floor!" I called from outside, rapping my knuckles loudly against the door on purpose. "I don't want to see you naked, so don't come out till I leave, okay?"

"Damn, Rory. I'm not deaf!" Peter yelled back from inside. "And how will I know you're gone?"

"How long do you think it will take me to walk across an eleven-by-twelve room?" I said, trying not to laugh. "Just wait ten seconds, okay? I'm leaving now!"

I grinned as I scurried across his room and closed the door. He was a funny guy!

I was in the living room with my notebook bag, ready to go to work, when Peter came out. His blue shirt looked good on him.

He gave a shy smile as our eyes met. "Thanks for the toilet paper, Rory," he said, taking his work shoes out of the hall closet.

"Sure," I shrugged, waving my hand. "Just don't forget to buy some for yourself, okay? There is a Target around the corner, or you can go with me to Costco—then we can split the cost of a bulk pack. Don't buy the hand towels or cleaning rags because I have plenty and will give you some."

"Thank you," Peter replied. "If you don't come home late, let's go to Costco tonight."

I nodded. "Sounds good. I need to buy some toothpaste and soap too."

Peter smiled and went out the front door, holding it for me as I followed him out.

CHAPTER 15

The team of five from White Water Inc. was finally in the office. On Friday morning, we had a quick introduction meeting in the theater room downstairs to accommodate almost thirty people, including the guests and Dwayne Bauer, the CFO of Myriad, who had flown in from New York and only came to Southern California for special occasions like this.

Val, Dwayne, some of the general managers, and the White Water team filled the first and second rows near the podium. There were a few whispers in the room, but most of us sat quietly. Dwayne seemed to sense the tension. When he was walking to the podium, he surprised us by smiling widely and waving his hands, which was out of character for him.

"Good morning, everyone. It's great to finally have a meeting where everyone can count past ten," he said energetically.

Everyone laughed politely.

Dwayne didn't seem satisfied and shook his head. "Now, tell me, does anyone know why God invented economists?" he asked, leaning forward.

Startled by the question, we looked at each other, shaking our heads.

"No one?" Dwayne prompted. Since no one said a word, he continued, "So we accountants could have someone to laugh at."

It wasn't that funny, but it was enough to melt the tension in the room. Most of Myriad's employees chuckled, but not the White Water team. They remained stoic.

After a brief introduction, Dwayne gave the podium to the White Water team leader. His name was Ruben Franklin, a big guy in his mid-forties. His suit jacket strained around his midsection. Lena whispered to me that she recognized a resemblance to Rowan Atkinson. I bit my lip to keep from grinning, since I'd watched my fair share of *Mr. Bean*. We had to lower our heads to hide our grins.

Ruben spoke about his business background and how long he had been working with White Water, then introduced the other members of his team: Kimberly Johnson, Vyhaan Jay, Samantha Darcy, and Phil Campbell. They would work with the finance and accounting department while Ruben worked privately with Valerie, Desiree, and Dwayne.

"The team looks tense. I've always thought Brits would be as lively as Mr. Bean," whispered Lena to me, crossing her eyes to imitate him.

I ducked my head again to hide my smirk.

After the meeting, we got an email from Dwayne saying that Myriad Beverage would work with the White Water team first. Desiree arrived at my desk with Vyhaan Jay. Vy, as he wanted to be called, was in charge of an account receivable I'd created and wanted to analyze the report. Vy was in his early thirties and had dark-brown eyes and a thin build, and he tended to rub his long, mussed-up hair whenever he was thinking.

I was in the midst of preparing the report for my meeting with Vy when Rowena called me to her office. As I reached to open her door, someone opened it from inside, revealing Lena with a crumpled face. She didn't look at me as she slipped out.

"Sit!" said Rowena sharply, pointing with her chin to the chair in front of her.

I obeyed, eyeing the two empty Coke cans and cookie crumbs on the paper plate beside them. Everybody knew Rowena had a sweet tooth.

"In the meeting room, I saw you and Lena giggling when Dwayne introduced White Water's team to us. Aren't you old enough to understand that this partnership is important for us? Do you think they didn't see you? What were you laughing about?" she asked in her condescending tone.

Scratching my temple, I looked at her with confusion. Everyone was expected to pay attention to the meeting. If she saw Lena and me giggling, didn't that mean she was watching us the whole time?

I started to get a bad feeling in the pit of my stomach as I realized Rowena was picking on us. *For what purpose?*

"Yes, I understand the importance of this partnership. However, I don't think our giggling could jeopardize it," I said carefully in a flat tone. "We were giggling because Mr. Franklin looks like Mr. Bean. Everyone could see that, and even Mr. Franklin admitted it, too."

Rowena seemed unsatisfied. Frowning, she flicked a lock of her auburn hair from her eyes. "No, I think you were giggling about something else. Maybe about Vyhaan's ugly hair or because Phil looks girly? Or maybe you were making fun of me because this red cardigan makes me look fat? I know I'm not like Lena, always skinny and happy. Now *you* tell me the truth!" Her deep, throaty voice sounded deeper as she growled.

Her words took me aback. For a long time, I'd trained myself to focus on my job and not on her attitude. I didn't understand her sudden paranoia. There were too many tasks on my plate to pay attention to her cardigan. And Vyhaan's hair? Or Phil? What was she even talking about?

"Well," I said, sitting up straighter, "I already told you the truth. I don't understand what you're talking about with your red cardigan or Vyhaan's hair or any of the rest of that."

Rowena's face flushed, and she abruptly turned to face her monitor.

I pressed my lips, maintaining my calm posture, and quietly left her office. Feeling baffled, I returned to my cubicle and sat staring at my computer for some time. *Rowena's lost it this time! What's wrong with her?*

I thought Lena would say something about her meeting with Rowena, but I was wrong. She was silent until the day was over and then left without saying good night to me or anyone else. I sent a text to her.

Are you okay?

But she didn't answer. She still hadn't responded to my text when Peter and I prepared to go to Costco that evening. Deep down, I hoped she wasn't so upset with Rowena that she would quit. If she did quit, I didn't know how I would handle Rowena on my own. My life in the office would be unbearable.

We arrived at Costco an hour before closing and found a parking spot quickly. Peter pushed the shopping cart while I flashed my membership card to an employee at the entrance.

"How much do you pay for membership?" asked Peter as we passed the electronics and moved to the fruit section.

"The annual fee is $65 for the basic membership, but my aunt pays for it," I answered. "I think I'll cancel it next year, though."

"Why?" Peter asked.

I shrugged. "Buying in bulk is expensive on the front end. Plus, I don't have anywhere to store it all. Most of the time, I only come here for toilet paper and gasoline, so I don't really save more than I would spend on a membership."

Peter nodded as he grabbed a bunch of bananas to put in the cart. After getting everything on our list, we split up; I went to the women's clothing section, and he went to the men's. We agreed to meet by the checkout lanes in ten minutes.

I was about to decide between a pair of shorts and a skort when I caught a familiar figure out of the corner of my eyes. It was Ben, my ex-boyfriend. He was perusing the electronics section across the aisle with a tall, thin girl with wavy blonde hair. She looked older than me and had high cheekbones and bright-blue eyes. Her slim figure looked perfect in the tight-fitting print dress she wore. She laughed merrily as Ben whispered something in her ear, his hand resting against her flat waist.

I swallowed hard. That was the type of girl he liked: thin and tall. I wasn't fat, but I wasn't skinny either, and nowhere near tall. Ben had said I was over-weight. Back then, I'd been foolish and tried hard to lose weight for him but couldn't get thin enough to please him, which had led to a ridiculous argument and his cheating on me.

My shopping mood dead on the floor of Costco, I dropped the items I was holding to go find Peter. Bumping into Ben and his new girlfriend was the last thing I wanted.

I found Peter standing with his back to me, holding a shirt. He turned as I approached.

"Are you done?" I asked, trying to sound casual. "I'm ready if you are."

"Okay," he said, putting the shirt back on the pile.

We walked toward the cashier, and along the way, I couldn't help glancing back to see if Ben was still in electronics, but he had disappeared.

Once we'd made it to Peter's car, loaded the groceries in the "boot," and gotten in, he looked at me and asked, "Are you okay? You've been quiet since we left."

"I'm good." I nodded and glanced out the window at the Costco building fading behind us as our car hit the main road.

"Who is he?" asked Peter.

I blinked and turned to him. "Who is who?"

"The guy with the blond in the electronics section." Peter glanced at me with understanding in his eyes.

I let out a breath, peered out the windshield, and glanced at him. "You saw it."

Peter gave a half shrug. "I was looking for you, and I saw you looking at them," he said in a matter-of-fact tone. "You looked like you were having some kind of inner battle."

His observation skills were sharp.

"Do you still like him?" asked Peter.

I lifted my head to look at his face. "Why do you ask that?"

Peter pressed his back against his seat. "I think it's normal if a girl still loves her ex-boyfriend after they break up," he finally said.

"I don't think I still love him," I said slowly, choosing my words carefully. "If I ever loved him. I just felt defeated. To be honest, I would've preferred him to tell me he was no longer interested in me rather than cheating behind my back. I know I'm not pretty or thin like his girlfriend now, but I wasn't stupid." I sighed, squeezing my shoulders up to my ears and letting them fall back.

"That's his loss," said Peter firmly.

I raised an eyebrow. "What do you mean?"

"He only looked at you physically. If I can say what I think honestly, you are a sweet and considerate girl. And smart, too, if a bit naïve. Overall, you are interesting girl to be with," he said.

Because of the street lights, my eyes tricked me into seeing his cheeks blushing. Was it the bad lighting, or was he really blushing?

"Don't cry over spilled milk. You deserve someone better than your ex," he added, tilting his head to me.

I chuckled. "Thanks for the vote of confidence, Roomie," I said, punching his shoulder playfully.

Peter smiled and looked back at the road, his long fingers gripping the steering wheel loosely.

I glanced at him before shifting my eyes to the window. Although he wouldn't be interested in me, it was nice to have his emotional support.

CHAPTER 16

The apartment was quiet Saturday morning as I folded my clean laundry in the living room. Peter had left early to pick up his friends to stay in Santa Monica for someone's birthday until Sunday evening. It sounded nice to have money and be able to enjoy privileges like that. I was jealous but didn't feel regret over the lifestyle I was used to. I preferred to save any penny I earned. With Peter's lump-sum rent payment, I'd paid off my credit card and saved some money to move to a one-bedroom apartment. I also still sold some stuff that I never used anymore through Amazon Marketplace and eBay. Better to convert the clutter into cash and increase my bank balance.

My phone buzzed with an incoming text. The name on the display screen made my heart jump: Jason.

Good morning, Rory, and have a fantastic Saturday.

He also asked if I had changed my mind about having brunch with him tomorrow. Jason was one of the politest people I'd ever met.

My lips curled into a smile, and I replied to his message.

Looking forward to it.

Another buzz alerted me to Jason's reply of a smile emoji.

Jason had been unusually nice to me lately and had sat with me during lunch on Friday. He might have been interested in dating, but for me, Jason was just a friend.

After finishing my laundry, I went to my room to find two long dresses I no longer wore, but they were still good enough to sell. I'd bought them a month after I'd started dating Ben. Those dresses would be better off in someone else's closet than mine. I hung them up to take pictures for posting on eBay. The doorbell rang as I was keying in their asking prices.

I found Lizzy standing in front of my door, smiling widely, with a backpack slung on her shoulder and a computer bag on her right side.

"Oh my God, Lizzy!" I cried as we hugged. "Why didn't you tell me you were in town again?"

She followed me inside, took off her shoes, and put her bags behind the sofa, then walked to the kitchen sink to wash her hands. "I'm sorry for this surprise visit. This is an unplanned business trip because my coworker, who was assigned to be here, had food poisoning the day before his flight. No one was available but me. So, I flew in Thursday night and worked like crazy until this morning. My flight home isn't till tonight, so I thought I could stop by and relax here for a few hours. Sorry for stopping by without calling," Lizzy explained, drying her hands on the towel.

"No, I'm happy you're here," I said, opening the fridge. "Orange juice or soda?"

"Do you have coffee?" asked Lizzy. "I need a boost."

"Got it," I said, closing the fridge, and then preparing to grind beans in the coffee machine.

"Hey, how's 'the dude'? Is he around?"

I laughed at her use of the nickname I'd given Peter the day he moved in. "Nope," I said, giving her a clean mug. "He is in Santa Monica with friends, celebrating one of his coworkers' birthdays. What a lucky dude!"

"Jealous much?" Lizzy smiled, gazing around the living room.

I nodded, pouring coffee into her mug. "Yup, I'm jealous." Then I told her about the boiled eggs, the blender, and the pancakes.

Lizzy snorted between her laughs as I told her about my embarrassing moment in my Hello Kitty sleep shirt.

"So you never wore it again?" Lizzy's eyes twinkled.

I nodded. "Not anymore, although I still keep it. That sleep shirt is old but so comfy."

"Wear it again when you live alone in your next apartment," she suggested.

Before I could reply, the doorbell rang.

"Is that Peter?" asked Lizzy.

I shrugged, glancing surreptitiously at the kitchen clock. "He won't be back until tomorrow," I answered, walking to the front door. "Besides, he has a key."

I shrieked at the sight of a middle-aged lady standing in front of my door with a Gucci bag hanging from the crook of her elbow. Next to her feet was a suitcase.

"Auntie?!?"

Aunt Amy had a bob hairstyle, stern eyes, and thin lips. Her poker face was usually perceived as cold or harsh, but deep down, her heart could melt ice.

"You don't look happy to see me, Rory," she said, entering. Her dark-brown eyes twinkled as she took off her jacket and hat and handed them to me.

I didn't understand why she was wearing a jacket on such a warm day.

She smiled at Lizzy, who was standing behind me.

"Of course I'm happy to see you, Auntie," I said, hanging her things in the closet. "I'm just surprised. If I'd known you were coming, I'd have picked you up at the airport."

Lizzy gave Aunt Amy a warm hug.

"I thought you moved out," said my aunt as Lizzy led her to the living room.

"Yes, Auntie, I've already moved to Seattle with Terry. I'm here for a client," Lizzy explained, sitting next to Aunt Amy.

Aunt Amy gave Lizzy a warm smile. "Should I expect an invitation soon?" teased my aunt.

Lizzy chuckled. "Maybe, but not too soon. We need to save up first," said Lizzy.

My aunt nodded, looking satisfied with her answer. "That's good. Never marry without savings," she said. She leaned toward me. "Rory could learn from you."

I groaned inwardly. My aunt tended to compare me with others. *Why can't she be satisfied with who I am?*

"Rory is smart. She would be better off than I am," said Lizzy, noticing a sudden change in my face. "Can I get you something to drink, Auntie?"

"Tea," Aunt Amy said as she looked around the living room. "You and your new roommate have kept this apartment well, Rory."

I forced a smile.

From the kitchen, Lizzy widened her eyes, titled her head to my aunt, signaled me to tell her about Peter.

"Speaking of your roommate," Aunt Amy said, turning to me, "how do you like her? What does she do for a living? Is she helpful?"

My cheeks warmed. "Uh…Auntie, about my that …" I paused as Lizzy brought a cup of hot green tea and placed it on the coffee table in front of my aunt.

"Thanks, dear," she said to Lizzy, then shifted her eyes back to me. "Yes?"

I wrenched my fingers, looking down at the floor. For a moment, I was pulled back to the moment I got a C-minus in eighth-grade science.

"Yes?" my aunt prompted again. She took the cup, brought it to her lips, and sipped expectantly.

"My roommate is a guy—his name is Peter Ryder," I said in one breath.

Aunt Amy froze for a couple beats before putting the cup back on the table slowly. Her eyes looked straight into mine.

My throat tightened as if someone were choking me.

"After I left, Rory tried hard to find a female roommate, Auntie," Lizzy defended me. "But no one was acceptable. Either a mom with a kid, a college student, or a—"

Aunt Amy lifted her hand to stop Lizzy. "Would you mind leaving us alone, Liz?" she asked in a gentle, soft voice that was certainly the calm before the storm.

Lizzy exhaled slowly as she stood and threw a glance at me before marching out to the patio. She sat on the outdoor chair, looking skyward as though praying for mercy for me.

"What happened?" asked Aunt Amy, folding her hands on her lap with her back straightened against the seat.

Managing to steady my voice, I told her what had been going on since Lizzy left—my ramen diet, connecting to Jane, and then her brother Peter.

Pride flashed in Aunt Amy's eyes as I admitted my fault. "So, where's Peter now? Can I meet him?" she asked.

I shook my head. "Unfortunately, no. He is in Santa Monica and won't be back until late tomorrow."

Aunt Amy leaned forward and picked up her tea again. Her face was placid, and it was hard to tell if she was upset or not.

"I'm sorry. I had no choice," I said, still trying to read her expression.

"You should've told me," Aunt Amy said in a flat tone.

I looked down and said, "If I had, you would have come to rescue me. Wouldn't you say I am a grown woman now and need to learn to manage my life? Besides, I didn't have the heart to ask for your help after you spent your time raising me."

We both stared across the room, silence filling the air for several moments.

"What did Rick say about Peter? He's already met him, right?" asked Aunt Amy.

I nodded. "Yes, he did. Rick was here when I accepted Peter's offer."

My aunt exhaled and said, "If Rick approves of him, and Peter already paid you for six months, there is nothing I can do."

I stared wide-eyed at her in disbelief and relief at the same time. She wasn't going to put up a big fuss about Peter! *Have I been overthinking?*

Aunt Amy gave a thin smile and signaled me to let Lizzy join us again. As Lizzy entered the room, she asked with her eyes if everything was okay, and I signaled that I'd tell her later.

"Will you stay here tonight?" I asked my aunt, glancing at her belongings again.

Aunt Amy shook her head. "No, I'm staying with Aunt Sophie in Ocean Island for a day before joining a group of teachers from my church in Baja. We're going to teach health education for young, poor, and pregnant teens there."

I wasn't surprised about her volunteer work, but I was surprised by the name she'd mentioned. "Aunt Sophie? Aunt Sophie *Kim*?" I asked.

Aunt Amy nodded.

"I didn't know she lived in California. Since when?" I asked. "I thought you guys lost contact when we moved back to Boston."

My aunt nodded again. "Yes. But thanks to Gail, who happened to know Sophie's sister, Sunny, we reconnected."

"I can drive you down if you'd like. I'd love to meet her too," I offered.

"No need. Sophie's son will drive me," Aunt Amy replied.

"Wait? Her son, you said?" I asked. "Do you mean Oppa Alfred, the Goose?"

Aunt Amy held her smile. "You still remember the nickname."

I chuckled. It would be hard to forget my childhood best friend: he was geeky and chubby with thick glasses and buck teeth. His eyes always widened and sparkled to see food in front of him, like Peter and his fried rice.

"Does he live here now?" I asked.

"Yes, in Los Angeles."

"Wow, I can't believe he moved to California too. It's been…what…ten or eleven years since the last time I saw him in Colorado?" I turned to Lizzy, who gave me a questioning look. "Remember the picture of a chubby boy with thick glasses wearing a pumpkin costume? That's Alfred, my childhood best friend."

Lizzy's mouth made a big O with crinkles around her eyes. At the time I'd shown her the picture, we were discussing the geekiest boys in our lives.

"Alfred will pick me up for dinner and then drop me off at his mom's house," said Aunt Amy. "Join us for dinner, Lizzy."

Lizzy shook her head. "I'm sorry, Auntie. I'll have to take a rain check. My flight leaves this evening. Maybe next time."

"Our restaurant won't be too far from the airport. I'll ask Alfred to drive you there."

"Thanks, Auntie. If it isn't convenient for Alfred, I'll take an Uber."

"Don't worry. Alfred won't mind. And I think he will be here soon."

CHAPTER 17

Alfred Kim arrived to pick us up for dinner at five o'clock, and I didn't recognize him because he was a foot taller than me, and there were no more thick glasses or bunny teeth. He'd turned into a handsome young man with an athletic, muscular build—totally different from the geeky boy I'd known.

"I wouldn't have recognized you if I bumped into you on the street," I said after Aunt Amy introduced him to Lizzy. I stared at him for a while, trying to find the old Alfred in him. "You look so different!"

"You mean handsome?" My aunt winked at me.

I laughed, nodding, and looked up at Alfred. He seemed happy to see me again and couldn't take his eyes off me.

"Yeah, I'm not a nerd anymore. You look different too, Rory—prettier, if I may say so. No more frizzy hair and braces," said Alfred, gazing at me in admiration, enough to make my cheeks warm.

"Sophie says you are a national champion in Tae Kwon Do. It is true?" said Aunt Amy with a smile. "Tell us about that."

Alfred smiled bashfully. "That was a long time ago, before I finished college. Now I'm getting fat from lack of exercise." His hand tapped his stomach.

Aunt Amy chuckled, her eyes brightening as she glanced back and forth between Alfred and me.

"What do you do for a living, Alfred?" asked Lizzy.

"I'm a senior IT analyst in the R&D department at Core Life Science. I worked in its branch in Colorado last year, until I got promoted and moved to the headquarters in LA," Alfred answered.

Lizzy's eyes widened. "You're working for my competitor in heart products. I'm working for R&D with Kambusha Science!"

Now Alfred's eyes got wider. "This is my first time meeting someone from Kambusha. People who work there are smart! By the way, I heard that at the beginning of next year your company is going to release the most effective heartbeat monitor on the market. Is that true?"

From the way Lizzy looked at him, I could tell her opinion of my childhood friend had changed. "You've already heard about that? You're very resourceful."

Alfred smiled. "It's brilliant! Most heart monitors get results from patients wearing them for a whole day, but this new product would get results in just an hour. That's amazing!" he said.

My gaze shifted from Alfred to Lizzy and back to Alfred again. I didn't have a clue what they were talking about but pretended with the occasional, casual nod.

"I don't want to interrupt the conversation, but we need to go. My reservation is at six," said Aunt Amy.

Alfred nodded, and we all headed toward the door. I retrieved my aunt's jacket from the closet and gave it to her.

"By the way, Alfred, would you mind dropping Lizzy at the airport so you can continue the conversation? She has a flight to catch at seven," said my aunt, slipping on her jacket.

"Airport?" Alfred raised his eyebrow and turned to Lizzy. "You aren't in Irvine? Oh, I get it—you are at Kambusha headquarters in Seattle, right?"

Lizzy smiled. "Yes, I just came down to troubleshoot a client, but I'm based in Seattle."

"Where are we going, Auntie?" I asked, finally getting the chance to speak. "Do we need to take two cars?"

Aunt Amy shook her head. "I don't think we need to take two cars. The restaurant and the airport are north and Aunt Sophie's house south. So, after we are done, we can drop you off back here on the way, right, Alfred?" My aunt turned to Alfred, who was still talking to Lizzy.

Alfred's head whipped around with a question in his eyes.

My aunt repeated the question.

"Yes, you're right on the way," he assured me.

"And what is the restaurant name?" I asked for the second time, feeling jealous of Lizzy talking so warmly with Alfred because they worked in the same industry. I wanted to ask Alfred many questions after we'd lost contact for so long. Perhaps he didn't miss me after all.

I sighed as I locked the door. My aunt, Lizzy, and Alfred were already walking toward the parking lot and hadn't even bothered to wait for me.

"Alfred is an amazing," Lizzy whispered to me when we were in the car. "At such a young age, he has deep knowledge about his work. Maybe I should hijack him to work with my company." She sat forward and tapped his shoulder, saying, "Hey, Alfred, are you interested in working with Kambusha?"

Alfred grinned at her in the rearview mirror.

"Maybe you should work with Lizzy, *Oppa*," I said, looking at Alfred through the rearview mirror.

"What did you call him?" asked Lizzy.

"*Oppa*," I laughed.

Alfred laughed too.

Then I explained to Lizzy that *oppa*, in Korean, was a term used by a girl for her older brother or boyfriend. Since Alfred was older than I was, it had been proper for me to call him *oppa* when we were growing up.

"Of course, I can't call him *Oppa* anymore because his girlfriend would be mad at me," I teased.

Alfred's ears became red. "I don't have a girlfriend yet."

"You are young and handsome. Girls will fall in love with you easily," said my aunt, chuckling.

Alfred smiled and said, "Thanks, Auntie."

Alfred's car slowed as we got closer to the John Wayne Airport. The traffic was heavy as we approached the drop-off area. A car honked behind us as Alfred tried to find a spot to let Lizzy out curbside.

"Unbelievable!" exclaimed Aunt Amy. She twisted her neck to see which driver had tooted his horn in all this traffic.

"Just ignore it. Always happens," said Alfred calmly, eyeing an open spot under the Southwest Airlines banner. After pulling in, he got out to help Lizzy with her bag.

Lizzy gave me a hug and whispered, "He is single, Rory."

She got out and gave Aunt Amy a peck on the cheek through the window, then shook Alfred's hand firmly and reminded him to contact her if he changed his mind. Then she waved to us and walked through the automatic door, into the airport.

"Lizzy is a smart and hardworking girl," commented Aunt Amy as Alfred drove toward the exit.

Traffic became less crowded as we moved away from the airport.

"Yes, she certainly is," he replied, glancing at me in the rearview mirror.

The food at the Moon restaurant wasn't bad but too pricey for the portion sizes. I didn't complain because my aunt and Alfred seemed to enjoy the food while taking a trip down memory lane.

Secretly, I glanced at Alfred sitting next to me. I was so happy to see him again. Listening to him and my aunt talking brought me back to the first time I'd met him. I was nine, and he was twelve. His parents' apartment was next to ours in Brighton. Uncle Kim and Aunt Kim were kind to me and treated me as their own daughter.

My aunt had never been married. Raising me alone and working full-time was tough for her. In her frustration, my aunt tended to yell at me, especially when I came back from school with my clothes torn. Without asking my side of the story, she would ground me to my bedroom. Little did she know that Alfred was being bullied and had been a crybaby back then. Despite being older than me, he had been short and chubby and didn't dare fight back against his bully. I wasn't afraid, and sometimes when I fought to defend him, my clothes ended up getting torn.

Once I'd attempted to run away from home, but my aunt and Alfred's parents found me. My aunt was furious, but Alfred's parents calmed her down. They asked my aunt to let me stay in their apartment after school, which she accepted happily. Since then, my relationship with my aunt got better over time because I was fed, and my homework was done before I returned to our apartment every night.

Two years after that, we moved from Brighton to Springfield, Illinois. Later, we moved to Boston, then to California because I was accepted as a student at the University of California, Irvine.

A gentle nudge on my arm brought me back to reality. I smiled at my aunt, who signaled me to take some leftovers home.

Well, Alfred was back. But this young man Alfred was different than the boy Alfred. I didn't see any familiar features except his comforting eyes. His personality had changed too. He was no longer a shy, skittish, stuttering boy.

Deep down, I missed the old Alfred. He may not have been brave, but he was my best friend and the brother I never had. However, this happy and confident Alfred wasn't bad either. At least he was a nice person to talk to.

CHAPTER 18

The following day, I met Jason for brunch. He didn't pick me up because I had an errand at the Fashion Island Mall. We met in Delissimo Café, not far from the mall, and spent two hours chatting over smoked salmon bagels and coffee. Talking to him had always made me feel good because he listened to me without interrupting. Peter was a good listener if you could tear his attention away from his video games. When I gave him my opinion, Peter proudly said he had multitasking skills and could listen to me while gaming.

After brunch, I headed to the mall to go shopping with Yoo-Shi. One of her best friends would be married in two weeks, and she didn't have a suitable dress for the occasion. I liked shopping with Yoo-Shi because she had an artistic eye for matching clothes with shoes and accessories. She should have worked as a clothing designer instead of becoming an accountant.

While waiting outside the fitting room, I texted Peter to tell him I would be home late, around 6 PM, because I didn't think Yoo-Shi would find a dress she liked any sooner. I didn't expect him to text me back, as I thought he would be having fun with his friends in Santa Monica.

Finally, after more than three hours in and out of stores in the mall, Yoo-Shi got a dress she loved. Then she took me to the shoe store where I could buy a new pair of work shoes with her membership discount. Yoo-Shi bought shoes often enough to have earned a forty-percent-off coupon.

It was 4:45 when I left the shopping mall. I was happy because I had enough time to cook meals for work, saving me more money.

Arriving at the apartment complex, I noticed Peter's parking space was empty. There had been a slight hope that I'd see his car there. It was silly, though, because he wouldn't be interested in me, anyway, with or without rule number nine. Sighing, I continued to my parking space.

My keys jingled as I took them out from my bag, and as I was about to unlock the apartment door, I heard muffled noises coming from inside. *Maybe I forgot to turn off the TV before I left?* I wondered. Grunting, I turned the key and pushed the door open. As I stepped into the hall, I froze. My keys and the shopping bag containing my new shoes slipped from my fingers and dropped to the floor.

In the living room, on the floor, Peter was sitting on a blue car simulator seat complete with a steering wheel, pedals, and gear shifters. I'd seen one about a month ago when Sylvia showed me her husband's new toy. It was called a Conquer Racing Simulator Cockpit. It was addictive because the person felt as if he were sitting in a race car but with no consequences if he crashed it in the game.

Peter didn't hear me enter because he was so absorbed by his racing game. One hand was busy turning the wheel while his other gripped the shifter, and he had his feet on the gas and brake pedals simultaneously. What surprised me most wasn't seeing a grown man playing so intently in a racing simulator but that he was half naked, wearing only boxer shorts.

If I were his girlfriend, I might be pleased with his current state of undress. Peter did an excellent job of taking care of his body. The muscles on his upper arms and torso created sexy curves. I closed my eyes as heat rushed through my body that had nothing to do with the heatwave entering the house through the open door.

Finally realizing he wasn't alone, Peter jumped up, turned to me, and froze. His eyes were wider than I'd ever seen. In the meantime, the game on the TV kept going.

I winced at the loud bang and crash coming through the speaker bar, then turned my back to him. "Oh man! What are you doing? Turn off the game!"

Peeking over my shoulder, I noticed Peter giving me an incredulous stare as he stood frozen in place. I slammed my foot down on the floor impatiently and pointed to the TV. "Turn it off!"

Startled out of his panic, Peter grabbed the TV remote and hit the mute button instead of turning off the TV.

I felt deaf in the sudden absence of sound. I turned and walked closer with a hand over my eyes. As I reached the coffee table, I peeked through my fingers, finding Peter sitting on the couch with a pillow pressed in front of his boxers. Looking at the pillow he was using, I dropped my hand and stood in front of him. "Don't use my TC to cover your crotch!" I shouted.

Bewilderment was written all over Peter's face. "Your…what?" he stammered.

"That pillow. Oh man, you used it to cover your—" I held both hands up like stop signs squeezed my eyes shut. *Oh God, why do you tempt me by letting this guy live with me?* "Why don't you put some clothes on?" I said weakly, staring at the *GAME OVER* message blinking on the TV.

From the reflection on the TV, I saw him dart to his room, dropping my dog-shaped pillow on the floor.

Damn Peter! Poor TC!

Swirling, I bent over and with my thumb and forefinger pinched its ear to pick it up. Then I noticed something blue, red, yellow, and green smeared all over the TV remote. With my other hand, I picked up the remote and felt that it was sticky all over.

"Peter!"

He came out wearing a T-shirt and shorts.

"What?" he asked.

I lifted the remote to his eye level. "What did you do to the remote? It's covered in something sticky!" I glanced at the big bowl on the kitchen countertop with only a few M&M's remaining. "Peter, I told you not to use the remote when your hands are dirty. You are so sloppy!" I frowned, extending the remote to him. "Clean it!"

"Okay, okay, I'll do it," Peter said, taking the remote and heading toward the kitchen sink. He dampened a paper towel with some water and leaned against the sink to wipe the remote.

I let out a heavy sigh and carried the pillow, my arm stretched away from me and my fingers holding it by the corner, to the laundry basket in my room. As I passed the sink, Peter rolled his eyes.

"Hey, what's the big deal? I'm wearing boxers," Peter said, obviously offended at how I'd carried the pillow.

"Still!" I shouted. In front of my laundry basket, I lowered the pillow gently. "Don't worry, I'm shocked too," I said to the pillow. "Aargh, that guy is something!" I scratched the back of my head and sighed. *I'll never look at him the same way after this.* Taking a few deep breaths, I walked back to the living room.

Peter glanced over his shoulder as he knelt on the floor to clean up his game simulation.

"I thought you would be home later," we spoke almost in unison.

I forced a smile as Peter chuckled, turning toward me. He gestured for me to speak first, so I repeated the comment.

Peter shrugged. "Last night, after the party, most of my friends were drunk. And I felt sick of it and decided to come back home early," he answered while dismantling his toys. "But you…you texted me earlier that you would be home late too?" he asked. "If I'd known you would be home earlier, of course, I wouldn't have dared to be dressed inappropriately."

I looked at him for a moment, not saying anything, and picked up the shopping bag and key I'd dropped earlier. "We got done earlier than I thought we would," I said.

Peter didn't say anything. The simulator cockpit was mostly dismantled, and he lifted the parts and carried them back to his room.

"Do you have a minute? I need to talk to you about something," I said.

"Sure, I'll be right back."

Several minutes later, we were sitting on the couch facing the TV that was off. Peter sat on the right end, and I sat on the left end like there was an invisible box between us.

"There are no rules about gaming while wearing only underwear," Peter said defensively. "I didn't do it on purpose. It's hot, and I was too lazy to turn on the air conditioning. If I'd known you would be home earlier, I wouldn't have done that. And you should believe me. I'm not a pervert."

My cheeks warmed a bit, recalling the incident earlier. It would be hard to look at him after that without thinking of his muscular physique. "I'm not talking about that. But I'll add another rule about being naked outside the bedroom," I said, glancing at him and turning my head to the TV again.

"I wasn't naked," Peter protested.

I shrugged. "Okay, half naked."

Peter rolled his eyes.

Leaning forward, propping my elbows on the knees, I massaged my eyes with my fingers. "My aunt was here yesterday, and I told her about you."

Peter shifted to face me, puzzled, which I'd expected.

In a clear voice, I reminded him that I should have found a female roommate.

"But you are a grown woman. Why do you still need your aunt's permission about your roommate?" Peter asked carefully, looking at me.

From his expression, I knew that whatever I explained, he wouldn't understand anyway. Yup, no one would believe that an almost-twenty-two-year-old woman still followed her aunt's advice.

"Peter, my mom was pregnant her first year of a college," I said, looking straight at him. "My dad left without marrying her. A young lady from a small town in Hokkaido got a scholarship to the University of Tokyo, but instead of finishing school, she returned to her hometown alone, carrying a baby. What do you think?"

Peter turned toward me, listening carefully.

I shifted my eyes to the coffee table because my heart jolted to see his tender eyes and thoughtful expression. I'd known Peter was a considerate person, but right now, he was exceptionally calm and mature, cocky yet vulnerable at the same time. I swallowed hard before continuing.

"Living in a small town, she became the topic of everyone's gossip and was shunned by my grandpa. My grandma, who grew up in Boston, had a different perspective than my grandpa, who had always lived in Hokkaido. So, my mom's pregnancy created a huge tension between them. In her anger, she took my mom to Boston, leaving my grandpa and my aunt. Later, my mom changed her last name to my grandma's maiden name."

"Arrington is your grandma's last name?"

"Yes."

Peter signaled me to continue.

"A few months later, I was born prematurely because my mother was under so much stress. She almost gave me up for adoption, but somehow, she changed her mind." I paused, swallowing what felt like sand in my throat. "A year later, my mom's older sister—my aunt—moved to Boston and lived with us. When I was three years old, my grandpa left Hokkaido and moved to the city to reconcile with my mom. But my grandma had already passed away by then, so she didn't see it."

Peter kept listening, nodding occasionally.

"My mom passed away from a car accident when I was nine years old, and my aunt took care of me after that," I said, taking a deep breath to relieve the tightening in my chest.

"I'm sorry you lost your mom at such a young age," Peter said sincerely. "How did your parents meet?"

"My dad was an international exchange student at the University of Tokyo, and he was a few years older than my mom. They met in one of the classes. I don't know much more than that."

"Have you ever met your dad?"

"He doesn't know I exist," I answered, looking at the floor.

The ticking clock on the kitchen wall was the only sound filling the room for several heartbeats.

"So, back to your aunt—will she let me stay here?" Peter asked, breaking the silence.

I nodded. "She seems fine with it, but she is still concerned."

"About what?" A deep crease appeared on his forehead.

"Peter, my mom's story…remember? My aunt has always watched me like a hawk."

"Why? We don't do anything, right? We even have rules about that."

I grimaced. *That's true.* "Well, if my aunt saw what I saw earlier, she would think there *is* something between us," I grinned.

Peter's face flushed. "Yeah, also when you wore your Hello Kitty nightdress. That would have freaked her out," he added.

Heat rushed over my cheeks. *Damn Peter! He still remembers that!* "Yeah, that one too," I groaned, covering my face with my hands.

Peter chuckled and tapped my back gently. "Let's find a way to make your aunt easy. To be honest, I can't move out right now. The project I've been working on is keeping me too busy. So, if you have any ideas, let me know. I'll do whatever you want."

I gazed at him. His words made me remember something that might make for a perfect solution, but I decided not to say anything.

Peter raised an eyebrow at me. "You had something in your mind just then, didn't you?" he asked, searching my face.

I shook my head quickly. "It's not a good idea," I said, avoiding his eyes.

"Spill it, Roomie." He nudged my shoulder gently. "I can tell you already have the answer. As I've said, I will comply."

"I do, but…," I looked at him doubtfully, "I don't think you'll like it."

"Try me," Peter said, spreading his arms to the sides.

"I'll tell her about your secret."

Peter seemed genuinely dumbfounded. "My secret? What do you mean?"

I looked down, rubbing my thumbs, struggling to create proper sentences in my mind. One or two classmates in college had been openly gay, but I didn't know if Peter had come out yet. If he hadn't, I couldn't guess his reaction. Carefully, in clear words, I told him about seeing him with a guy and hearing his confession of love that night.

Peter's mouth slowly dropped open as he listened. Slowly, the corner of his lips curled into a smile when I tried to comfort him that I would keep his secret. He surveyed my face for a moment before his head swirled to the front door, covering his mouth to cough several times before turning back to me with his solemn face.

"Well," Peter said, clearing his throat, "if that will set your aunt at ease, let's do it."

I was taken aback. "Are you sure?"

Peter nodded and looked sincere.

"Thank you. Maybe it's uncomfortable for you, but I'm grateful for your understanding," I said, gazing at him.

The corners of his eyes crinkled as he leaned toward me and whispered, "Is there any discount for being nice to you?"

"No. I'm broke." I laughed and pushed his shoulder away playfully.

Peter grinned. "So, everything is clear now?" he asked, looking at me.

"Yes, but I still have one thing to tell you."

"What?"

"When you play your game, don't turn up the volume too loud. The neighbors will complain." I pointed in the direction of the upstairs neighbor.

Peter's cheeks flushed. "Sorry."

"Just please remember that we have neighbors around us."

"I'll remember."

"Hey, let's have supper. I'm hungry. Where should we go?" I asked.

Peter's face lit up. Smiling, he pointed at a flyer on the refrigerator. It was for a new Popeye's Fried Chicken near our apartment.

"The grand opening is today. I bet you forgot." He gave me a wink.

I tsked at him, folding my arms. "Peter Ryder, that's my favorite fried chicken place. Of course I remembered. But I don't want to go there on grand-opening day. The line will be around the block."

Peter looked dismayed. "Come on, Rory. Where's your sense of adventure?" he said, pleading with his sparkling eyes. At that moment, his face looked innocent, like a child begging for an ice cream. "It won't be that busy at this hour."

Rubbing my face, I considered it. Maybe he was right. I sighed and nodded. "Let's go."

"That's my Roomie," Peter said, wrapping his arm around my shoulder.

I wanted to protest the invasion of my personal space but bit my tongue instead. Peter looked happy, and I liked seeing his big smile.

We slipped on shoes and headed out the door. Outside, dark clouds hung low in the sky, but I doubted it would rain. After a few years of living in California, I knew a dark sky didn't mean we would have rain anytime soon.

Peter almost bounced the whole walk out to his car.

"Look at you! So happy over fried chicken," I teased as we got into his Tesla.

"It's my first time having fried chicken. I'm excited," he said with his forefinger lifted to the sky.

I snickered and shook my head.

The restaurant's parking lot was packed, and the line of people waiting to order extended out the doors, wrapping around one side of the building.

"No line, you said," I grumbled, pointing as the car rolled to a stop in the parking lot. "That's a long line. How long will we have to wait?" I turned to Peter. "We can't go now. Maybe sometime this week."

Peter shook his head, then peered out the windshield, concentrating on finding a parking spot at least somewhere near the restaurant.

"You're crazy, Peter. It's only fried chicken, for God's sake!" I exhaled.

"Do I need to add another house rule about making your roommate happy once a week?" He chuckled.

I rolled my eyes. And then I saw a Chrysler Town and Country backing out of a parking space. "Peter, look!" I said, pointing at the van.

Peter followed my finger and nodded. "Teamwork!"

He laughed as I made a face at him, then whipped into the space and gave me a huge grin before jumping out.

Peter nudged my arm as we walked toward the long line. "We were lucky to get this spot. We'll be lucky to get our food faster too."

I gave him a weak smile, impressed by his enthusiasm but doubtful things would go the way he expected. "We'll see," I said.

Peter paid no attention to my pessimism or the twenty or more people in front of us in line. I was surprised to see everyone's enthusiasm at that hour and struggled to imagine the line during lunchtime. It had to have been much worse!

Peter took out his cell phone and asked me to turn around.

"For what?" I asked, looking at him.

"Selfie with the sign behind us." Peter pointed at the big Grand Opening sign hanging above the entrance. "Smile, Roomie!" He leaned to the left and touched my shoulder with his, then stretched his hand out above us to snap the photo.

I forced a smile just as his finger pressed the button.

"You need to smile bigger," Peter protested while reviewing the picture. "Let's take another one."

"No, I won't. I don't think your friends in London know about this restaurant anyway. Why bother?" I said, crossing both arms over my chest.

"They will," he said stubbornly. "Come on."

I let out a sigh, dropped my arms, and lifted the corners of my lips for a big smile. This time he looked satisfied at the result.

"Are you going to post the picture on your Instagram, titled 'My First Fried Chicken in California'?" I stretched my palms apart like I was opening something in the air as I mocked him.

"Heck, yeah! But the title will be 'My Sulky Roommate and Me, Waiting in Front of Her Favorite Fried Chicken Place.'"

"I'm not sulking," I protested.

I tried to snatch the phone out of his hands, but Peter was quick. He hid it in his back pocket, a big grin splitting his face.

"Childish!" I hissed at him.

He beamed as he gave me a mischievous look.

Finally, after my feet had grown tired of standing and Peter's stomach had begun rumbling like rolling thunder, we got our turn to order. Luckily, it only took them five minutes to serve the order, and we found a two-seater table opening up by the window very quickly.

"This is *so* good!" Peter said through lips shiny from the juicy fried chicken. "Tastes different from the fried chicken in London. No wonder you like this!"

"Yup, and tastes better because you paid," I teased, waving a chicken leg at him.

He had ordered a big meal for both of us. I'd warned him that I would only eat maybe three pieces of dark meat, but he had smiled and assured me that, between the two of us, we could finish the meal.

"By the way, where do you work, Roomie? I don't think I ever asked," asked Peter, dipping two Cajun fries into a small cup of tomato ketchup.

"Myriad Food and Beverage, as an accountant," I said, wiping my mouth. "It's a private company that belongs to Samuel Hamilton. Have you heard of it?"

Peter coughed wildly, like a piece of food had gone down the wrong pipe. His face turned red, and his eyes teared up.

I leaned forward to pat his back, trying to help. "Are you okay?" I looked at him, concerned and pushing his drink closer to encourage him to take a sip.

Peter nodded and drank half of it. "Swallowed wrong," he croaked as he tapped his fist against his chest.

Once he settled back down, we focused on eating our food slowly for a bit.

Sitting back from his empty plate, Peter said, "So, tell me about Myriad." His face was not red anymore, and his voice had returned to normal.

Nodding, I began telling him a little more about working at Myriad. I tore a buttermilk biscuit into four pieces and ate them one by one as I went on about my job. Peter nodded and asked a question here and there, but it seemed like his mind was preoccupied. He didn't hear a question I asked him until I waved my hand in front of his face.

"Sorry, what?" he asked.

"You said you work for your family's company. What type of business is it?" I repeated.

He looked down and wiped his greasy hands slowly with a wad of napkins. Eventually, he said, "Not my parents' company, per se, but my extended family's business. It's an investment company."

My mouth agape, I exclaimed, "Wow, that's awesome!" Leaning closer, I asked, "Are you hiring?"

Peter crumpled the napkins and dropped them onto his plate, then leaned toward me. That close to him, I could see his long eyelashes. "I don't know, but why do you want to quit your current job?" He looked serious.

I wrinkled my nose and leaned back in my seat.

Peter tilted his head but didn't move.

"I don't like my manager. She is bitchy," I pouted, then I told him about what had happened in the last week. "Can you believe it? I didn't laugh about her *or* White Water's team, but she just accused me like that." My stomach hurt as the image of Rowena's censure flashed through my mind.

"Does she always act like that?" Peter asked, propping his chin with an elbow on the table.

I tucked a lock of hair behind my ear and said, "That's been my experience. My coworker, who has been working for her for a while longer, said Rowena has always been that way."

"And why doesn't anyone complain about her? Couldn't you tell your general manager?" Peter asked again.

"Desiree used to work with Rowena, so they are friends, and she always listens to Rowena—gives her special treatment. One time, Rowena and Christine, another accounting manager, went to Desiree about some issues. In my opinion, Christine's idea was the same as Rowena's, just in different words, but Desiree accepted Rowena's idea and even said 'Why didn't anyone think of that before?'" I wrinkled my nose. "So, if there is an opening at your company, let me know, please? Especially in accounting," I begged, pressing my palms together in front of me. "Please?"

"I won't hire you," he said calmly, drinking his water.

"Why?" I said, dismayed, then saw a smile tug at the corner of his mouth.

"One thing you need to know when you have an interview for your next job is don't ever say bad things about your boss," he explained. "You should focus on why you want to move into your future company and what skills you can contribute."

For a moment, Peter appeared mature and charismatic as I'd never seen him before. The way he talked sounded like he had many years of experience in hiring people.

"All right. Noted," I said. "How about my reason to move is because I've never been to London?"

Peter grinned and slapped the table suddenly, making the people nearby turn and look at us. "Ha! That's failed answer number two," he said, pointing at me.

I rolled my eyes.

Peter gazed at me and said, "Well, I can't make any promises, but I'll let you know if there is an opening."

"Yay! Awesome!" I cried, raising my palm to give him a high-five.

Peter smiled and tapped my palm with his.

"Can I get a higher salary too?"

Now Peter rolled his eyes, but he chuckled. After that, I asked him about Jane, his sister. Peter's face turned gloomy as he told me about the possibility that she needed to have a third surgery. My chest ached for her and their family having to deal with stomach cancer.

But Peter was Peter. He never sank into sadness for long. He leaned back and smiled, rubbing his full belly, and said, "Ready to go home?"

Looking down at the empty plates and containers, I couldn't believe we'd finished off nine pieces of dark meat, two large Cajun fries, and four buttermilk biscuits. Peter had an amazing appetite—he had eaten six pieces of chicken and cleaned up the leftover fries and biscuits. My stomach was stuffed, but he seemed fine and even asked if I wanted to stop for ice cream.

A single raindrop fell on top of my head as I followed Peter out of Popeye's. Stepping back by the door, under the overhang, I said, "It's raining?" Leaning out, I looked up at the sky, catching several more raindrops on my cheeks. "Really? We rarely have rain in May!"

"*Rarely* doesn't mean you won't have it at all, right?" said Peter, glancing skyward while stretching his hand out to feel the rain. "It's just light rain. But if we walk, we'll be drenched. Are you okay if we run to the car?"

"Um …" I looked down at my three-inch heels. They weren't that high, but running in them would be murder.

"Would you mind if your roommate runs across the parking lot barefoot?" I looked up at him.

Peter blinked, not understanding until I pointed at my feet and then bent to take off one of the shoes.

"Not at all. It'll be a first for me. Most girls would ask me to get the car and pick them up," Peter said, grinning. He threw his head back, laughing, as I lifted the shoes with both hands and twirled them like baton sticks.

"Ready?" he asked.

I nodded.

"Go!" he shouted.

I shrieked as my bare feet touched the rough, warm asphalt. Peter could run faster, but he was pacing his steps with me and watching out for the cars moving around the parking lot. Once or twice, he pulled me closer to him whenever a car got too close to us.

As we approached the Tesla, Peter sped ahead and opened the car door for me. I laughed and slid inside. The rain hadn't gotten too heavy yet but was enough to make my face, hair, and shoulders wet.

"That was fun!" Peter exclaimed, glancing at me.

I turned to him and nodded, drying my face with some Kleenex from my purse. "No one knows when rain will fall in California," I giggled.

I moved aside when Peter twisted around to reach something in the back seat. He pulled a navy-blue jacket up to the front seat and offered it to me.

"What is it for?" I asked, half smiling, looking at the jacket and at Peter. "I'm not cold."

Peter bit his lower lip and cleared his throat before pointing to my chest.

I looked down and shrieked, grabbing the jacket from his hand to cover my front. We had run against the rain, and my front was soaked all the way through my light-colored blouse. Way too much of my chest was exposed for all to see. Feeling embarrassed, I turned away to look out the window while clutching the jacket against me as if my life depended on it.

"Don't worry. No one saw," consoled Peter as he managed the car through the parking lot.

"But you saw it," I mumbled as the heat rushed to my cheeks.

Peter remained quiet for a moment, focusing on the road as he drove us home. Clearing his throat, he said, "Well, just remember what you've seen about me, and you won't need to be worried, right?"

After a long pause, I turned to him and nodded slowly.

The rain came down harder as we entered the driveway at Pacific Hills.

CHAPTER 19

I'd intended to return Peter's jacket before he left for work the following day, but he had already left and locked his bedroom by the time I came out. The jacket had become damp from my wet blouse, so I used a hairdryer to dry it. By the time I finished, his room had already turned dark.

He must have been tired. For the past couple of nights, whenever I couldn't sleep and went to the kitchen for some warm milk, I'd seen his light still on from underneath his bedroom door and faintly heard him talking on the phone. Working for a family business wasn't as easy as I'd thought.

I brought the jacket back to my room and laid it on my bed. Sighing, I caressed the material before grabbing my bag and heading out to work. Part of me felt crazy for liking him, unreciprocated, but I couldn't lie about my feelings—not even to myself.

My phone buzzed as I locked my apartment door. While walking to my car, I took it out and checked who had texted me at that hour. There were two texts: one from Lena and one from Aunt Amy. Debating which I should read first, I decided to read the text from my aunt.

> *Rory, I'm leaving Baja in two days, but I won't fly back to Boston. Instead, I rerouted my flight to John Wayne Airport so I can stay with you for a night. Would that be okay?*

I sighed and texted her back. My aunt still wanted to meet Peter. I felt thankful that Peter didn't mind my sharing his secret with her.

Sure. Tell me your flight number, and I'll pick you up.

Before I forgot, I texted Peter to let him know about my aunt staying for a night.

A minute later, Peter replied.

Not a problem.

Then I checked Lena's message.

Rory, the witch wants us to finish the reconciliation reports. Are yours done?

I frowned and replied to Lena.

It's not even the fourth week of the month…why is she rushing? We've been busy preparing for the WW team, and I'll have a meeting with Vy today after lunch. That lady is really something!

Less than a minute later, I got her response.

I've told you she is crazy! Just do what she wants, or she is going to accuse me of something ridiculous. Did you know that she accused me of laughing at her and the WW team at the introductory meeting? CRAZY BITCH!

I couldn't agree more. Exhaling loudly, I yanked the gear stick in reverse, backed out of my space, then shifted into drive and rolled slowly toward the exit gate. It was not going to be a good day for Lena, Rowena, and I. Lena had already been throwing tantrums since last week, and now I was upset too.

I smacked my steering wheel hard when I was about a mile away from the office on the I-5 North freeway. The freeway was congested, and somehow the traffic app hadn't alerted me earlier about the accident at the entrance of Winnebago, the main street I needed to take before reaching Harbor Circle.

"Dammit! Shouldn't you tell me earlier, before I get on the freeway?" I yelled. "Ugh!"

While sitting at a stop in traffic, I checked to see if there were alternative routes, but the app seemed to have given up. All the options gave me the same length of drive time, anyway.

By the time I arrived at the office, there were no parking spots left, and I had to go to the extra parking area in the next building. *What a bummer!*

A loud thud came from Rowena's office as I sat down on my chair and turned on my notebook computer. I could feel her eyes on me as I logged into my computer. At that moment, a message popped up on my Skype window from Lena.

Rowena asked about you five minutes ago. She was upset. Did you text her about the accident?

My shoulders slumped as if someone had put heavy stones on them. I replied to the message.

I did. But you know her.

Taking a deep breath and holding before releasing it helped the tightness in my chest. Slowly, I got up, walked to Rowena's office, and knocked on the door.

Rowena glanced up with her usual "come in" glare, so I stepped in.

"Sorry I'm late. There was a huge accident on the freeway," I said, maintaining a smooth tone.

Rowena scoffed. "Our freeways are always backed up. Leave earlier next time," she said, waving her hand to signal me to leave.

"Be patient, Rory. Be patient," I said to myself while walking back to my cubicle.

Trying to ignore her attitude, I focused on my work and shut out the rest of the world.

Since Rowena wanted everything done by the end of the day, I worked on finishing the reconciliation report while eating lunch at my desk. For once, I felt happy when Vy postponed our meeting, because now I could focus on the task I was doing right now.

After another two hours, I felt my shoulders tense. I lifted my arms and stretched my back.

"Maybe I need to take a break," I mumbled. Pushing away from the desk, I stood up and headed toward the lunchroom on the first floor.

There were only a few people in the lunchroom, and I recognized an Indian lady who worked as a business analyst. We had sat next to each other during employee orientation. Her name was Anaya Dara. Anaya seemed to recognize me, too, because she waved as I entered the room.

"I haven't seen you for a long time! How are you?" she greeted me.

"Good. Just busy counting beans," I said, half joking. "How about yourself?"

"Same old, same old," she answered.

"I hear you. Hey, sorry, I can't chat. I'll catch up with you later. Have a great day," I said, pacing to the cabinet where the coffee was kept.

After inserting a pod into the Keurig machine, I pressed the start button and waited as it brewed my coffee. Just then, my phone buzzed with a new message. I glanced at it and saw that Peter had sent me the message.

Rory, I have a lot of things to do in my office and have to stay very late. See you tomorrow night.

No worries. Thanks for telling me. See you tomorrow,

I responded.

In less than a minute, he replied.

Don't forget to latch the door tonight, okay?

I chuckled and nodded, knowing he couldn't see me. It was sweet, and his thoughtfulness made my heart warm.

I won't,

I texted back.

Feeling giddy, I took my mug from the drip plate and tossed the used K-cup into the trash can. From the corner of my right eye, I caught a shadow standing near the water dispenser. Twirling, I saw Jason standing there with a coffee tumbler in hand.

He gazed at me with a strange expression on his face as he walked over to me. *How long has he been standing there?*

"Sorry, I didn't realize you were here." I offered a smile.

Jason smiled back. "Just got here, but I didn't want to bother you. Your daydream looked so happy," he said, putting his tumbler on the counter next to the coffee machine. "Care to share?"

"Uh, my roommate sent me…a joke," I lied, waving the phone in my hand.

Jason nodded and plopped a K-pod into the coffee machine. "So, did you like the breakfast place we went to yesterday?"

"Yes, I did! The price was reasonable, and the food was delicious. I really liked the mocha latte. Not too sweet like in other coffee shops," I said matter-of-factly.

Jason glanced at me sideways, took his tumbler from under the coffee machine's spout, and tightened its cap. "Would you like to go out for dinner tonight, maybe?" His voice was soft, and he was slowly closing the gap between us. "There is a new place not far from here that I'd like you to try if you are free," he added, tilting his head.

I sensed subtle coercion in his tone that I'd never heard from him before. He'd always been so soft-spoken, timid even. Composing myself, I cleared my throat and said, "Maybe another time. I have some errands to take care of tonight."

Disappointment flashed across Jason's face, but he forced a smile. "Sure, no problem. Next time then," he said, and headed toward the door.

I nodded and followed him. We walked down the hall and turned left to take the stairs. When I was about to ascend, Jason touched my elbow lightly to stop me. I turned to find his bright-green eyes looking straight at mine tenderly. I'd always thought of him as a friend; still, my heart skipped a beat from the way he looked at me.

"Yes?" I asked, gazing up at him.

Jason sighed, ducking his head before looking up again. "I forgot what I wanted to say, but …" His fingers tightened a bit on my elbow before releasing it. "Have a good day, Rory." And he continued heading to his office without glancing at me again.

CHAPTER 20

The following day, my meeting with Vy went smoothly, and I admired his humility despite being a senior manager. He spoke in a friendly tone and listened to my explanations attentively.

After our meeting, we chitchatted for several minutes. Vy shared about his last vacation with his wife to Switzerland and his opinion on the beautiful California weather. He asked me about local places to eat and to visit that he and his coworkers could go on foot. He'd heard about famous sites like the Hollywood Walk of Fame, Disneyland, and Universal Studios, but he didn't know of any places nearby.

I wrote down some places for him on a piece of paper. "By the way, may I ask if you've ever met the founder's son?" I asked, gathering my documents from the meeting.

Vy shook his head slowly, rising from his seat. "I've never met him personally but have heard he is a nice guy who loves his family."

"How old is he?" I asked.

"Um…around sixty, I think," Vy answered before extending his hand to me. "Thanks for your explanations, Rory. I'll read the reports, and if I have a question, I'll let you know."

"Anytime." I shook his hand, and we left the conference room together.

Vy turned to the left to go back to his office, and I climbed the stairs, excited to tell Lena that the founder's son wasn't in his forties as people said. Distracted, I didn't pay attention when someone racing down the stairs bumped my shoulder. Staggering, I grabbed the rail and looked down to see who had knocked me. It was Lena, red-faced and crying.

"Lena!" I called.

She halted and looked up, tears still streaming down her cheeks.

I descended the stairs and stopped in front of her. "Hey, what happened?" I tilted to see her face clearly.

Lena looked away. "I'm not…Just leave me alone, okay?" Without waiting, she rushed down the stairs, pushed open the door, and walked out of the building.

Dumbfounded, I gazed after her, trying to guess what had happened. Our beloved manager was most likely the nuisance.

Rowena was in her office with the door shut when I got back to my cubicle. Sylvia sent me a message after I turned my computer back on.

> *Lena and the witch had a heated argument. Don't say anything, and act as if nothing happened. If you aren't busy, let's grab dinner with Lena after work.*

The vein on my temple throbbed after reading the message. What would happen to us if Rowena never stopped being a jerk?

> *I'll go with you guys,*

I replied via messaging.

After work, Lena, Sylvia, and I rushed to the Irvine Spectrum Center, which was far enough from the office for us to be sure we wouldn't see anyone from work. Yoo-Shi couldn't join us because her family was visiting her from Korea. We sat under a big yellow umbrella in the outdoor dining area.

Between tears, Lena filled us in. As we'd expected, Rowena had ripped into Lena harshly.

"'You keep asking questions about simple things. As an accountant who has been here longer than a year, I expect you to know everything by now. If I have to review your work and keep fixing your mistakes, I can do the job without you!'" said Lena, mimicking Rowena's deep, throaty voice. In a normal situation, we would have laughed because Lena could mimic Rowena perfectly, including the disgusting snort she used whenever she looked down at someone.

Sniffing, Lena wiped her swollen eyes with some Kleenex, then took a deep breath as our eyes met. "Myriad's accounts are so detailed. Each item has its own account that we record only once every year. The item that made her upset was recorded last year by her because I wasn't in the office at that time, but she didn't want to accept that she'd made a blunder and just blamed me for not thinking as an accountant. Whatever I do, right or wrong, she will never be happy anyway," Lena sniffed. "She is so arrogant, always thinking she can do the job better than everyone else. So, why doesn't she do it by herself? Why does she bother to hire staff if she thinks others are stupid?" Lena swallowed, wiping her tears again. "Working with her for two years has made a big hole in my heart. She really hurts my confidence." Letting out a heavy sigh, Lena tugged a lock of her golden hair behind her ears.

I sighed, patting her shoulder gently. I'd never seen her cry like this. It must have been hard for her to face condescension every day for so long.

"I quit," Lena blurted out. "I called my husband earlier, and he gave his approval. It is a bit tough since my kids are still in school, but we can manage on one income. I'm glad I'm not a spender. With the salary I've earned, I'll be fine not working for at least a year. And yes, I already gave my resignation to the witch and the bitch," she said, referring to Rowena and Desiree, respectively.

"No! Please don't go. Without you, I'll suffer even more," I said, feeling a twist in my stomach. If she left, I'd be the one working most directly for Rowena.

Sylvia gave me a sympathetic look.

"I'm sorry, Rory. I've tried to hang in there," Lena said in a little voice. "My last day will be two weeks from now."

Two weeks wasn't long enough for me to learn her work!

Lena sighed and looked skyward. Her face crumpled. "Desiree is a sick person too. When I told her I quit, she didn't show any concern. She even smiled widely and told me to email my resignation letter to HR. That's it!"

Sylvia's face turned red, and her voice rose as she said, "That's the worst thing I ever heard!"

The server brought our orders, interrupting the moment. Sensing tension, he left quickly after putting the food on the table, not even bothering to ask if we needed anything else.

"I can't believe those two devils treated you like that." Sylvia curled her fingers into fists. "Rowena and Desiree are evil. I hope there is a special place in hell for those kinds of people!"

She was the oldest and calmest among the four of us. While I understood her reaction, I was surprised at her anger. Behind the massive, well-designed office building, those cruel and abusive managers continued to work without any repercussions. They were fortunate none of their staff dared report them to HR, fearing they would be perceived as disloyal or complainers. The only ones who would speak up were those who had quit, during their exit interviews, but even then, their claims were often dismissed. Those who remained had to endure unfair treatment day after day.

"You'll be the sixth person who has left Myriad within the last three years." Sylvia exhaled loudly. "I wish we could prevent this from happening again."

Lena smiled bitterly. "To be honest, I regret ever working here. But I'm glad I met you, ladies." She glanced at Sylvia and me. "Maybe I won't find a job very easily, leaving this way, but for sure I'll find a way to ruin them." Lena's soft features looked vicious, and her eyes seemed to be afire.

"Just don't do anything stupid, okay?" Sylvia said with concern.

Lena chuckled. "No, I won't. Don't worry," she said, then turned to me. "Don't resign like me. If you have any issues, go to Sylvia, okay?"

I nodded.

Sylvia gave us a sympathetic gaze. For a moment, each of us was busy with her own thoughts. In the meantime, the moon had become brighter in the sky, and a beautiful halo hung around it. Unfortunately, it would take a lot more than the moon and sparkling stars on a beautiful California night to transform our gloomy hearts.

On the way home, I couldn't stop thinking about my future at Myriad without Lena. It meant that each time Rowena was in a bad mood, which was most of the time, I would be her victim. I shuddered at the thought and wished to find a new job soon.

Sighing, I parked my car and picked up the plastic bag with a half-gallon of milk and some oranges from the passenger seat. Almost to my front door, I noticed it was ajar. Then Peter came out, followed by a tall man. Peter hadn't come home yesterday, which he had told me beforehand, but I didn't recall him informing me about bringing his friend to our apartment.

I smiled when Peter waved to me, then shifted my gaze to his guest, who looked familiar.

"Rory," Peter called, "I didn't know you would be home so late. Was your boss upset again?"

"Something like that." I chuckled at his comment. "Also, I stopped by the grocery store for milk and some oranges."

Peter snapped his fingers. "Speaking of milk, I forgot to text you that I'd already bought milk on my way home."

"You shouldn't have," I looked at him, "but thanks for buying. I appreciate it."

"Nah, don't mention it. I use some milk, too, for my tea," he said.

My eyes shifted to his guest, standing slightly behind him. His ginger hair was cut in a high and tight style and looked perfect on his long face shape. He nodded at me as our eyes met.

Suddenly, Peter slapped his forehead. "Ah, my bad. I should've introduced you," he said in an apologetic voice. He waved his hand to his guest and then to me. "Tom, this is Rory. Rory, this is Tom. She already knows about us," he added, tilting his head and widening his eyes slightly at Tom.

Tom's mouth made an O, and then he smiled while extending his hand to me.

Now I remembered who Tom was—the ginger-haired guy from that night in the yard.

"Nice to meet you," he said.

"Nice to meet you," I responded as I accepted his hand.

Looking up, I could see Tom's face clearly under the moonlight. His eyes were blue, and his high nose sat perfectly on his face. I had to admit that Tom was quite good-looking.

Peter stood next to Tom, eyes twinkling mischievously, and the corners of his lips curling up in a smile. He put his hand around Tom's shoulder, but Tom moved slightly forward, and Peter's hand fell from his shoulder.

"Where're you guys going?" I said, keeping my voice cheerful.

Before Peter opened his mouth, Tom answered, "We're going to the new Avengers movie. But before that, we are going to stop for some In-N-Out Burgers. This man," he pointed at Peter, "has never tried it, so he wants a burger for dinner. I've lived in California awhile, so I can get one anytime. Care to join us?"

"I wish I could, but I've promised to call Alfred in…," I glanced at my wristwatch, "ten minutes. There's something we have to arrange together."

"Alfred? I didn't know you had a new boyfriend, Roomie," Peter said, smiling, but a crease also appeared between his eyes as if he were gazing at me curiously.

"No, he's just my childhood friend. We met again after more than a decade on the day my aunt was here. I didn't think it was important enough to share."

Peter's smile faltered.

"By the way," Tom said, looking at me, "my company has a lot of projects with Disney, especially with these Marvel projects, and we get free movie tickets, so let me know if you need one or two."

"Aww, thanks, Tom. I appreciate it!" I beamed. "Well, I'd better go in. Enjoy the burgers and the movie, guys!" I waved my hand.

Peter and Tom moved to the side so I could pass. "Oy, Rory!" Peter called.

"Yes?" I asked, turning to meet his gaze.

"If you'd like, I can tell you all about the movie tomorrow morning," he said, a big grin appearing on his lips.

"Noooo! Don't you dare!" I yelled. I had been trying to avoid any spoilers about the movie until I could see it, and as popular as it was, that had been really hard to do.

"Just a little," Peter said, raising his hand with his thumb and forefinger an inch apart.

"Peter Ryder, if you do, I won't let you back in the apartment," I threatened.

Peter laughed and turned to Tom, then said something that made Tom glance at me and smile.

"Don't worry, I won't let him ruin it, Rory," said Tom, placing his hand over his heart.

I smiled and waved to them as they turned toward the parking lot.

Inside the apartment, I opened the fridge and put the milk I'd bought next to the milk Peter had bought. It was kind of him to remember, although I hadn't expected him to do that. I was lucky to have had two good roommates. Lizzy was like the sister I'd never had. Putting aside my romantic feelings toward Peter, he was like a best friend who cared about me. Sometimes he was childish, but overall, he was a good and responsible man.

When I closed the fridge door, my ears picked up soft swishing sounds near the kitchen window. When I whipped my head to look out the window, I saw a shadow. *Maybe Peter forgot something?* I wondered, walking to the front door to open it.

The evening breeze whipped locks of my dark-brown hair behind me gently. I didn't see anyone except an older man walking his Chihuahua on the green belt at the right corner, but I knew him, and he wasn't close enough to have caused the shadow at my window.

Scanning the courtyard and the parking lot, I didn't see anyone. Shrugging, I walked back into my apartment and closed the door. Maybe my eyes had been wrong.

CHAPTER 21

My aunt's flight from Baja California was scheduled to land on Thursday afternoon. I'd already sought Rowena's permission to leave early to pick her up.

As I expected, my bitchy manager didn't approve it quickly, especially after learning I would also take the next day off. Since Lena had submitted her resignation and then took a few days off, Rowena's bad mood was skyrocketing. She didn't want to take over Lena's tasks and shoved them to me. Unfortunately, my knowledge wasn't adequate to handle the tasks, and I started asking her for guidance. Her attitude bothered me so much because whenever I left her office, Rowena would slam anything available in front of her: her Coke can, her Longchamp bag, her office phone, a thick folder, anything. Oddly, Desiree didn't say anything even when she heard the tantrum from Rowena's office; she pretended nothing was happening. Sylvia gave a disgusted expression behind Desiree's back after she spoke nicely to Rowena about the soccer club she'd recommended for Rowena's boys.

Finally, near lunchtime, Rowena gave her approval along with a note stating that I should complete the inventory report soon.

I left the office and drove to John Wayne Airport. Although the airport was crowded and my car was crawling through the entrance, it was still a better option than driving to Los Angeles Airport where the streets were tangled with cars.

My eyes scanned the area in search of my aunt. She had texted me to pick her up on the arrival curb, saving me the need to park.

In front of me, a Hyundai Sonata slammed on its brakes to avoid a couple dragging their luggage across the street although the light for pedestrians was red. I slammed mine quickly as well, wondering if the pedestrian would get fined, since I noticed one or two police cars along the curb.

As traffic resumed, my eyes caught a tiny lady in a green pastel dress, complete with its cardigan, standing elegantly on the curb below the Southwest Airlines sign. A standard piece of luggage was standing near her shoes. Her angular eyes were watching the cars pass by. I pulled over and shifted into park in front of her. Aunt Amy smiled as I got out and opened the door for the passenger front seat and put her luggage in the trunk. We gave each other a quick hug before entering the vehicle.

"How was your flight?" I asked, glancing at her as I shifted my car into drive and it rolled slowly away from the curb, heading toward the exit.

"Tiring. There is no direct flight from Baja to here. We also had an issue at La Paz International. But overall, this trip was worth it, and my heart was touched to see people from different places gathered with the same mission to educate these poor pregnant young ladies to be good, independent moms despite their situations," said Aunt Amy, adjusting her seat belt.

I could see a glimpse of emotion in her eyes before I turned my focus to finding the entrance of the I-405 South freeway. After my mom's pregnancy, Aunt Amy had a soft spot for pregnant teens.

"That's good that you enjoyed the trip," I said.

"So, how's Peter? Have you gotten along well?" Aunt Amy asked after we merged into traffic on the freeway.

"Yes, I'm surprised we've gotten along well," I answered, peering through the windshield. "Initially, I was afraid we wouldn't because I've never had a roommate other than Lizzy. But then I found out that my fear was unfounded. He's followed the roommate rules that make my life easier. But he is clumsy in the kitchen and with any household chores. Do you know he hired a cleaning lady to clean his room twice a week and do some household chores?"

"Really?" she asked, her head tilted to the side. "That's expensive!"

I laughed and nodded. "Yup, he is here for his family business, so all expenses must be reimbursed. As long as his room is tidy and he does his weekly chores, I'm good."

"So, are you going to find a new studio after this?" asked my aunt.

"Yes, I've saved enough for the deposit," I smiled, glancing at her.

My aunt gazed at me before looking out the window.

The flight must have been tiring for her. She dozed off with her head leaning on the window, and her breath was even. I was touched, noticing soft wrinkles in the corners of her eyes and across her forehead. Most of the wrinkles there must have been caused by me. She woke up as we pulled into the Pacific Hills entrance. Jose, the longtime security guard, recognized my aunt. He smiled and waved at her.

As I parked in my assigned spot, Peter was just leaving to catch a flight for a business trip to New York.

"Nice to meet you, Ms. Ishida," Peter said as I introduced my aunt to him. "I'm sorry I couldn't stay longer to know you better. I hope we meet again."

I was surprised to find how well-mannered he was, as if he had plenty of experience dealing with different kinds of people. He looked comfortable talking to my aunt and even offered to take her luggage to my room.

A few minutes later, a silver Honda Civic with an Uber emblem on the top right corner of the windshield arrived. That was his transportation. Peter waved to us as he got into the passenger seat.

"Your roommate's manners are incredible. I've never met a young man with such confidence, who treats people with deep respect," my aunt said as the car was rolling slowly toward the exit gate. "How old is he?"

"Twenty-three," I said, following his Uber with my eyes until it turned the corner.

"Very young, but he has charisma," said my aunt, entering the apartment. I followed.

For dinner, I cooked simple dishes, mostly vegetables: stir-fry vegetables and pan-fried tofu with garlic and soy sauce. My aunt wasn't a vegetarian, but she preferred vegetables to meat.

After dinner, we sat on the couch, talking about her trips, Aunt Sophie, and Alfred. I shared with my aunt about my attempt to reconnect with Alfred after we'd first met, but we had grown apart as we grew up. There was no "click" feeling anymore as we used to have. My aunt comforted me and reminded me

I shouldn't have expected that Alfred wouldn't change. Eventually, everyone changed, including me.

We continued chatting until almost eleven and then went to bed. I let my aunt sleep in my bed while I slept on the carpet in my sleeping bag.

"Rory, I'm going to be honest about your living together with Peter. I'm worried," she said as she lay down. "Your mom's experience was enough for me. She was impregnated and left behind like a cheap skank."

From the way she spoke, I could hear the spark of bitterness in her voice. I bit my lower lip. Each time she brought up my dad, she was always angry.

"Don't worry, Aunt Amy. That won't happen to me," I maintained, my voice flat. Sometimes, I didn't know how to respond to her with a cool head. It always felt like she was mad at me or blamed me in some way for what my father did.

"If you were still with Ben, you could have lived with him and not had to worry about finding a new roommate," said Aunt Amy.

Glancing up at her, I rolled my eyes and turned my back to her. My aunt had liked Ben a lot. In her eyes, he was perfect: a handsome gentleman with a good career and mature personality. She was upset when I broke up with him. If she'd known why, she would have been more shocked, so I'd never told her.

"I don't want to talk about Ben. Good night, Auntie," I said, pulling the sleeping bag over my head.

"Let bygones be bygones, Rory. Wouldn't it be better to be back with him?" my aunt asked, pressing the issue.

I let out a sigh and rolled on my back to stare up at her. "Could we drop the topic, please?" I said tiredly. "I broke up with him. End of story."

"But Ben is a good guy. He would forgive you, wouldn't he?" my aunt persisted.

I pulled down the sleeping bag from over my head and slammed my hand on the carpet with a loud thud. "Why have you never asked why I broke up with him? You've just assumed I am the one who made a mistake. No. I broke up with him because he isn't a good guy like you think he is. Do you know what he thought of me? In his mind, I'm too naïve and clumsy. He always criticized my fashion choices, calling them tacky. He suggested I should lose weight, and foolish me, I listened and even fulfilled his wishes."

There was a slight movement on the bed, but my aunt didn't say anything. The room became quiet except for my heavy breathing.

"Do you remember when Lizzy and her fiancé took me to the emergency room?" I continued. "It was because I was on a strict diet to lose weight. The

ER doctor was upset to hear what I did, but Ben—do you know what he said to me? He laughed at me and said that if I had eaten properly, I wouldn't have suffered. Terry would have punched Ben in the face for laughing at me if Lizzy hadn't stopped him. I had been so foolish! Behind my back, Ben was cheating on me while I starved myself for a thin body to make him happy. Now, tell me, do you still say that Ben is the perfect guy for me?"

I could hear a strangled sound coming from my aunt's throat as she sat straight up on her bed and came down to crouch on the floor next to me. I pushed myself up to a sitting position, gazing at my aunt. In the dim light from the moon shining through my window, I could see her eyes were wide and glassy.

"Why have you never told me this?" Her voice was quiet, slightly shaky.

"How could I? You're always worried about me, always watching me closely, and even moved to California to accompany me throughout my four years of university. I've known you intended that I wouldn't experience the same mishap my mom did and that I would get a bachelor's degree that my mom couldn't. So, why would I burden you by telling you that unpleasant story?" I said quietly.

Aunt Amy hugged me and tightened her arms around my shoulders, making me wince. No one would believe there was so much hidden strength in her small body!

"I'm sorry for what you've been through," she cried softly.

My shoulder became wet from her tears, the first tears she'd shed in front of me since my mom had passed away. "I'm sorry for the pressure I've put on you. But for now, you should tell me anything, everything. Yes, I'm not your biological mother, but I *am* your mom," she choked out, biting her lips. Her chin trembled. "I know I'm not good at showing my emotions, or maybe my reactions aren't exactly as you expect, but you are my forever daughter, one and only."

I blinked rapidly at the sudden warmth behind my eyes, and a tear escaped. "I promise to tell you things from now on," I said as my aunt pulled back to gaze at me.

"I'm silly and shouldn't have worried about you. You are an adult now. Be free; make any decision you want to make. But whenever you need help, I'm here for you." She caressed my cheek, then wiped her tears and moved back up to the bed.

She smiled at me as I stretched my hands up to hold her hand.

"I have something to tell you—about Peter," I said, wondering if I should just blurt it out or tell the whole story from the beginning.

Her eyebrows knotted, but she waited patiently for me to continue.

"Peter…," I paused for a moment, "is a wonderful person. He is a good roommate, although sometimes he drives me crazy by teasing me or his silly behavior, acting like a little boy. I really enjoy his company. But…he isn't a guy who would appreciate having a girl standing next to him. He…has different opinions about dating a girl."

Aunt Amy blinked a couple of times, and a deep crease appeared on her forehead. Slowly, she lowered her eyes to our hands. "I see," she nodded. Sighing, she tapped my hand gently before releasing it. "Well, if that's the case, I certainly don't have to be worried about any funny business. Good night, dear."

"Good night, Auntie," I replied.

For some time, we lay on our beds, staring at the ceiling in silence. Neither of us fell asleep very quickly, but I heard her breathing became heavy and even long before I drifted off. Sighing, I turned to lie on my side and closed my eyes.

The next morning, I woke to find the bed next to me empty. The blanket was folded neatly at the end of the bed like my aunt always did. I glanced at the alarm clock; it was six thirty.

I got up and washed my face and brushed my teeth. After changing from my pajamas, I walked down to the kitchen to find my aunt sitting on one of the tall kitchen chairs, enjoying some tea. In front of her was a plate of toast, scrambled eggs with sausage, and a small bottle of jam.

"Ah, you woke up," my aunt said with a smile as I emerged into the kitchen. She pointed to another plate across from her. "Grab your breakfast, Rory."

I sat down across from her, and we ate in silence.

"Auntie, I'm off from work today and can drop you at the airport," I said, looking up from the sink of breakfast dishes I was washing while she sipped tea at the counter.

Aunt Amy waved her hand dismissively. "No need, dear. I'm going by Uber. You know I don't like depending on people. Why don't you enjoy your day off while you can?" She studied my face. "I'm fine; don't worry."

I knew her mind was made up.

At ten o'clock, the Uber came to pick up my aunt. Before getting in the car, she reached up and cupped my face in her hands as I leaned forward to hug her.

"I'm proud of you, Rory, my beautiful daughter."

My eyes swelled as she tiptoed to kiss my forehead gently.

CHAPTER 22

When I got back from the library on Saturday afternoon, I heard laughter coming from the living room. As I pushed the front door open, I wasn't surprised to see Peter and Tom there. Last night, Peter had texted that he was already back from his business trip but staying overnight at Tom's apartment.

"Hi, Roomie," Peter said with a wave.

Tom nodded and smiled at me.

"Hi, guys. How was your trip, Peter?" I asked. Dropping my books and my bag on the kitchen countertop, I walked to the fridge to get some water.

"Not too bad. It would have been better if the trip had been a vacation," Peter sighed. "By the way, Tom wanted to wait for you to give you some movie tickets."

"Awesome!" I brought my water to the coffee table and sat on an ottoman across from Tom.

Tom fished out the tickets from the front pocket of his light-green shirt. "My company only allows four tickets per employee per movie, and as you know, we already used two of them, so I only have two for you," he said, holding the tickets out to me. He smiled as my face lit up.

"Two are enough. Thanks," I said, putting the tickets on the table. I turned to Peter, who looked relaxed in his beige khakis and an indigo T-shirt. "So, what are you guys up to?"

"Nothing," Peter shrugged. "We are going out for dinner. Would you care to join us? My treat."

I glanced at Tom quickly before turning back to Peter. "I'll have to pass this time. Thanks, though."

"You shouldn't turn down his offer," Tom smirked.

I felt my eyebrows wrinkle as Peter hung his head and ran a hand through his hair. I followed him with my eyes as he got up from the sofa and walked around before leaning against the kitchen countertop.

Tom stood and moved to stand next to Peter. "This guy is rarely nice to a girl. Come and join us. Don't make him sad."

"Don't listen to him, Rory. He likes teasing people," said Peter, casting a hard look at Tom, trying to tell him to shut up. Afterward, he placed his hands on Tom's shoulder and steered him toward the door.

Tom chuckled, winking and waving at me.

"See you tomorrow, Roomie. Don't latch the door like last time, okay?" said Peter, turning back to me.

Tom froze and whipped back around toward the door. "She did what? Locked you out?" he asked.

Peter nodded, rubbing a hand over his eyes and letting the corner of his mouth droop like he was crying.

"That's not true." I glared at Peter.

"Security found me and beat me up." Peter leaned on Tom's shoulder, wailing.

I shook my head as he winked at me.

"Really? Wow, how could you mistreat him, Rory?" Tom implored, joining the charade.

I rolled my eyes.

"Yeah, she abuses me. Now you see what it's been like to live—"

"Stop it!" I cried, lunging forward and covering Peter's mouth with my hands.

I was taken aback by my own reaction, but it was too late to withdraw my fingers from his lips. My heart leaped into my chest as I felt the warmth and softness of Peter's lips against my fingers. Both Peter and Tom were shocked. Tom's mouth hung slightly open as he stared at me.

The awkwardness was shattered when Peter gently grasped my hands to pull them down, revealing the broad smile he had been hiding underneath them.

"Are you going to cover your crime now?" he said, throwing his head back and laughing hard.

Tom raised his eyebrow and glanced at me and shifted his eyes to Peter and back at me.

"I never locked you out on purpose!" I said, curling my fingers as the sensation lingered on my palms. "I forgot that you said you'd be home late."

"But you made the neighbor call security when I tried to get in!" Peter protested, still holding my hands. "They thought your apartment was being burglarized." He turned to Tom and said, "You should be happy to see me in one piece. The security dog almost pulled my leg off."

I grimaced because that was true. "But I cleared it up with them, didn't I?" I said, jerking my hands free, and he released his grip.

Peter chuckled, inserting his hands into his back pockets. "Yeah, yeah, yeah." He rolled his eyes. "But you hurt my reputation, Rory."

"What reputation? You didn't have one until then, and now the neighbors know you, and everyone seems to like you." I wrinkled my nose at him.

Tom leaned toward me and said, "I think that's a juicy story and deserves to be told over dinner. Come with us. I'd looooove to hear that story from the beginning," he sang.

"But—"

Tom hooked his hand around my arm and took my bag off the countertop as he steered me out of the apartment.

"My dear Rory, let's hear your story." Tom smiled widely at Peter and gestured toward the door. "You can lock the door, mate, but don't latch it." Cackling, he dragged me with him as Peter rolled his eyes and turned back to lock the door.

The burger restaurant was crowded, but we didn't have to wait too long. Ten minutes later, we were placing our order.

I ordered a salad and a small chocolate shake while Tom and Peter each ordered fries and two burgers. I looked at them with envy. If I ate that many burgers, I would be fat in a short time.

We found a table after grabbing our trays, and Tom quickly reminded us he wanted the whole scoop. His eyes soon teared up from laughing as Peter told him about attempting to break into the apartment and getting accosted by security while waking up the entire building.

Poor Peter! He had tried and tried to call my phone, but I didn't answer. After that, he'd decided to climb over the patio fence, hoping I'd forgotten to lock the sliding door. Unfortunately, Leo, my next-door neighbor, had insomnia and happened to see Peter climb up the fence. He'd called security, and they'd rushed over with a dog and caught Peter at the top of the railing. The dog had desperately tried to bite his dangling leg, and its bark had woken the neighbors.

I explained that it was all a misunderstanding. That night, I'd come home late from work and thought Peter was already in his room. I'd forgotten he'd told me he would be back very late, so I'd bolted the door and gone to bed. He had called my phone, but I always put it on airplane mode before going to bed, so I never heard it ring.

Peter was upset with me after the incident and didn't talk to me for a whole day. He even went out and bought a small chalkboard and hung it behind the door. The board's purpose was to leave each other notes whenever we planned to be home late.

In his delight, he'd also added rule number 14R: *"Make sure to read notes on the chalkboard before bolting the door."* And *R* meant it was just for me, as his revenge for rule 12P that I'd written primarily for him.

My cheeks warmed as I covered my face with my hands.

Peter smiled and put his arm around my shoulder when Tom couldn't stop laughing, his face redder than his hair and tears streaming down his cheeks.

"That's okay, Roomie. It's over now. Just Tom…and he is heartless," he said, pointing at Tom with his chin.

Peter let his arm hang on my shoulder even as the food server came and filled up our glasses with ice water. The server was a girl about my age, and she couldn't take her eyes off Peter's face. Her eyes narrowed at me as Peter offered me the glass she'd just filled. I refused because I wasn't thirsty, so he brought the glass to his lips and drank one-fourth of it. I knew Peter did it on purpose, and it worked. The girl scoffed softly and left our table. Soon, Peter lifted his arm from my shoulder, leaving me cold from the sudden absence.

You shouldn't have used me, Peter. I glanced at Peter as he told Tom a joke.

But I didn't want to overthink it and joined them in the conversation.

CHAPTER 23

From: Pacific Hills Management
To: All tenants
Subject: Power outage and BBQ party tonight

Dear valued tenants,

Due to the extreme heat wave happening in Southern California, two utility poles in our neighborhood blew up at 9 AM, causing a blackout that affects our apartment complex. The electric company was notified and has been working on the issue. However, the transformers need to be replaced, and we were informed that it may take a while for the power to be restored.

So, if you have any meat in your fridge, please bring it over to the main club-house for our impromptu BBQ party. Better to share than let it spoil. Bring your favorite drinks. The management will provide salad, plates, plastic knives, and forks.

Further, for those who have medications that need refrigeration or have baby food, please contact the management so that we can store them in our office refrigerator, which is powered by a small generator.

Sincerely,
Lynette Reed
Leasing Manager
Pacific Hills Apartment.

"Oh man!" I groaned, recalling our full refrigerator. "Why is this happening when I'm busy?"

This morning, Desiree was pushing us to finish our financial reports because the White Water team wanted to see the current report as well as the reports from the last six months for trend analysis. The reports should have been done quicker. However, Lena hadn't taught me yet, and I was having a hard time finishing my part.

Since submitting her resignation letter, Lena didn't seem to care about her job anymore, took a few vacation days, and had only been in the office five days out of her last two weeks. I was upset that she was acting so unprofessional, leaving burdens on me like that. Although she wanted to punish Rowena, I wished Lena would have been more considerate to me as her friend.

"Maybe I should text Peter to see if he could save our food," I wondered, taking out my phone to send him a text.

> ***Peter, I'm going to forward you an email from management about the power outage. I wish I could go home earlier, but I can't and will be home late. Is it possible for you to go back earlier and take the meat from the freezer up to the office?***

At the same time, Rowena's message popped up on my Skype.

> ***Rory, come to my office!***

I grunted silently. After closing my eyes and taking a few deep breaths, I stood up and walked to Rowena's office.

She was busy typing as I entered. Without saying anything, she signaled for me to sit down. I took one of the empty chairs and waited until she finished typing whatever it was. I sat in Rowena's office for ten minutes, watching her type. Didn't she know I was busy too?

Finally, she stopped and let out a big sigh before looking at me.

"You've known Lena's last day will be in two days for the past two weeks. I expected you to learn her tasks quickly," Rowena said in her condescending tone. "I've checked the reserve analysis report, and you did it wrong. Redo it and give it to me by the end of the day; I need it for my analysis." And she turned to her screen and continued typing.

That's it? After waiting ten minutes?

"Okay," I said, standing up to leave.

My phone rang at the same time I closed Rowena's door behind me. Her head jerked up, and she narrowed her eyes at me. I turned and walked toward my cubicle, looking at my phone's screen to see who was calling.

"Hi, Peter," I said in a low voice.

"Is this Rory?" an unfamiliar voice said.

"Yes. And who is this? How did you get Peter's phone?" I asked, feeling panic rising in my chest.

"This is Mac Patterson, Peter's coworker. Peter is in the hospital with some stomach pain, and your name was marked as his contact person. Could you come to the hospital?" the man said.

"Oh no," I muttered, clenching my phone tighter. "Is he okay?"

"The doctor is with him now."

"I see." Then I remembered something. "Uh, wait, are you sure Peter put my name as his emergency contact? I'm only his roommate," I said, feeling confused. "Can you find Tom's name in his phone?"

There was a pause.

"Sorry, there is no other name but yours. Could you come now?" Mac said.

I let out a breath, lifting my hand to scratch the back of my head as I pondered why Tom's name wouldn't be anywhere in Peter's phone. "Uh, I'm—" The word *busy* was already on the tip of my tongue, but I stopped. Peter needed me. "Yes, I'll try. Please text me the hospital's address."

"I will." Then he hung up, and soon after, my phone buzzed with a text.

Hoag Memorial Hospital Presbyterian, Newport Beach. Please meet me in the ER. Mac.

I rushed back into Rowena's office. She was staring at her computer, munching a chocolate chip cookie. She pouted as she looked up at me.

"Sorry, Rowena, I have an emergency. My roommate has just been rushed to the hospital, and I'm the emergency contact. Can I leave now and work from home after that?" I said, maintaining a calm voice so as not to sound rushed.

"Why did your roommate call *you*? Doesn't she have family to help?" asked Rowena, her eyes glittering with disbelief.

"Well, his coworker called me because I am his *emergency contact person*," I repeated.

"*His* coworker?" Rowena's voice rose, and a mocking smile appeared on her face. "So, you live with a guy? Since when?"

"Can I leave now, please? It's an emergency," I said, controlling my tongue to keep from saying, *"It's none of your business!"*

Rowena scoffed and flapped her hand. "Make sure to submit your work today," she said coldly.

I gave her a nod and closed the door quietly.

Yoo-Shi's head popped up over my cubicle, and she whispered, "Is everything okay? I saw you rushing back to Rowena's office."

"Peter is in the hospital, and my name was listed as his emergency contact, so I need to get to the hospital now," I said, saving my work and then turning off my notebook.

"I hope he is okay," Yoo-Shi said, giving me a sympathetic look while I tidied up some papers and piled them on the corner of my desk.

"I hope so too," I said, inserting my notebook in its bag. "See you tomorrow."

I rushed downstairs and pushed the big door open just as someone yelled from behind me, "Hold the door, please!" My mind was on Peter, and it was too late for me to hold the door, anyway. I glanced over my shoulder. It was Lisa. I would hear she'd complained about that tomorrow, but now, I didn't care much.

CHAPTER 24

The traffic from Myriad's office to Newport Beach was light since it wasn't a rush hour, but for me, it seemed to crawl along. I knew switching lanes on the freeway didn't make the trip any faster, but I did it anyway. In about twenty minutes, I was searching for a parking space in the visitor parking lot at the hospital, but none were empty.

Finally, I found a spot at the end of the lot, which required me to walk a long way to the emergency building. I closed my eyes and took a deep breath before getting out of the car. The last time I had been at the hospital was when my mom had her car accident. I didn't like hospitals since then. The cleanest smell made my stomach fluttery and nauseous. However, my roommate needed me.

Gritting my teeth, I got out of the car and half-jogged to the emergency wing. Passing by a couple of empty spots in the emergency parking lot, I wanted to slap my forehead for not thinking clearly. Of course, there was a special parking lot for emergency patients. *Duh, Rory!*

I almost bumped into a man in a white knee-length overcoat coming out of the building.

"Whoa, take it easy!" cried the man, shifting quickly enough to prevent us from colliding.

I glanced at his name tag. Edward Martin, MD. He looked young for a doctor. "So sorry. I didn't see you." I lifted my hands.

"Are you okay?" he asked, adjusting his glasses.

I shook my head. "No, my roommate is in the ER, and they called me about coming down to confirm something," I said quickly, then continued walking toward the main lobby. "Sorry, I have to go."

"I'm an ER doctor. Maybe I can help. What's your roommate's name?" he asked, catching up to me.

"Peter Ryder," I answered.

His eyebrows knitted together as if he recognized the name. "I think he was admitted about forty-five minutes ago." He motioned for me to follow him.

"Thank you," I said, trailing behind him.

The young doctor smiled over his shoulder.

We walked across the main lobby to the front desk, where two of four nurses behind the counter were busy talking with patients. One was on the phone, perching it between her shoulder and her head while she busily typed on the keyboard, and the other was reading something on the clipboard in her hand. She looked up and offered a smile when Dr. Martin approached the table.

"What can I do for you, Doctor?" she asked, glancing at me.

"Kathy, could you give me information about a patient named Peter Ryder? If I'm not mistaken, he was admitted thirty to forty-five minutes ago," he said. "This is his roommate—" He whipped his head around and asked me, "What's your name?"

"Rory Arrington."

Turning back to the nurse, he said, "I think Rory here was called about confirming something. Could you give us an update on him?"

The nurse nodded and moved to an empty monitor. After several clicks, she looked up at him. "Yes, I found his information. He was admitted with stomach pain. We did some bloodwork but are still waiting for the results," she answered, straightening her back. "Someone—"

"Rory!" I heard someone call out from behind me.

I turned and focused on a guy of medium height with short, blond hair waving at me as he approached. His buttoned-down shirt, navy-blue pants, tie, and blazer made him look out of place.

"Rory?" he asked, studying my face. "Hi, I'm Mac, Peter's assista—er, coworker." He extended his hand.

I shook his hand gently. "What happened to him? And why am I needed here?" I asked, feeling butterflies in the pit of my stomach.

"The doctor said he has appendicitis and needs surgery. Peter insisted I call you. He wanted you to be here," said Mac, wiping his clammy forehead.

Now I understood why Peter only had me as his ECP. He wanted to hide his relationship with Tom. I nodded and turned to Dr. Martin. "Doctor, is it possible for me to see Peter before the surgery?" I asked, even though I figured the answer would be no because I wasn't a relative.

Dr. Martin gazed at me, seeming to be having a debate with himself. "Well, you aren't family, but Peter wants you to be here. Um, let me see. Why don't you take a seat?" He pointed at the array of hard chairs in the waiting room.

I nodded and followed Mac to a row of seats looking out the windows.

Dr. Martin disappeared through two big swinging doors with an Emergency Personnel Only sign on them.

"Do you need anything? Coffee or tea or water?" asked Mac, sitting next to me.

"I'm good, thank you," I answered, holding my purse on my lap.

Mac nodded and sat quietly.

The waiting room was full of people. Two young moms held crying babies in the corner. Across from Mac was a guy in his twenties, cradling a bleeding arm. In another row, a plump lady around fifty sat with her hands clasped tightly in her lap. Her eyes kept glancing at the swinging doors where Dr. Martin had gone. Maybe she was waiting for a loved one.

I pressed my back against the seat as I felt nauseous, and my heartbeat was raging in my ears. Squeezing my eyes shut helped a little, but the septic smell and mumbles from people around me made me dizzy.

I'll be fine. I'll be fine. I'll be fine.

A soft touch on my shoulder brought me back, and I looked up at Mac's concerned face.

"You look pale. Are you okay?" he asked.

I gave a soft chuckle and rubbed the middle of my forehead with my fingers. "I'm fine. Just…," I lifted my shoulders and looked around, "I'm a bit dizzy with all the commotion."

Mac nodded and reached into his blazer pocket to take out a roll of candies. He handed the roll to me. "Want a peppermint? I heard it's good for calming your nerves."

"Yes, thank you," I said, picking one of the candies out of the roll. The minty flavor was refreshing in my mouth, and I felt a bit better. "How long have you worked with Peter?"

"Well, not too long. Maybe—"

My gaze quickly shifted to Dr. Martin emerging from the big doors and walking toward us.

"Peter is waiting for his blood test result, so I can let you in for a short time," he said, jerking his head toward the doors.

I nodded and rose from my seat.

Mac said, "You go ahead. Tell him I'm here if he needs anything."

I nodded again, still in a daze, and turned to follow the doctor.

"Only five minutes, okay?" Dr. Martin reminded me as we passed through the doors.

"Thank you, Doctor," I said.

"Call me Edward," he smiled at me.

"Thank you, Edward," I said again.

Edward nodded and led me to a large room with a row of five beds on each side and a green curtain between them. He stopped at the second bed on the right and pulled the curtain aside.

My hand flew to my mouth at sight in front of me.

Peter's face was ashen as he lay on the bed with an IV attached to each arm. His shirt was open, and two electrodes were stuck on his chest to monitor his heartbeat. His forehead glistened with sweat, and his breathing was labored.

"He isn't in pain. We already gave him morphine. He is going to be a little out of it," said Edward. "But you—don't stay longer than five minutes, okay?"

I nodded, never taking my eyes off Peter.

Peter stirred as I approached his bed. His eyes fluttered and slowly opened.

"Hi, Roomie," he croaked.

"I'll leave you guys alone," Edward said, placing his hand on my shoulder. "Five minutes."

"Okay." I nodded, watching him pull the curtain back into position.

"You seemed okay this morning," I said. "When did you start feeling pain in your stomach?"

Peter exhaled slowly before forcing a thin smile. "I thought I had a regular stomachache, but the doctor said my appendix is about to burst. They already took a sample of my blood, and once that test comes back, they will do surgery." His eyes turned gentle as our eyes met. "It's good to see you before the surgery. I'm glad you came. And by the way, don't tie your hair up like that. It looks like a ducktail."

I couldn't believe my ears. He was in the ER and still in the mood to tease me.

Peter smiled mischievously as I scowled at him and pulled the tiny hairband from my hair. The AC at the office was broken again. Although the General Affairs department had provided us with some standing fans, the air in the room had still been stuffy. My hair wasn't too long, just above my shoulder, but it was too hot to let it down. Tying it up was a good way to cool off my neck.

"Does Tom know you are here? I didn't see him in the waiting room," I said. "Your coworker, Mac, called me because you put my name as your emergency contact."

Peter cleared his throat. "Yes, he'll be here shortly. I already asked a nurse to contact him."

I heard someone approaching, and then the curtain was pushed aside. I turned to see a female nurse about my height with a clipboard in her hand. Her smile widened as she looked at us—at Peter, to be exact. She looked cheerful compared to the stern-looking nurses at the front desk.

"Well, Mr. Ryder, my name is Lindsey, and I'm going to review your blood test and CT scan results, because there is something I want to tell you before we open up your stomach." She shifted her eyes to me and then back to Peter. "Is she your family? If not, I'd like to give you this information privately."

"I'm not. I'm going back to the waiting room now," I said, turning to Peter. "Good luck with your surgery."

Peter grabbed my wrist and pulled me closer. "She can hear. I want her to be here," he said to the nurse, ignoring my puzzled look.

His fingers around my wrist were cold. *Is he afraid?*

Lindsey looked at him thoughtfully and nodded, glancing at his fingers around my wrist as she said, "Well, if you prefer it that way …" Slowly, in plain English, she explained that there was a small growth in his intestine that the doctor wanted to remove to see if it was benign while he was in there taking out his appendix. "But don't worry; it's just best to check."

Peter nodded, seeming preoccupied and nervous.

"When will he have surgery?" I asked.

"Soon. We've contacted the operating room, and I believe in one or two more hours, we can take him up for the surgery. You'd better wait in the waiting room while we prep him," she added with a smile, pushing the curtain aside. "See you later, Mr. Ryder."

Peter looked pale and swallowed hard as he stared off into space beyond the curtain. For once, he looked like a boy who was scared to sleep in the dark. He released his fingers from my wrist, leaving pink marks behind.

I placed my hand on his shoulder. "Don't be afraid. I believe you'll be fine. Tom and I will be waiting for you outside, okay?"

Peter blinked and turned to me. He winced as he sat up. His IV tubing was a bit tangled under the blanket. When I came closer to adjust it, I felt his eyes on me. I looked up to find something in his look that made my pulse thud at the base of my throat and ears. I didn't know what to do but look down and pretend to adjust his blanket again.

"Rory, it sounds stupid, but I'm scared," he said without letting his gaze drop. "Now, listen, there is something I want to tell you just in case I don't wake up again."

"Don't be silly. You'll be fine," I comforted while patting his shoulder. "How about telling me later, after your surgery, okay?"

Peter grabbed my wrist and squeezed. Not hard, but enough to make me stop smiling. "I'm serious. I have to tell you this because it is important, so you don't hate me later." His voice trembled. "Between Tom and me, we are—"

Peter's words were cut off by the curtain being pushed aside again. Two male nurses, one tall and one short, appeared in front of Peter's bed. The short nurse pushed a cart with a syringe, a long needle, a scissors, a tiny bottle with a metal cap, and a pair of gloves. He stopped halfway, his slanted eyes widening behind his glasses.

"Who is she? Why is she here?" he asked the tall nurse.

"Sorry, miss. You shouldn't be here," ordered the tall nurse. His hand waved sharply to force me out.

"I'm sorry," I said, looking at them and turning to Peter quickly. "I'm waiting outside." And I hurried toward the door that led to the waiting room.

Back in the waiting room, Mac was still there, but Tom hadn't arrived yet. *Where was he?*

Mac rose from his seat, then sat again as I sat down next to him.

"They are preparing him for surgery," I informed him. "Listen, Mac, I'm going back home, but I'll be back later. Is it okay to leave you here alone?"

"Don't worry, I'll be here until everything is done," he said calmly, as if it were part of his job.

"Um, don't you have to go back to work?" I asked in disbelief.

Mac shrugged. "This is my job too." And his face flushed as if he were saying something he shouldn't have to say. Clearing his throat, he rose from his seat and said, "I need something to drink. See you later, Rory."

I returned to the hospital an hour later. I'd taken the liberty of getting some clean clothes for Peter, just in case he needed them, and thanks to Sunshine Cleaners for delivering his clothes, including underwear, while I was home.

After putting a rolling suitcase in the back seat, I closed the door and went to the driver's seat. I sensed that I was being watched. With a hand on the front door, I looked around, but there was no one in the parking lot or the courtyard or greenbelts. Maybe I was anxious because of Peter's condition. Taking a deep breath, I slid into the seat, closed the door, and started the engine. Slowly, I left the parking lot through the main gate and rolled onto the main street.

I parked my car in the regular lot because Mac had texted me that the doctors had moved Peter to the main hospital for surgery. I took out the luggage and dragged it behind me. The automatic doors opened as I stepped in front of them. An elderly lady in a flowered blouse greeted me and gave me directions to the waiting room for surgery.

I passed one corridor after another until I noticed a chapel near the gift shop inside the hospital. I entered the chapel. It was dark there. The only light came from some candles in front of a statue of Mother Mary in the corner and a few dimmed lights on the ceiling. I sat on a pew and clasped my hands in a prayer position.

I wasn't a regular churchgoer and prayed only if I remembered. I wasn't sure if God would listen to me for Peter's surgery, but it didn't hurt to try. I closed my eyes and said a short prayer for Peter and then left the chapel, heading toward the waiting room.

The waiting room in the main hospital was smaller than the waiting room in the emergency building. Mac was there and had already taken off his blazer and tie and folded them next to his chair. He was typing on a notebook sitting on his lap.

Tom was also in the room and talking to a guy with a blond, slicked-back hairstyle. He turned his head in my direction as I entered.

"Rory!" Tom rose from his seat and walked over to greet me.

"How's the surgery?" I asked, glancing at the blond guy. My eyes widened as I recognized Phil Campbell, one of the five team members from White Water. *What is he doing here?*

"Hi, Mac," I greeted as he looked up from his computer to smile at me.

Phil recognized me and looked surprised to see me there. He gave a nod of acknowledgment as Tom led me to take a seat next to him.

"The surgery just started twenty minutes ago," Tom said. He caught Phil and me exchanging glances. With a smile, he turned to Phil and shifted his eyes toward me. "Rory, this is Phil Campbell. Phil, this is Rory, Peter's roommate, who happens to be a Myriad employee. I bet you have met in the office. Phil is my—our friend, so I hope this meeting won't make things awkward at work." He chuckled.

"Yes, we've met at the office, but he has been working closely with the finance department, so we haven't had a chance to talk yet," I said.

Phil offered a smile. "Yes, we've met." His eyes fell to the luggage standing near my feet.

"Oh, I almost forgot!" I turned to Tom and gave it to him. "This is clothes for Peter. I had hoped you'd take care of this, but I don't know your phone number, and Peter couldn't tell me either, so I took the liberty to bring these. I hope you don't mind."

Tom took the carry-on from my hand, his eyes sparkling. "Thanks. You sure are nice to him," he said, putting it on the floor in front of his seat.

"Peter is my roommate. When he is in trouble, of course I want to help him," I said brightly.

"Do you want anything to drink?" asked Phil. His voice was gentle, almost like a whisper.

"I'm good. Thank you," I said, taking a Kindle from my bag.

He nodded and turned to Tom with the same question. Tom said he would go with him, and they went to the snack area next door together.

I was on the tenth page of my book when two doctors entered wearing their surgical uniforms. As they removed the masks from their faces, I recognized one of them as Dr. Martin, who had let me talk to Peter before his surgery. He smiled at me from behind the older doctor.

Mac and I rose from our seats almost in unison as the doctors approached us, and Tom and Phil returned just as the older doctor started speaking.

"The surgery went well, and the appendix was removed, including the growth. We just sent the growth to the lab for further testing. I don't think it is dangerous, but we have to test it to be one-hundred-percent certain. Dr. Martin will go over the results with you later. In the meantime, Peter is still under sedation, but you can see him when he wakes up. Any questions?"

Tom asked, "About the surgery report and the test results, is it possible to send those to his family in London?"

The doctor nodded. "Yes, I'll make sure we fax it to the number you gave us earlier," he said, then he lightly bowed to Tom before leaving us alone.

Edward followed the older doctor out of the room.

A heavy burden lifted from my shoulders with the good news. Tom and Phil clasped hands to show their relief.

Mac exhaled slowly, closed his notebook, and put it into its case. "I'm going to the administration office to arrange everything," he said to Tom. "Have a good night, gentlemen." He nodded to Tom and Phil. "Rory," he said as he turned to me.

I nodded at him as he left the waiting room. My eyebrows knitted as a sudden thought flashed in my mind: Why did Mac, Peter's coworker, have to deal with the administration office? But my thought was interrupted by Tom.

"So, Rory," he said, turning to me, "everything turned out well. I think it's better you take a rest, and I'll give you an update as soon as possible."

"Yes, thanks," I said, feeling grateful for being able to go back home. I still had to finish the reports for Rowena. She'd only said "by the end of the day" but hadn't mentioned what time, so I assumed any time before midnight should be sufficient. "Bye, Tom. Bye, Phil. See you in the office."

It was almost seven in the evening when I walked to the parking lot. The sky was still as bright as it had been at four. Suddenly I stopped walking and turned around to scan the parking lot. There was an elderly lady in a wheelchair with her son pushing her to the car. There was a young couple, and the husband carried a baby seat in one hand and held his wife's hand with the other. So sweet! However, they were not my reason for stopping. I felt like someone was watching me again, although I didn't see anyone suspicious in the parking lot. Shuddering, I walked faster to my car.

CHAPTER 25

Tom called before I left for work the following morning, giving me an update that Peter's condition was stable. The growth they had removed was benign. Although he was past the critical hour, his condition needed to be monitored a little longer, so he would have to stay in the hospital for another three or four days. Peter's family had requested he be transferred to a rehab facility they'd chosen for his recovery, and Tom suggested I visit him if I was free in the afternoon.

Before hanging up, he gave me the address and instructed me to tell the front desk that I needed to go to room 808, and someone named Marcus would accept me.

"Yes!" I pumped my arm up into the air. I couldn't forget the panicked expression on Peter's face when they'd told him about finding the growth. Now, he could focus on healing and go back to work peacefully.

I parked my car in the additional parking lot across from Myriad's main building due to the ongoing semiannual sales meeting that had occupied the regular parking spaces for the entire week. Despite the early hour, there were no available spots due to the crowded event.

"Rory!" someone called from the direction of the back entrance.

I looked over as Jason waved and jogged toward me.

"Good morning," he greeted as he stopped in front of me. As usual, he was dressed nicely for work. Jason's clothes always fit perfectly, as if made by tailors instead of from a regular department store, and his shoes were always shiny.

"Good morning." I smiled at him, swiping my employee card to open the back door. A soft click sounded to inform us that the door was unlocked.

Jason held the door for me. "I was looking for you yesterday, but Yoo-Shi said you left early. Is everything okay?" he asked as I passed him.

"Yes, everything is good. Nothing to be worried about," I answered, heading toward the foyer.

"Good. I'm glad everything is okay," said Jason, giving a quick look to the left before turning back to me.

"And why were you looking for me yesterday?" I asked, gazing at him.

Jason shook his head. "Nothing important. I just wanted to tell you there is a seafood place I think you may like. Do you want to go with me this weekend?"

"Maybe not this weekend. I've been busy with the White Water project, and I may have to work Saturday. Sorry," I explained. Maybe my eyes fooled me, but I thought I saw some coldness in his eyes for a second. Then I blinked, and those eyes were as warm as usual.

"Well, maybe in another week, if you are free," Jason offered with a smile. "Have a good day, Rory. See you around."

"You, too, Jason," I said, turning to climb the stairs to the second floor.

"Hey, Rory," Jason called again as I was halfway up the first flight.

I looked down to the first floor.

"If your roommate happens to move out, please let me know. You don't mind taking a guy roommate, do you? I am still looking for a place," he said.

I tucked my eyebrows together. *Why did he say that?* But I didn't want to overthink. "Uh, yeah," I answered quickly, and continued climbing the stairs.

Hoping not to be noticed, I walked across the hall and passed Rowena's office quietly. Her office was still dark. Feeling relief, I sat on my seat, took out my notebook, and turned it on.

"Rory, are you there?" Yoo-Shi whispered.

"Yes, I'm here," I answered, typing in my password.

Yoo-Shi came to my desk and glanced at Rowena's office before saying anything. She looked tense.

"What happened?" I whispered as Yoo-Shi crouched next to me.

"I thought only Sylvia, and Lena, and I knew your roommate is a guy. I didn't know Rowena knows too. How did she find out?" Yoo-Shi whispered back.

I blinked fast as I tried to recall yesterday. Once I remembered, I told her in a low voice, "I was in a panic yesterday and slipped when telling her that *his* coworker called me, and I needed to leave for his emergency. Damn!"

Yoo-Shi nodded slowly. "Yes, so damn! Well, after you left, Jason came and looked for you. At the same time, Rowena was bad-mouthing you in front of Desiree about having a male roommate who was in the hospital. You know how loud her voice gets when she's excited about something." She bit her lower lip as she took a breath. "I've noticed Jason seems to like you, and he obviously heard the conversation. I don't know how to describe it, but his expression was strange. Without saying anything, he abruptly left." Yoo-Shi snapped her fingers. "When I tried to find out where he went, someone said he left early with a stomachache. I hope he isn't mad at you," Yoo-Shi said, pressing her lips together.

Her explanation made me understand why Jason, out of the blue, had said that I was fine to have a male roommate.

Sighing, I closed my eyes. The milk was already spilled; there was no reason to cry over it. "Thanks, Yoo-Shi. Yeah, I met Jason this morning, and he didn't seem upset," I said.

Yoo-Shi nodded in relief. "I'm glad he is still nice to you," she said, standing up. "I'd better get back to my desk before the witch turns me into a rat."

I chuckled. "Thanks again!" I whisper-shouted to her.

"Don't mention it," she whisper-shouted back as she tiptoed to her cubicle.

I headed to the printing room and returned fifteen minutes later with two inches of paper, noticing Rowena had come in while I was gone.

"Rory! Come to my office!" she yelled as I passed her office.

I sighed and put the papers on my table. "Yes?" I said, entering her office.

"What did I tell you about the reports yesterday? I wanted them by the end of the day. And when did you send it to me? At 11:00 p.m.? Do you think our office is open until 11:00 p.m.?" She slapped her hand down hard on the table. "Now, how do I have time to review them?" A deep crease on her forehead got deeper, and she pouted as she glared at me from behind her glasses.

"I'm sorry, Rowena. I'd tried to finish them as fast I could, but I didn't leave the hospital until late."

Rowena scoffed. "You care about your roommate, but you don't care about your job? Did your roommate give you money, so you preferred to help him instead of doing your work?"

That was an unfair accusation! Anger bubbled in my chest. Clenching my fingers, I tried to control it. "With all due respect, Rowena, it has nothing to do with money. We help each other because neither of us has family in California." I was half-lying because Peter had Tom and I had Rick. "So, we agreed to put our names as emergency contacts for each other just in case something happened. And he had to have emergency surgery yesterday," I said, maintaining my voice and looking straight at her. "I don't think I broke any rules except to send you the report later than your expectation."

Rowena's lips got thinner, and her eyes flashed. "But you could work at the hospital while waiting for your roommate, right?"

I bit my inner lip tighter to stop me from saying something stupid.

"I did take my notebook to the hospital, but the hospital blocked any internet connection to prevent interference with their medical devices, so I couldn't access Myriad's network," I said. "I had to do it at home, and I got it done as quickly as I could."

Rowena snorted, looking at me in disbelief. "Don't expect me to forget to write this tardiness on your performance review, Rory," she said haughtily.

My chest tightened. I was so tired of her bullying. "If that happens, I apologize if I have to bring this up to HR. I left early from work because of an emergency, not for some frivolous leisure activity."

For a few seconds, we stared each other down until Rowena backed down. She turned away and flapped her hand to shoo me out.

Without saying anything, I turned and returned to my desk, completely fed up with the unfair treatment. I figured it was time for me to find another job. I couldn't handle that crazy bitch anymore. Sylvia was right—there had to be a hell for someone like her.

After work, I decided to visit Peter because I missed my goofy roommate. It took me an hour to reach his rehab facility.

"No way!" My jaw dropped as my car rolled slowly through a broad, elaborate metal gate and onto a long gravel driveway with beautifully manicured hedges on each side. The driveway circled a large fountain with a turnoff for the parking area at the back of the building.

Cruising slowly down the aisle in search of a parking space, I admired the many expensive cars there. I parked my Ford C-Max, the cheapest car to ever park there, between a Bentley and a Jaguar. Then I dialed Tom's number because he must have given me the wrong address. Peter had come to the US for his family business, and from his lifestyle, he must have been from an affluent family. But this place was *too* expensive for him.

After two rings, Tom picked up his phone. "Hey, Rory."

I raised an eyebrow at the unusual, slightly sharp tone in his voice. "Hey, Tom. I arrived at the address you gave me, but this place doesn't look like a rehab facility. Did I miss a digit of the address number?" I asked carefully.

He didn't respond, but in the background, someone was talking to him, and then I didn't hear anything. I pulled my phone away from my ear to see if I was still connected to Tom.

A minute later, Tom spoke again. "That's the correct address. His family chose this place." His voice was gentler than before. Listening to him, I glanced at the expensive cars around me. "Just go to the front desk, then tell them you need to go to room 808. And sorry, love, I have to deal with something."

Without waiting, he hung up, leaving me amused with the disconnected tone in my ears. Shrugging, I put my phone in my bag and got out of my car.

Along the way to the front of the building, I couldn't stop admiring the enormous complex. The main building of gray stone was impressive. Walking through the tall, double front doors, I took in the main lobby. It was a luxurious space with cushy sofas decorated with pillows and faux-fur throws.

My steps echoed on the marble floor as I walked toward the long reception desk along the right wall.

A middle-aged lady greeted me, her eyes squinting as she smiled sweetly. "What can I help you with, dear?" she said softly.

"Good afternoon. I'm a guest for a patient in room 808," I said.

The lady's face changed. With a slight bow, she asked me to wait and walked over to the mahogany desk behind her and picked up the only phone there. She pressed one button and had a brief conversation with someone. Her salt-and-pepper wavy hair bounced as she nodded, then she put the receiver back before writing something on a piece of light-yellow paper. Finally, she returned to where I was waiting.

"Here are the directions to the room," she said, giving me the paper with both hands.

Thanking her, I took the paper and followed her pointed direction toward the elevator. As I walked there, I read the instructions she'd written in such neat handwriting.

Use the middle elevator to reach the 3rd floor. Then walk straight until the end of the corridor, turn left, and then turn right. You won't miss it because there is a security guard in front of the room.

"A guard? Really?" I paused and reread the instruction.

Shrugging, I pressed the button and waited for the elevator in the middle to open. It was a short ride to the third floor. Once the door opened with a soft ding, I stepped out into a long beige corridor decorated with huge paintings and elaborate flower arrangements on antique console tables along the far wall. The carpet had an elegant curving pattern, and I was tempted to run barefoot across its plush surface.

On the last turn, I saw a slender man in a black suit standing tall with his hands behind his back in front of the room ahead. His gaze locked on me as I walked toward him.

"Good afternoon. My name is Rory Arrington, and I'm here to visit Peter," I said.

The guard gave me a nod and signaled me to wait while he entered the room. Within a minute, he returned and held the door to let me in, then closed it behind me.

My mouth rounded as I took in the sight of a rectangular room designed like a small waiting room with two plush sofas, two straight-backed chairs, and a marble coffee table positioned between them. From the big window on my left, I could see Catalina Island. This luxurious room looked more like a penthouse than a hospital room, featuring a beautiful kitchen complete with a dinette and four chairs. There was a large landscape painting hung between two sets of doors.

Looking at the expensive furniture in the costly rehab facility, I was genuinely curious about Peter's background. We had lived as roommates for four months, but we'd never openly spoken about our lives in detail other than his job, my job, my ex-boyfriend, my aunt, and his secret relationship with Tom because we simply honored each other's privacy.

If his family chose this place for his recuperation, his family business must have been bigger than I thought. *Or maybe Peter is doing illegal business.* Come to think of it, his reason to stay in my house was vague.

My wild thought made my heart pump faster. Good thing it was disrupted by the presence of a gray-haired man in a suit coming out of the nearest door and approaching me.

"Miss Arrington? My name is Marcus. Young Maste—eh, Peter has been waiting for you, but could you wait here for a few minutes?" he said in a thick British accent, pointing to a chair.

I nodded and took a seat, my stomach twisted with confusion as Marcus went through the other door. Grabbing my phone out of my bag, I open a browser to search something on the internet but stopped short at the sound of raised voices. At first muffled, the voices quickly got louder.

Before long, I recognized the voices—Peter and Tom—and they were having a heated argument.

"Don't be a jerk, Peter!" Tom yelled. "You should tell her the truth!"

"No, I won't! Just wait until everything is done. You've known the reason for this and promised to back me up. Also—"

"Prick! God, I never would've believed you would have the heart to hurt an innocent person. You're even worse than Dad! Screw you for doing this, Peter!"

The door on the right flung open, and Tom stormed out and slammed it behind him. His face and neck were crimson. Startled by my presence, he froze mid-step.

"Hi," I said hesitantly.

"Hi," Tom greeted me, forcing a smile.

"Is everything okay?" I said just above a whisper.

Tom exhaled and shook his head. "Sorry, love. I have to leave. I'm sorry," he mumbled as he rushed out.

Uncertain what would happen next, I sat watching the two doors with a million questions running through my mind. Before any paranoid thought could worry me further, Marcus came out the same door Tom had just burst through.

"Peter is waiting for you, Miss Arrington," he said, gesturing toward the door.

"Thank you," I said, rising from my seat. Walking through the door, I was greeted by the smell of jasmine as I stepped inside the room.

Peter was sitting up against the headboard of an enormous bed and smiling at me. His smile wasn't wide as usual, but he was genuinely happy to see me.

"Thank you, Marcus." He nodded to Marcus, who was standing behind me. Then he beckoned me to an armchair next to his bed.

As I came closer, I noticed the healthy pinkish color of his cheeks. He looked better, totally different than when he was in the ER.

"Oy, Roomie, do you miss me?" he teased.

"Not for a second." I grinned. "But you look better." I circled my finger in front of my face.

"Yup, feel like a new man." Peter stretched his arms to the sides.

I pulled the corners of my mouth up and sat on the chair. "Wow!" I yelped a little, looking at the seat cushion.

"Are you okay?" Peter's eyes widened as he threw the blanket to the side.

"Young Mast—please stay put." Marcus rushed to Peter, preventing him from stepping out of bed and then looked at me. "What happened, miss?"

"Nothing. Just…this chair is so soft and bouncy." I bounced slightly in my seat.

Peter rolled his eyes as Marcus pulled the blanket back over his lap.

Turning to me, Marcus gave a faint smile, clasped his hands together, and asked, "Would you like anything to drink?"

"Water is fine. Thank you, uh, Marcus," I said, moving a decorative sofa pillow to the empty seat next to mine.

"You're welcome, miss," said Marcus, backing away a few steps before turning and walking to the door.

Stopping him, Peter said, "Oh, Marcus, we have some strawberry-vanilla cake, right? Could you bring her some? And the chocolate bar."

"Yes." Marcus gave him a nod and exited.

The way he walked so elegantly, his body straight as a board and his hands at his sides, reminded me of the butler in *The Fresh Prince of Bel-Air* from the '90s, less the tuxedo and white gloves.

I giggled and leaned toward Peter. "Who is he?" I whispered.

He waved the question aside as if saying, *"I'll tell you later."*

"It's nice to hear your laughter again, Roomie. But why are you giggling?" Peter glanced at me, leaning back against his pillow.

"Have you ever watched the old American series called *The Fresh Prince of Bel-Air*? Marcus reminds me of their butler, Geoffrey."

Peter shook his head. "Is it good?" he asked.

"It is funny. Lizzy and I like it," I said.

"Awesome. Let's watch it together once I return home, okay?" Peter said.

"Sure."

"Could you adjust these pillows for me?" he asked, pointing behind himself.

I nodded and rose from my seat. "When I was sitting outside, I overheard you and Tom arguing," I said, adjusting his pillow. "Is everything okay?"

"Did you hear the whole conversation?" His voice sounded strained.

"No," I said, shaking my head.

"I see," Peter nodded, letting out a huge breath. "We just don't agree about something. But everything will be fine soon."

Our eyes met, and from the way he looked at me, I knew he sensed that I didn't believe him.

Avoiding my eyes, he ran his hand through his hair. "Hey, by the way, we had a blackout at the apartment complex the day I went to the hospital, right?" Peter said. "'Has the power come back yet? Have you been able to save the meat in the fridge? Sorry, I feel bad because I couldn't help you that day."

"Honestly, I was so rattled yesterday. When I finally got home, I was busy with my work. By morning, it was all thawing, so I threw it away." I shrugged, standing next to him. "I should have given the meat to management for their BBQ party when I came home to get your clothes."

Peter's neck flushed. "I'm sorry," he said.

"Nah, don't be sorry. No one can predict when an appendix will burst," I said, nudging his shoulder with my forefinger.

Lowering his eyes, Peter gave a little smile. "Let's go shopping after I get out of this place," he said gently, meeting my gaze.

"Great! You are going to buy some good meat for me, right? How about filet mignon? Or Kobe beef?" I grinned widely.

Peter chuckled, then turned his head to look at the open door. Marcus entered, carrying a tray with a bottle of Evian water, an ice-filled glass, a thick slice of cake on a plate, a chocolate bar wrapped in golden paper, and a bowl of Jell-O. I sat back in my seat and observed as he pushed an over-the-bed table on wheels closer to Peter and put the bowl of strawberry Jell-O on it.

Peter's nose wrinkled. "Again?" he groaned.

"Doctor's orders," said Marcus flatly, placing a teaspoon on a thick white napkin. Next, he put the cake, water, glass, and chocolate bar on the table next to me. "Please enjoy," he said gently, nodding to me before turning and treading to the door.

I took a bite of the cake, and it melted right away in my mouth. The tangy and sweet taste of the cream topping blended perfectly with the cake.

Peter struggled to get a spoonful of Jell-O into his mouth, past the clear disgust painted all over his face.

I smacked my lips. "Mm. Yummy!"

"Stop rubbing it in!" he scowled.

"Maybe you should imagine the Jell-O as the food you like. Like, let's see… In-N-Out Burger? Fried rice?" I suggested.

Peter made a face. "Yeah, right. Strawberry-flavored burger?"

Nodding, I stretched the corners of my lips up to a big grin.

Peter rolled his eyes but stopped pouting.

"Marcus?" Squinting, I waved my spoon toward the door. "Is he your butler?"

Peter almost choked on his Jell-O but nodded slowly after considering. "Marcus worked for my family even before I was born, and he is someone who assists me with many things. I could say that he is one of the most important people in my life." He stopped eating and stared at his Jell-O. "I barely knew my parents. They were always busy with their clients or attending social events or whatever reasons they made up. But I'm glad to have Marcus by my side. He is always with me—on my birthday, at my graduation, and even on Christmas—while my parents just sent me gifts or money on those occasions. Ironic, isn't it?" His face became gloomy as he watched his finger run around the bowl's edge.

I felt a pang of pity for him. After my mom passed away, I wasn't alone because I'd had Aunt Amy. But Peter only had Marcus, who acted as a personal assistant.

Peter wiped his mouth with a napkin and pushed the table away. A deep crease appeared on his forehead. He looked sad.

"Hey!" I called out, hoping to distract his attention.

Peter looked up at me.

"It sucks to have parents who don't care about you," I said, "but when you get older and have your own family, you can do things differently than your parents did. You can be with your kids for every important occasion, right?"

A smile appeared on his lips as his eyes came alive again. "I didn't know you could sound like such an old lady." He chuckled. "How old are you? Fifty-two?"

I rolled my eyes, grabbed the sofa pillow from the other seat, and threw it at him.

"Hey, hey, stop! I'm the one who got stitches, remember?" Peter laughed, ducking the pillow that bounced once before disappearing off the other side of the bed.

"Can I ask you a question?" I said.

"Sure."

"Before you were taken to the operating room, you were about to tell me something about you and Tom. What was it?" I studied his face.

Peter blinked, giving me a blank look. "What? Did I say that? I don't recall."

My mouth slightly opened. "You don't? Really? You were fully conscious at the time."

Peter scratched his head and shrugged. "Sorry, Roomie. I really don't remember. I must have been talking nonsense because of the painkiller," he said solemnly.

"Hmm." I narrowed my eyes, inspecting his face while Peter chuckled softly and gave a shrug. I was a hundred-percent sure he had been alert and conscious at the time.

Peter seemed relieved as Marcus entered the room to collect the dirty plate and bowl from us, then told me that visiting time was over. His eyes were on me for a while before telling me to come back again tomorrow as I waved and left the room.

CHAPTER 26

Fridays were usually my favorite day, but not this Friday. Today was Lena's last day. I hadn't learned any of my new responsibilities from her because she'd deliberately taken vacation days to punish Rowena, assuming she would be stuck with the work. Lena hadn't known I would inherit her tasks.

Lena and I went over as much as we could that last morning, and all the while my chest ached at the thought of doing her tasks with such limited knowledge and working for a narrow-minded woman who already rejected my every effort. My fists itched to punch something, to release the tightening in my chest.

Before her exit interview with HR, Lena asked if I'd like to join her to go down to the lunchroom. She'd felt terrible all morning, having realized the predicament she was leaving me with. Lena had always been helpful to me, and I wanted to keep our friendship outside the office.

Entering the lunchroom, I grabbed a seat as Lena stood almost in the middle of the room and looked around ruefully.

"I've worked at this company for two and a half years. I love the people here. I've made many friends from different departments. Quitting like this really hurts. I don't want it to end like this." Her voice sounded choked.

Lena was a strong lady, and she had finally broken down after two years of working for Rowena. What about me? What would I become?

"On my first day here, I sat at that table alone," Lena continued, running her fingers over the surface of the booth table at the corner, next to the refrigerator. "One by one, people approached and sat next to me: Andrew, Ted, Camilla, Sylvia. They treated me like I had been here for a long time. Since then, each day for lunch, we've gathered here. Then Yoo-shi came aboard, and then Geoffrey." Lena chuckled, glancing up at me. Her fingers curled into fists, and her eyes brimmed with tears. "Then Rowena joined Myriad. Since her first day, I haven't gotten along with her. The more you obey her, the more she steps on you. When Geoffrey left, I was miserable. Good thing you came aboard, so my life wasn't so bad," she said.

"Yeah, too bad she is a horrible manager. You'll be free from her after your exit interview. And if you find a new job, please remember me," I said.

Lena nodded, pressing her lips together. "Yes, for sure," she said.

I forced a smile and felt my steps becoming heavy as we walked back to our cubicles.

Around noon, I walked Lena out of the building. Sylvia and Yoo-Shi wanted to join us, but they had a meeting with Christine.

"Take care," said Lena, looking up at me through her car window.

"You too," I said, waving as her car rolled slowly toward the front gate.

Suddenly, her car stopped moving, rolled backward, and stopped in front of me.

"What happened? Did you forget something?" I asked, leaning down to see her clearly.

"Rory, listen—I'll only share this with you." Lena popped her head out of the window.

I nodded. "What is it?"

"I told HR everything. *Everything.* I even showed them some nasty emails Rowena sent me. HR promised to do something to prevent losing more good employees. But we'll see. People can promise anything. When Geoffrey left, HR promised to do something, but nothing happened. So, we'll see," she said, waving her hand. "Bye now, Rory!"

I watched her car roll out to the main street and then disappear. Heading back to the office, I felt dismayed when I heard my phone buzz in my pocket. Expecting a message from Peter, I found it was Jason reminding me about dinner with him tomorrow. I didn't feel like going, but Jason was my friend, and I didn't want to let him down.

CHAPTER 27

I spent my Saturday morning at home, attempting to complete the analysis of AR reports. Lena's helpful notes made it easier for me to understand the reports. The main problem was the significant amount of time it took to check each of the clients that had overdue payments for more than a year. Obviously, Rowena had forgotten that Myriad Beverage had seventy-five overdue clients.

Around four in the afternoon, I stopped. Standing up, I looked down happily at my work spread over the coffee table. I'd already analyzed half the overdue clients and felt confident that I could finish the rest tomorrow.

"I'd better get ready for dinner with Jason," I mumbled, walking to my closet and pulling out a white blouse and jeans.

Once I was ready, my doorbell rang. Opening the door, I saw Jason standing there, dressed up nicely.

"You look great!" I said, gazing at his clothes.

Jason beamed. "Thanks! And you too," he said, smiling.

I looked down at my jeans and blouse. "Should I change? I look shabby compared to you."

Jason shook his head. "No need. You look good in anything," he said thoughtfully.

"Thank you. Hey, wait a minute—let me grab my bag, okay?" And I turned to get my handbag from my room.

When I came out, Jason was in the living room, holding Peter's gaming headset up for inspection.

Damn, I should have moved it to my room.

"I didn't know you were into online gaming," he said, pointing at the headset. "I love this SteelSeries Arctic Wireless Headset. This is the best for gaming because it is sweat-free and very comfortable."

"Oh, that belongs to my roommate," I said. "Let's go. I'm ready."

Jason didn't seem to be in a rush as he kept staring at the headset. "I love online games too. Hey, ask Peter about his username, and what game he plays so we can play together," he said casually, putting the headset back on the table as he looked straight at me.

My eyebrows wrinkled. "How did you know his name?" I asked, searching his eyes.

Jason lifted his chin, showing Gwent, the Witcher card game, with something written on the tiny label.

To Peter. Happy Birthday. Love, Jane.

"I see. Sure, I'll let him know," I said, turning toward the door.

Jason followed. "Great. Let's get some dinner."

In the parking lot, he opened the car door for me.

"Thank you!"

He nodded and closed the door, then walked around the front to the driver's side.

"Where are we going?" I asked as he buckled his seat belt.

"A surprise. But I promise this place is wonderful, and you won't forget it," Jason said, smiling.

I grinned widely. "Okay, then. I love surprises." Noticing his knuckles were red and bruised, as if they'd been used for punching something hard, I looked up at him and asked, "What happened to your hands?"

Jason glanced at them and shrugged. "That's nothing. Just from exercising."

I didn't ask more.

The weather was perfect, and the freeway was not too crowded. In this warm weather, the beaches were usually packed with people.

Jason took me to a seafood restaurant right on the beach at Crystal Cove. It was a perfect place to have a drink, unwind, and enjoy the beauty of the orangish sky before sunset.

I was overwhelmed by the list of foods on the menu. Jason noticed and suggested I try the pan-seared striped sea bass. He ordered the Scottish wild isle salmon for himself and a bowl of jumbo shrimp cocktail for both of us. When he offered to order a bottle of white wine, I refused gently.

After a delicious meal, we sat on the beach and watched people light up the bonfire. The sky darkened, slowly revealing the stars that were always seen more clearly at the beach.

"What a lovely evening, don't you think?" asked Jason, looking around with a smile as he slid his arm around my shoulder.

Surprised, I felt uncomfortable. Jason was a friend, and I didn't want our friendship to change. Trying not to be too obvious, I leaned forward and picked up a shell from the sand. "Look! What a beautiful shell." I showed it to him.

Jason's arm fell away. "Ah, yeah, that's pretty," he said a little too enthusiastically. His ears turned red as he looked at the shell.

After that, we walked along the beach and let the waves wet our bare feet. Jason laughed each time I shrieked when a wave brushed my feet. The weather was warm, but the water was ice-cold. Before we left, we ordered ice cream and enjoyed it while watching people singing and dancing around their bonfire.

I enjoyed going out with Jason; he was a gentleman and knew how to treat a lady. When the weather turned a bit colder on the beach, he ran back to his car and offered me his jacket. Peter was a nice person, but sometimes he was childish too.

"Thanks for tonight," I said, looking down through his car window. "I really enjoyed it." Under the bright sky, I could see his eyes sparkling.

"Likewise. Could we do it again?" he asked.

"Sure," I nodded.

Jason smiled and started backing his car out without letting his gaze drop.

"Bye!" I waved.

Jason waved back and then drove slowly toward the exit gate.

When I was about to turn back to my apartment, my eyes caught a lady standing behind the maple tree, about thirty feet from me, and she was looking at me. Intrigued, I walked toward her.

The lady took a startled step backwards.

"Hi, can I help you?" I asked, walking closer to see her clearly. Under the garden path light, I could see her face. She was a petite girl with an oval, pretty face and long brown hair cascading over her shoulders. Her big eyes looked at me sorrowfully.

"Are you Rory?" she asked timidly.

"Yes," I answered. "How do you know my name? Have we met?"

"Don't go out with Jason anymore. He is not who you think he is," the girl said and then turned away quickly.

"Hey!" I called, but she ran to a blue Toyota Avalon and got in. I was too stunned to chase her.

"Remember what I said!" she called as the car passed me by.

CHAPTER 28

I couldn't shake off the warning from the girl the night before. It had loomed in my mind the whole night, interrupting my beauty sleep.

My phone buzzed on the kitchen counter.

"Hi, Peter!" I spoke.

"Hi, Roomie! Do you miss me?"

"Nah," I chuckled.

Peter blew a raspberry at me. "Hey, I just wanted to let you know I'll be home Monday. Yes, the doctor said I can go back home. Finally!" he said, letting out his breath. "God, I can't stand this place."

"Why?" I asked, sipping my coffee slowly. "Don't you get pampered there? You have Marcus to take care of you, and maybe he assigns a masseur to come and give you a massage."

"Humph! That old man!" Peter grunted. "He always said he cares about me, but then he gives me nothing but Jell-O each meal. I thought he was my mate."

I snickered. "If he gave you everything you wanted, you wouldn't be healing so quickly, dude!"

Peter scoffed. "You should be on my side."

I laughed at the grumble in his voice.

"Hey, someone will come to the apartment today and clean my bedroom. Is that okay?" Peter asked. His voice sounded unsure because he knew how I hated for strangers to come to my house.

"Oh, come on! Not again. Rule number thirteen!" I said, rolling my eyes.

"But my bedsheets need changing," he protested.

"I'll do it for you," I said stubbornly.

Peter scoffed again. "I locked my room, and you don't have the key. Besides, you aren't a maid, you are my roommate," he said.

I could imagine his expression at this moment. He sounded annoyed.

"Okay, call Tom and let him change them for you," I suggested, biting my lower lip to hold my laughter.

"Not Tom. He won't do it for me."

"But he is your boyfriend. Couldn't he help you with that?" I said, starting to feel annoyed.

"He isn't my—"

He stopped abruptly, but I'd already heard him clearly. "He isn't your what?" I asked, half-teasing, half-curious.

"For goodness' sake, Rory. Why are you making things so hard?" Peter said, raising his voice. "Fine, I don't want to argue with you anymore. Have a good day!" And he hung up.

I tsked and put my phone down on the countertop. What an irritable person he was! But I was happy about seeing him again. The apartment was too quiet without him.

Sunday afternoon, Peter sent Marcus to clean his bedroom. He was aware that I wouldn't be happy with yet another stranger entering my apartment, but since I'd met Marcus already, I couldn't argue the point.

Marcus was an efficient person. I was amazed at how quickly he changed the bedsheets and cleaned Peter's room. After he was done, I offered him something to drink, which he accepted gratefully.

"Thank you for letting Peter stay here," said Marcus, gazing across the coffee table at me. "He couldn't wait to get back home. I didn't understand why every day he asked the doctor when he could leave. Now I know the reason. This place feels like home." His eyes scanned the kitchen and living room.

"Thank you," I said, pressing my knees together while forcing a smile. "This place must be small compared to his home in England."

Marcus nodded. "That's true. This place is as small as his playroom when he was little."

What? His playroom was as big as this apartment? I cleared my throat, clamping my agape mouth shut. The more I knew about Peter, the more he became a stranger to me. "No wonder he always makes a mess in the kitchen," I said, half-joking.

Marcus's eyebrows furrowed. "Peter? In the kitchen?" he asked, shifting his body slightly toward me.

I nodded.

"What did he make? Boiled eggs?"

I chuckled. "Yes, that was his first attempt. And he burned them."

"Ah," Marcus nodded, pressing his lips as if trying not to laugh.

"Then, he wanted to make smoothies but forgot to secure the blender lid. Fruit juice flew all over the kitchen," I grinned, remembering that moment. "The third one was pancakes. He wasn't patient enough to use a fork to whisk the egg, so he used a hand-mixer."

Marcus tried not to look surprised and even lifted his eyebrows to encourage me to continue.

"He turned it on at the highest power, splattering flour and eggs everywhere. After that, I forbade him to cook unless I'm around. I bet he never cooked in his entire life."

Marcus seemed to consider this before saying, "Well, it must be unusual for you to see a man his age that can't cook something simple like pancakes or boiled eggs. Peter did learn to boil eggs, though. And that was it. After that, he never stepped into the kitchen or showed any interest in cooking anymore. He never told me why. But," Marcus tilted his head, his eyebrows pinched together in a frown, "listening to you, it seems to me he is interested in learning about cooking again. Hmm, it's fascinating!"

He shook his head in amazement and then lifted his gaze, smiling. "I ought to be going now. My *patient* is waiting for me. Thanks for the refreshment, Miss Rory. It is a pleasure to talk to you, and I hope we can meet again," he said, giving me a wink while rising from his seat.

I smiled at him. "Likewise, Marcus."

I walked him to the front porch, and Marcus bowed slightly before turning toward the parking lot.

CHAPTER 29

Though I'd wanted to be home when Peter arrived on Monday, my work had already been piling up, and I was overwhelmed. I'd gone into the office early and had to stay late. I hadn't been sleeping well because, each time I closed my eyes, Rowena's face flashed behind my eyelids, and her condescending tone rang in my ears.

I was typing an email to Vy when my phone blinked. I'd been keeping it on silent mode since Rowena had complained about hearing too many buzzes lately. I looked down at my phone. Peter had texted me.

> *Rory, I'm not going to be home today. Something happened in London, and I have to fly out tonight. See you in two weeks.*

My heart sank. I rose from my seat and stole a glance at Rowena's office to make sure she wouldn't see me leaving my cubicle. Rowena was focused on her computer, munching chocolate chip cookies as usual.

I went outside the building and dialed Peter's phone. "Come on…come on…," I mumbled, breathing faster as I waited to be connected.

"Hello?" Peter said.

"Peter, thank God you picked up. What happened?" I asked.

My eyes widened at the sound of a muffled cry.

"Hey, Roomie, can you tell me what happened?" I said softly.

"It's Jane," his voice croaked as he struggled to control his emotions. "Her third surgery didn't go well. Rory, she is dying!" he wept.

Peter! Carefree Peter—crying!

"Oh, Peter! I'm so sorry. Where are you now?" I asked. "When do you leave for London? From which airport?" I almost slapped my forehead. *What a dumb question!* He'd have to leave from LAX.

Peter sniffed. "I'm still at the rehab facility. My flight is from LAX—British Airways at seven thirty. That's the earliest flight I could get. How I wish to get a flight now," he said ruefully.

"I hear you," I said, my throat closed from the sudden news. "I'm so sorry, Peter."

"Yeah." Peter inhaled.

Neither of us said a word for several moments.

"Rory, could you come to LAX?" Peter said, breaking the silence first.

"Do you want me to?"

"Yes."

"Why?"

"I just need someone to talk to."

"I wish I could, Peter, but…I'm not sure if I can leave the office in time today. The earliest I could leave is at five, but by the time I arrive, you will already be boarding."

"Yeah, the traffic to LAX is always worse during rush hour." Peter sighed.

"I'm sorry. But Tom will be there, right?" I said quietly.

I could hear Peter huff on the other end. "Hey, I have to pack my stuff. I'll see you in two weeks, maybe?" he said in a hurry.

"Yes, and I'm sorry about Jane," I said.

Peter hung up.

I stared at my phone. *Poor Peter!*

The traffic to LAX was crowded. I drummed my fingers on the wheel as I noticed the time was already 5:45. I'd sneaked out of the office a few minutes early, while Rowena was in a meeting with Desiree, hoping to get ahead of rush hour.

After driving in bumper-to-bumper traffic for almost two hours, I finally parked in the Tom Brady International Airport's parking lot. I didn't know why I was driving to LAX, knowing Peter would be boarding by the time I got there.

The dashboard clock read five to seven. I ran across the parking lot to the terminal among people who were about to travel. They were steering an airport cart with piles of their luggage toward the airline's ticketing counters. I noticed a grandma busily cooing a crying little girl as I passed the counters, heading toward the TSA passenger screening area. I was feeling pretty foolish for doing this. Then I heard the first boarding announcement for British Airways to London. Peter's flight would leave in thirty minutes, so he was probably boarding.

Not sure why, I kept looking at the queue of people on the second floor, taking their turn through the last security checkpoint. Five more minutes, and if I didn't see him, I would leave. Finally, I spotted a tall guy with a blue backpack, wearing a Popeye's Fried Chicken hat like the one Peter had bought from eBay. He was a weirdo and didn't care when I teased him that no one would buy such a thing for even a dollar, and he'd paid $11.

"Peter!" I called out, waving my hands in the air. "Peter!"

However, the guy didn't budge. Maybe another eccentric guy with a similar hat. Nevertheless, I had to make sure. With my hands, I cupped my mouth and screamed louder. "Peter! Peter!"

From the corner of my eye, I saw a security guard approaching me.

"Excuse me, miss, is there anything I can help you with?" he said firmly, his hands perched on his belt. At the sight of my desperate expression, his face softened.

"My friend is up there. I got here as fast as I could, but I'm going to miss seeing him before he flies to London. Do you see the guy with the orange hat up there?" I said, pointing to the second floor. "Sorry, I don't mean to make a scene, but I have to see him." I put my hand over my head, glancing up again.

"Well, instead of screaming like that, why don't you just call him?" he suggested.

His words clicked in my mind.

"That's right! Thank you!" I said. Taking out my phone, I dialed his number.

Just one ring and the man with the orange hat put his phone to his ear. I was right: he was Peter.

"Rory? Is everything okay? Why is it so noisy?" he asked while stepping out of the queue, giving his place to a middle-aged couple.

"No...yes...everything is okay," I said, still gazing up. I didn't want to tell him that I was looking at him while we talked. I was afraid if I faced him, he would see my feelings, and our relationship would change. No. I wouldn't let it happen. "Are you already boarding?"

"My flight was delayed to 8:30, but they just gave the boarding announcement," he answered, leaning his back against the railing.

"That's good that you are already at your gate," I said, fixing my eyes on him.

"Not yet. I'm still at the security checkpoint."

"Why aren't you at the gate yet?" My breath stopped. *Is he waiting for me?*

"Well," Peter finally said after a long moment, "I hoped …" He sighed. "Well, I don't know what I hoped, but …"

"I see," I said, not sure what to say. "Have a safe flight, Peter. Let me know when you arrive in London."

"Yeah, sure," he answered.

Neither of us hung up, and there was silence on the other end.

"See you in two weeks," I said, breaking the silence.

"Yes," he nodded.

"Bye, Peter. And I'm so sorry about Jane," I said, forcing a smile.

Peter nodded and sighed. "Take care, Roomie. And don't forget to bolt the door, okay?" he said. In the meantime, the airport intercom announced boarding for Japan Airlines to Singapore.

"Don't worry, I won't forget. Bye now," I said quietly, biting my lower lip and sighing before I pressed the button to hang up.

Peter looked at the phone for a moment before putting it back in his jacket. He remained in the same position as I exhaled and turned toward the exit.

A transport cart picking up an elderly couple beeped, startling me. The driver smiled and signaled for me to continue. Lifting my hand to thank him, I ran toward the exit. By the time I reached the automatic sliding doors, I thought I heard my name called twice, but I dismissed it. I must have misheard.

Getting in and out of LAX was tough. It took me twenty minutes to get out of the parking structure and onto Sepulveda Boulevard. I felt relieved as I hit the I-105 East ramp and found that traffic wasn't bad after that.

I had just passed the sign for the I-405 South freeway when my phone rang. My heart hammered in my chest as I saw it was Peter calling.

I swallowed before pressing the button on my steering wheel. "Hi, Peter," I said, trying to control my voice. "Are you already at the gate?"

"Yes, I am," Peter said. "Are you at home?"

"Hmm, no. I'm…on my way back from the grocery store. I needed some fruit," I lied, biting my lip. "What's up?"

"I just wanted to check if you were back from wherever you were."

"I see. Thanks."

"Don't mention it."

And then neither of us said anything. I could hear his breathing on the other end.

"Hey, Roomie," Peter finally said.

"Yes?"

"I need a favor," he said hesitantly.

"Sure."

"Could we add one roommate rule to the list?" he asked.

"Did you really call me for this?" I scoffed. "Couldn't you text me later or wait until you returned from London?"

"I'm afraid I'll forget. But would you mind?" He sounded urgent.

"Of course not. What this is all about?"

"Rule number fifteen: Forgive each other for any mistakes made intentionally or unintentionally. Could you add it to our list?" Peter said.

"I'm suspicious now. Are you planning on doing something illegal?" I said jokingly.

Peter gave a chuckle.

"All right. I'll add it later."

"Take a picture of that rule and send it to me."

"You must be joking."

"No, I'm serious."

I let out an exaggerated sigh. "Fine, I'll do it."

"Thank you, Rory."

In the meantime, I could hear the last boarding announcement in the background.

"Hey, got to go. See you in two weeks?" he said.

"Do you want me to pick you up the day you return?" I offered.

"Thanks, but I don't know when I'll return, though."

That makes sense. "Okay," I said.

"Bye, Rory."

"Bye, Peter."

CHAPTER 30

A few days after Peter left California, Lizzy and I found ourselves at the Blue-Silk-Satin boutique. Lizzy had made a reservation for Saturday morning to try on wedding dresses. She had flown in from Seattle, and I picked her up from John Wayne Airport after work last night. She would be staying with me for the weekend.

Lizzy and Terry had decided to move their wedding up a month because Lizzy's mom had been diagnosed with late-stage liver cancer, and the doctor said if the chemo treatment went well, she might have two years at most or, if it failed, she would live maybe six months.

"What did you think about the dresses?" asked Lizzy as she came out of the fitting room in her street clothes.

I'd taken pictures of each dress she tried on so we could review them together.

She sat next to me on the long couch in the middle of the dressing-room area.

"Okay, I already connected my phone to my tablet so we can see better detail on the larger screen," I said, turning to Lizzy.

She nodded. As she leaned forward to the screen, she placed her elbows on her knees.

"This dress"—I pointed at the halter-style gown she'd tried on first—"is no good. I don't like the way the straps wrap around your neck, leaving your back strapless."

Lizzy smiled. "I could tell you didn't like this one," she said, nodding at the dress. "Yeah, I don't feel comfortable in that one. Next."

My finger slid to the right to show the next dress. "Dress number two: I like the A-line silhouette, but I don't like the straight-across neckline, and it's strapless too."

Lizzy nodded. From her expression, it seemed that she liked that one. "Next."

I nodded and swept my finger to the right. "Definitely not this one! It seemed like you were drowning in this gown!" I said, grinning at the sweetheart neckline with the ball-gown skirt.

Lizzy squinted and nodded, grinning as well. She was skinny and tall, so in this gown she'd looked like a feather duster!

"Ah, I like this one!" I said, showing the next dress. The sheath dress draped across the bodice with a soft scoop from one shoulder to the other.

Lizzy tilted her head, thinking, then nodded.

"And the last one," I said. "The short-sleeve A-line style. I'm neutral about this one, meaning you look good in it because it's elegant and bit more modest."

Lizzy nodded and turned to me. "Thanks, Rory. You did a good job taking those pictures from different angles and giving me your advice. If you are tired of working as an accountant, maybe you need to consider becoming a wedding dress consultant."

I laughed and turned off the tablet. "Let me think about that," I said, winking at her. "So which dress will you choose?"

Lizzy sighed. She gazed off into the distance. "Which dress do you think my mom will like best?" she asked quietly, as if talking to herself.

I wrapped my arm around her shoulder. Lizzy leaned her head on my shoulder, tears rolling down her cheeks. "Lizzy, it's your wedding. I understand that you want to make your mom happy, but you are the one who has to live with the memory of your wedding day. You should choose the dress you like. Just like you told me to start living for myself, not for my aunt."

Lizzy drew her head away, sniffing. "I think you are right. Well, I still have time to decide, maybe after a good night's sleep. For sure, dress number three is eliminated, and also number one, so I only have three dresses to think about tonight."

"Why don't we watch a movie?" I said, hoping to lighten her mood. "Tom, Peter's boyfriend, gave me two free tickets …" My voice trailed off as I watched Lizzy's eyes widen.

Damn! I revealed Peter's secret to Lizzy.

"Now I understand why you've kept ducking the question about why Aunt Amy allowed you to live with Peter because you'd told her," Lizzy said softly.

I nodded.

"And you couldn't tell me, Rory?"

I glanced at her, feeling guilty. "I know. But just …" I shrugged and inserted the tablet into my backpack.

Lizzy squinted, tilting her head to see my face clearly. "You like him, don't you?"

I froze and watched as she leaned back in her seat, a thin smile playing on her lips.

"I lived with you for two years, Rory. I'd know when you feel happy or sad or fall in love. Maybe I don't see your face, but your voice is…always excited when you talk about Peter. And I don't hear the same excitement when you talk about Jason, although you claimed you went out with him a few times."

I tsked, shaking my head. "We must have been sisters in a past life," I said, looking at her. "You seem to know me better than anyone else."

Lizzy grinned widely, then rose and shouldered her bag. "Come on, let's get some food and then watch a movie. But you have to tell me about Peter," she said, leading the way to the lobby.

Felicia, the owner, finished talking with another customer and turned to Lizzy. "How're things going?" Her brunette hair was pulled into a bun with a lovely crystal hair stick.

"I liked all five, but I narrowed them down to three. I'll call you soon when I decide," Lizzy said.

Felicia nodded. "Don't worry. Once you confirm, I'll put the dress aside and ship it to you with the veil and the gloves."

"Thanks, Felicia. Have a great day!"

"Thanks, Lizzy. Looking forward to hearing from you."

The next morning, after attending Sunday's church service, Lizzy accompanied me to look at a few apartments I could afford by myself. Peter had known about the plan. Besides, I didn't mean to move right away, since he would be staying for another two months. I just wanted to prepare sooner than later to make sure I could get a studio apartment by the time he left.

It would be hard to leave Pacific Hills because I really loved the place. But I had to think more practically. Living in a less expensive studio apartment would help me in the long term. And I had enough money for the deposit now that the balance in my bank account had been increasing from selling my bags, shoes, and clothes I never used. My closet was also more spacious.

We spent the entire Sunday at the Irvine Spectrum Mall, reminiscing about our past when we used to live together. The mall had been one of our regular hangouts, especially when Terry had to work on a weekend.

At my favorite bookstore, we bumped into Jason. For a moment, I couldn't help but wonder why I'd been bumping into him almost everywhere I went. I didn't think he lived around here. If I was not mistaken, he lived in Orange with his brother.

Jason kindly invited Lizzy and me to have coffee with him. I wasn't eager to go, but Lizzy wanted to rest her legs, so we agreed and went to the small coffee shop until it was time for Lizzy to head to the airport.

CHAPTER 31

It had been more than a week since Peter had left and his last text had been sent upon his arrival at London Heathrow Airport. Since then, I hadn't received any further texts from him. I speculated that his heart must have been broken to see Jane's condition. It was possible Jane had already passed away. Poor Peter. I didn't know Jane, but from the short conversation between Peter and his sister, I could tell they had a close relationship.

I was stepping out of the ladies' room when I heard footsteps behind me, echoing in the corridor. Looking over my shoulder, I saw Sylvia walking toward me.

"Hi, Syl, wha—"

Sylvia grabbed my elbow and dragged me to the stairs leading to the rooftop, where the company sometimes hosted parties. Sofas, tables, and umbrellas filled the space, and it was nice to sit on the rooftop and enjoy the breeze sometimes.

"Sorry, we have to go outside before I can say anything," she hissed in a low voice, pushing open the door.

No one was on the roof. Sylvia stopped just outside the door and released my elbow.

"What happened?" I looked at her with a quizzical expression.

Facing me, she said, "Lena is suing Desiree and Rowena."

"What?" I couldn't believe my ears. "Where did you get that news from?"

Sylvia walked closer, whispering. "Remember Aileen? The lady in the legal department I told you was my friend in college?"

I bobbed my head.

"This morning, her boss said an ex-employee from accounting took out a lawsuit against Desiree and Rowena yesterday. And later on, Desiree and Rowena came to the legal department so they could get advice about finding a good lawyer. It's purely a personal lawsuit, so no reflection on the company."

"But that lawsuit will cost Lena tons of money. You know how it works: the court, the attorney's fees. They even charge for reading a simple email! How does she have the money to pay a lawyer?" I said.

Sylvia shrugged. "I guess her parents are helping her. They have a successful construction business, and if I'm not mistaken, they recently sold it for a huge chunk of money. I think that's why she decided to take the unfair treatment from Desiree and Rowena to court."

I gave a half shrug in response. "That's possible."

Sylvia gazed at me. "I'm not a person who wishes bad things for people, but I'm truly glad Rowena and Desiree will get something for their bad behavior, especially Rowena. That woman needs to learn to appreciate people. This lawsuit will cost them money too."

I wasn't convinced, and Sylvia seemed to notice. She asked, "Don't you agree?"

"Well, the witch's husband works for a big supermarket in California, so I bet they also have money for a lawyer."

Sylvia tilted her head, thinking. "Maybe. But what I heard is that Lena's lawyer is one of the best. God, I cannot wait to see the end of this. I'll pray for Lena and hope she wins the case."

I nodded. "Me too."

"By the way, I heard you'll have a new coworker to replace Lena soon," said Sylvia as I stretched my hand to push the exit door open.

My hand stopped a few inches before the door. I turned to her. "Really? I didn't know that," I said, raising my eyebrows. "How do you know?"

Sylvia looked at me, confused. "Why don't you know? Didn't Rowena take you with her during the interview process for the new candidates?" she asked.

I blinked and shook my head.

"I wouldn't be surprised if she intentionally didn't tell you about that," Sylvia exclaimed. "You should've been in the loop because you're the one who has to work with them. If your voice is not counted, how can they expect you to work in harmony with that person?"

Rubbing my eyes, I looked at her, feeling heavy in my stomach. "Rowena doesn't look at me as her subordinate, merely as her enemy. Don't ask me why, because I don't know. Maybe she is upset that I can't do Lena's job or because I'm Lena's friend. That lady is something. She glared at me when Valerie praised my presentation for the White Water team. It seems to me she doesn't like people outshining her on anything, even our own jobs." I sucked my lips in, shaking my head. "Doesn't she remember the days when she worked as a lower-ranked employee? When tiny little praise mattered? And why does she bitch at me no matter what I do? She's always saying, 'Hi, buds, how're thing going?' to the refund clerks, but when she talked Lena or me, she always used that condescending tone. What does she think about us?"

Sylvia gazed at me in sympathy and patted my shoulder gently.

"If she is jealous of Lena, that's understandable, because Lena's rank was only one below hers. But me? My rank is *three* levels below hers! What is her reason to be jealous of me, and what the *heck* have I done wrong? I can't do Lena's job because no one taught me how!" I clenched my fingers into fists as my heart pounded.

Sylvia's jaw dropped. She'd never seen me like this before. But it was nice to vent after so long dealing with the unfair treatment day after day.

"I understand," she said, clearing her throat. "I've felt sorry for you and Lena having to deal with Rowena, but please don't quit, Rory. Please endure a bit longer. And feel free to come to me if you need to vent," Sylvia said. "I can tell you aren't happy, especially after Lena ditched you during her last weeks here. To be honest, I think that was a really unprofessional attitude, as if she threw you under the bus. But at that time, she had assumed Rowena would take her tasks, not you."

I sighed. "Well, I'm trying to look for a new job, but I keep getting rejections because I don't have a lot of experience yet," I said, studying Sylvia's face. "Thanks for your advice. Of all of us, I think you deserve to be a manager."

Sylvia offered a smile. "Thanks for your confidence in me. Too bad those words won't come out of Desiree's mouth. Are you okay to go down now?" she asked, looking at me.

"Yeah," I nodded. I pushed the door open, and we descended the stairs. "Thanks for listening to me."

Sylvia nodded. "But please don't quit. If you quit now, she will be happy and use that to convince Val and Desiree that you weren't a capable person," she said gently. "Hang on a little longer."

"I'll try," I said, forcing a smile.

CHAPTER 32

Upon the White Water team's arrival at Myriad's office, Val had instructed her executive assistant, Theresa Cortez, to convert a large meeting room on the first floor into their office while they were in California. The room had everything from a couple of armchairs, a coffee table, small fridge, a coffee machine, and a 62-inch TV that could be used for teleconferencing or watching the daily news.

I had a meeting with Kimberly Johnson around noon to discuss the current reconciliation reports. Rowena had been overwhelmed since Lena left and assigned me to handle the task. I was happy to take it because it would look good on my resume, showcasing my involvement in the partnership project.

The meeting lasted an hour. Like Vy, Kim was also a nice person to work with.

"Thank you for your time, Rory. I really appreciate it," Kim said, gathering the papers I'd provided into one tidy pile. "Now I understand how to read and analyze Myriad's reports."

Vy entered the room just as she finished her sentence. "Kim, we *have to* listen to this evening's news," he said, picking up the remote control and turning on the TV.

A big bald guy in an expensive suit came into view, standing at a podium in a room full of reporters.

"The Board of Directors for RTC had a quick meeting this morning, London time, about the new CEO—" Vy stopped when he realized I was in the room. "Oh, hi, Rory. Sorry I didn't see you."

"Hey, Vy. No worries," I said quickly.

Noticing him exchange glances with Kim, I understood that whatever the news was, they didn't want me to be there. With a smile of understanding, I rose from my seat. "If you have any questions, please let me know," I said to Kim.

"Thank you," she answered, giving me a nod before turning her attention to the TV.

As I walked to the door, my ears picked up the news about RTC's plan to extend their wings in Canada and the USA under White Water, Inc., but Sarah Jane Alexandra Ryder, who was being considered for the CEO position, had passed away two days ago. Since RTC was a private investment company of the Sandridge family, the RTC Board of Directors had agreed to give the position to her sibling.

My hand froze on the doorknob as the bald guy announced the new CEO's name: Frederick Peter Alexander Ryder. My jaw dropped at the familiar face standing at the podium, giving his speech eloquently, with his voice full of authority that I'd never heard before.

A gentle tap on my left shoulder startled me. Phil was standing in the middle of the doorframe, with his hand on the knob.

"Why didn't you tell me?" My voice came out weird, sounding like I was choking or something.

"He forbade me," he said in a low voice, glancing up at Peter giving his speech. "He said—"

I pushed Phil aside and ran back to my cubicle with my heart pounding so hard my chest hurt. Sitting in my cubicle, I clenched the desk's edge tightly until the tips of my fingers turned white.

Peter is the new CEO of White Water for the US and Canada.

My mind wandered off, making it hard to concentrate on work. I couldn't stop thinking about Peter and Jane, and I was startled when the phone's alarm buzzed to remind me of a dentist appointment in one hour. I felt relief knowing I could stay home after the appointment, giving me enough time to digest the shocking news alone.

Returning from the dentist's office, I sat on the couch with my laptop and started searching for Peter. *So many Peter Ryders!* When I typed his full name as I'd heard it on TV press conference, the results amazed me.

Peter, or "Wild Fred," as social media called him, was acknowledged as a wild young man who loved parties and spending sprees. Social media stated that his potential as the fourth family member in the line of succession to lead RTC was doubted because he partied so hard and was often spotted drunk. One picture showed him drunk at a party, having fallen into a swimming pool fully clothed.

There were some more photos that showed him running around in his underwear. I discovered that he was arrested for DUI on his twenty-first birthday. After his twenty-second birthday, he seemed to disappear from social media altogether. No one knew where he was. Some said he'd passed away from drinking, some said he went to Tibet and became a monk, and others buzzed about things he'd done that made my jaw drop.

Jane, on the other hand, was described as a capable person for the third in the line of succession, though she was known as an eccentric woman. She liked working and focused on her job, but she didn't like being a public figure. Among other successful young women, she was the only person who didn't have Instagram or Twitter accounts. She loved living in a quiet area and even went to India to meet the Dalai Lama for enlightenment. Whenever she went anywhere, she was always in disguise. For her recent trip to California, which she couldn't make because of her illness, no one knew where she had planned to stay.

Feeling lightheaded, I closed my notebook and buried my face in my palms. My mind was rewinding each moment I'd had with Peter in a logical way, desperately searching for any signs or cues that could explain why I hadn't seen it coming.

I thought I knew him.

CHAPTER 33

I still hadn't received any communication from Peter after the shocking news. However, I didn't have time to worry about that because, the following day, the office gossip emerged, and to my surprise, I found myself involved in it.

Someone released nasty pictures of Peter and me to all the office email addresses and social media. They were all coming from an Instagram user ID, @youngandwild, which was linked to an individual who went by the initials WF rather than using their full name.

The pictures portrayed Peter and me as party animals and heavy drinkers in bars, nightclubs, and other places I had never been, wearing revealing clothes I had never owned. Without confirming any facts with me, people in the office looked at me like I'd committed a crime. I couldn't go anywhere without being stared at and hearing jealous or degrading comments. Sylvia and Yoo-Shi deliberately avoided me. The office became a nightmare place to work.

How desperately I wanted to talk to Peter and seek clarification.

A couple days later, Peter finally came home. He entered while I was sitting on the couch in the living room and stood in the doorway, looking at me. Phil must have told him about me watching his speech.

"Hi," he greeted me quietly, closing the door carefully.

I glared back at him, clenching my book tightly.

Peter stood in the hallway and took a deep breath before walking across the living room. Stopping in front of me, his fingers entwined, he said in a low voice, "I have something to tell you."

"And I've been waiting for it," I said sharply, closing my book louder than I intended and dropping it on the coffee table with a thud.

Peter exhaled and sat on the ottoman across from me, then leaned forward with his elbows on his knees and his gaze fixed on his clasped hands. He looked exhausted. "I…I don't know how to start, but …" He looked up at me and then down again since I was sitting straight and glaring at him. "I'm sorry. I didn't like to hide everything from you. Things weren't supposed to turn out like this."

I swallowed hard and continued staring at him.

Shifting on his seat, Peter cleared his throat. "You've known that I work for my family business, but I never wanted to be a CEO. My grandfather had never considered it, anyway. But Jane is—*was*—different. Since she was young, my grandfather had high hopes for her and my two cousins to lead the company one day. Although Jane was smart, she had a unique personality and never liked being in the limelight, which would be hard, since a person who manages a company, small or big, has to be in the spotlight. She preferred a small city and a quiet life and hated staying in hotels. As a member of the Sandridge family, she couldn't avoid her duty. During the California project, Marcus suggested staying in someone's house instead of a hotel and then gave your advertisement to her. After making sure you didn't have any criminal background, Jane agreed to stay with you.

"You know the rest of the story. I came here initially to accompany her so she wouldn't feel overwhelmed, then thing changed and I had to replace her. Marcus had already placed me in a hotel, but I changed my mind and wanted to stay in your apartment." Peter stopped, crossing his ankles and uncrossing them again a few seconds later. With a sad smile, he cleared his throat and continued. "Afterward, I was busy learning her tasks and duties, then found out you worked for Myriad. I couldn't tell you White Water is part of RTC. However, it never crossed my mind that I would be assigned CEO because Jane would…pass away. When I gave the speech that day, I hoped you wouldn't see or hear about it until I could get back and explain everything to you." Peter rubbed his eyes with his hand and gazed at me. "I didn't mean for everything to happen like this. Trust me."

"Things weren't supposed to turn out like this," I repeated, looking at him sadly. It surprised me that I felt more sad than angry at him. "Are you using me, Peter? I thought we were friends."

"I'm not using you, and we *are* friends," he answered.

Heat flushed through my body. "Friends—good friends—don't lie to each other. You lied to me and tarnished my reputation, Peter!" I yelled.

He blinked, confused. "What do you mean, I tarnished your reputation?"

I forced a bitter smile. I couldn't believe Peter had been such a liar. The pictures of us had been circulated on social media, and it was impossible he didn't know. Phil or someone must have told him about them.

Letting out a heavy sigh, I took my phone from my pocket and slid my finger across the screen. "Look at these pictures. Do you think I'm a clown now?" I handed it to him.

He appeared puzzled, and his mouth hung open while he scrolled through the photos. I watched his Adam's apple bob up and down. He shook his head as he lifted his eyes from the screen.

"Rory, I swear to God that I never posted any pictures on social media. These pictures…those aren't mine. I would never do anything to humiliate you. The only pictures I have on my phone are these." He set my phone on the table and took out his own. His expression changed as he went through the photos on his phone.

"I never had those pictures, I swear!" His voice trembled.

Our eyes met, and I didn't see any deceit there, only shock. I took the phone from his hand and saw the same pictures that had been posted on Instagram.

"Not your pictures, huh?" I threw his phone back to him, but Peter let it fall on the carpet. "Because of those pictures, everyone stares at me everywhere I go, like I'm some kind of leper! Val called me into her office to clarify if I had been living with you. Rowena and Desiree sneered at me. Before I left work today, I was called by the legal department to sign a conflict-of-interest disclosure agreement."

Peter's hand twitched as I continued.

"The worst part is that I also started getting phone calls from the media asking me if I am Wild Fred's new girlfriend and how many times had I slept with you to get a job at Myriad. Some callers even asked my rate per day!" My voice trembled. "They even asked—"

"Rory, stop." Peter lifted his hand, his eyes wide in horror. "Please…stop."

I sniffed and shuddered.

Peter's face was pale as he shook his head. "I never gave your phone number to anyone. I didn't have anything to do with those filthy pictures either," he pleaded. "Please believe me."

My head was spinning. "No, I don't! You had posted to your Instagram whenever you went to wild parties, and I also found out you did fabricate a picture of a poor girl who refused to be your girlfriend. Remember that?"

Peter's hands dropped to his sides. "Yes, I did post about my wild parties. Yes, I did like her and begged her to be my girlfriend when we were in ninth grade. But she lied to everybody about the picture. We *did* fabricate one of her pictures for a harmless prank on her parents so she could get their attention. However, I shut down all my social media because I swore on my mom's deathbed that I wouldn't humiliate our family again. Don't you dare accuse me of something I didn't do, Rory! And ask Marcus. He knows me well!"

"How could I ask him if he is working for you?" I shouted.

Peter closed his eyes and took a deep breath. No one said a word because we were busy calming ourselves.

"Peter," I broke the silence, taking an envelope out from between the pages of my book. "I enjoyed living with you for the last four months. You and Jane were very generous. I'm so grateful for your kindness. And by contract, you still have two more months to live here, but," I pushed the envelope toward him, "this is a check for the last two months of rent. I'm returning it to you, and please find somewhere else, because I already signed an agreement to lease a studio apartment starting next month."

Peter's eyes widened. "Rory…," he begged me.

I shook my head. "You have more than a week to find a new place, and I don't believe it will be difficult for you. Please move out before the end of the month," I said, clenching my hands to control my voice. "And for tonight, I want you to sleep somewhere else."

Peter looked at the ceiling, his lips thinner. His hand ran over his hair as he lowered his head and looked back at me. "Please keep the money," he said, pushing the envelope back to me.

"I'm not your charity case!" My voice sounded louder than I'd meant. I cleared my throat, pushed the envelope toward him again, and said in a gentler voice, "Just take it, Peter."

For a few seconds, he gazed at me, studying my face. Exhaling, he lowered his eyes and took the envelope from the table.

I offered a thin smile, but my eyes widened in surprise as Peter tore the envelope into pieces.

"You don't owe me anything, Roomie. My gratitude for living with you these last few months is worth more than money. And now I've caused you misery. No, you don't owe me anything." He stood slowly, regret all over his face. "Let me grab some of my clothes, and I'll pack the rest and get out of here as soon as possible."

A sad smile appeared on his face as he stared at me for a moment before going to his bedroom. Ten minutes later, he came out with a backpack on his shoulder and a duffel bag in his left hand. His eyes were slightly red.

"I'll stay in a hotel. But if you have any problems tonight, just call me. I'll come right away," he said softly.

"No need." I shook my head slowly.

He let out a sigh and nodded, then headed toward the door and turned the knob. "Rory," he called, turning back to me. I could see a dejected look on his face. "Remember rule number fifteen? About forgiving each other? Could we apply it now so we can still be friends?"

I fought back the lump in my throat as I finally comprehended why he had insisted on adding that specific rule. *Peter, how could you?!?* I shook my head again, feeling utterly betrayed.

Peter sighed and gently closed the door behind him. I blinked faster, trying to hold my tears as I watched his figure disappear through the door.

CHAPTER 34

I didn't know what woke me at first, then became aware of my phone buzzing. I'd been so upset that I'd forgotten to put it on airplane mode. It was one in the morning as I glanced at my desk clock and reached to turn off my phone, but I stopped when I noticed Peter's name on the screen.

"Ugh. Doesn't he know I don't want to deal with him anymore?" I sighed, letting it drop to the carpet.

A few minutes later, it buzzed again.

This guy is driving me crazy!

"Peter, do you know what time it is?" I snapped as I picked up the phone.

"Hi, is this Rory?" a strange male voice asked.

"Who is this?" I asked, sitting straight up in bed.

"My name is Mike. I'm a bartender at JW's Bar and Grill. Your friend Peter is drunk, and he is too intoxicated to drive. I found your name in his phone, could you pick him up?"

I pressed my forehead with my palm. "I don't know why he gave you my number," I said, slightly annoyed with Peter. "Let me call his—"

"I'm sorry, but we are going to close soon. We need you to pick him up now." Mike's voice sounded urgent.

I bit my lower lip and said, "Okay, what's the address? Could you text it to me?"

"Yes, absolutely. Please be here in thirty minutes. If not, I'll call a taxi for him." And he hung up.

A few seconds later, I got a text with the address. I copied and pasted the address into Google Maps, which predicted my trip would take fifteen minutes to reach the bar. In less than five, I'd changed my clothes, grabbed my bag and my car keys, and stepped out to the parking lot.

The moon was hiding behind thick clouds. It was summer, but at this hour there was a slight chill in the air. A chirping sound came from my car as I pressed the unlock button on my key fob.

The road was nearly empty when I merged onto the freeway. My tired brain couldn't help but think how nice it would be if morning traffic were like that. With my free hand, I pressed a call button to dial Tom. After two attempts, I let it drop and focused on my driving. He must have been fast asleep at that hour. "Why didn't he call Tom for help?" I wondered.

Twenty minutes before two, I arrived at the bar.

Someone—presumably, Mike—peeked out the door as soon as I pulled in front of the entrance and got out of my car. "Rory?" he asked.

"Yes."

"Please open the passenger door, and I'll bring Peter out for you," he said.

"Okay," I said, heading toward the passenger side.

Mike nodded and disappeared behind the tinted glass doors. He emerged a minute later dragging a stumbling Peter, his arm draped across Mike's shoulder. Carefully, the bartender maneuvered Peter's body into the passenger seat, pulled the seat belt across his chest, and buckled it. It was apparent that Peter wasn't his first drunk customer.

"Thank you, Mike," I said, opening my purse to give him a tip.

Mike shook his head. "No need. It is our policy to make sure drunk customers get back home safely," he said, smiling.

"I see. Thanks!"

"Drive safely," Mike said, waving as he turned back to the bar.

Peter snorted when the car moved. Under the streetlamps we passed on the way to the freeway, I saw how awful he looked. I'd never seen him like that before.

"Where am I?" he croaked as he tried to open his eyes.

"Somewhere in Huntington Beach," I said, pressing the brake at the last traffic light before the interstate.

"Rory?" he asked, turning his head and leaning closer to me.

"Sit down." I pushed him back in the seat. "Gosh, you smell awful!"

"Why are you here?" he slurred.

"You are drunk, and the bartender called me to pick you up," I said, rolling my eyes to myself because, in this wasted state, he wouldn't understand or remember my words, anyway. "You should have given Tom's number to the bartender."

Peter grunted, mumbling unintelligibly, and curled up toward the window. "Don't drive too fast. I'm feeling sick," he said, groaning as he turned his head toward me. "My stomach hurts."

The expression on his face suggested he was about to vomit.

I tapped Peter's shoulder hard. "Don't you dare throw up in my car. Let me pull over."

Peter nodded and groaned again. He leaned forward as I pressed the gas pedal to accelerate toward the first parking lot I could get into. But the acceleration didn't help. I heard a gag from Peter's mouth.

"No, no, no, don't throw up now, okay?" Panic rose in my chest as Peter leaned forward again. "Peter, don't!" With my right hand, I pushed him back.

In one sudden movement, Peter bent forward and vomited on his feet.

"Eeeeew! Damn you, Peter!"

My nose wrinkled immediately in disgust, and I pressed the button to lower all four windows at the same time. Fresh air rushed into the car, thankfully lessening the smell.

I spotted a convenience store a few hundred yards away. The parking lot was empty, but it had bright lights over each fuel dispenser, and there was a nice hotel across from it. After making a quick decision that it looked safe, I whipped into the parking lot and pulled to a stop between the front door and the gas pumps. I dialed Tom's number. After the fifth attempt, he picked up his phone.

"Hey, Rory." His voice sounded sleepy. "What's up? Why are you calling at this hour?"

"Peter. He is drunk, and I just picked him up from a bar in Huntington Beach," I said matter-of-factly.

"Peter? Really?" Tom said. From the change in his voice, I could tell his sleepiness had been swept away by the news.

"Tom, Peter is really drunk and just barfed in my car. I can't bring him with me. Can you come get him?" I begged.

"Doesn't he live with you?" Tom said.

Hearing him breathing heavily, like he was rushing to get out the door, I sighed and pressed my forehead against the steering wheel. "It's a long story, but not as of last night."

"Oh."

"How long before you can get here?" I asked.

"Text me your location, and I'll be there as soon as I can."

"Okay, I'll do it," I said, feeling relieved. "Thanks Tom!"

"Don't mention it," he said before hanging up.

I opened my Google Maps to locate where I was and shared the location with Tom. Sighing, I rubbed my face and went into the store to buy a pair of gloves and a roll of paper towels. The middle-aged guy behind the counter suggested I use water from the spigot outside.

I drove to the corner where the clerk had indicated the spigot was and started cleaning the carpet at Peter's feet. He snored loudly, deeply asleep the whole time. Under the dim sky, his face was peaceful like a baby's.

It took me twenty minutes to clean the mess. After I was done, I washed my hands and leaned back against my car, waiting for Tom. It felt like forever until he arrived.

"My God!" Tom exclaimed as he gazed down at Peter passed out in the passenger seat. "I haven't seen him drink like this for years. He's been sober. What happened to him?"

I sighed, scratching my temple with my finger. "I can't tell you right now. I'm too tired. Could you move him to your car?"

"Yeah, sure," Tom said, bending over to slip his arm under Peter's and around his back. "Okay, brother, work with me," he said to Peter. "One, two, three!"

In one jerk, Tom had Peter out of my car and almost standing upright. I slipped my arm under Peter's other arm to help Tom.

"Thanks, Rory," he said as we maneuvered Peter's body into Tom's car.

My shoulder hurt. Peter was heavy.

"Rory, let me pay for your car wash," he said, looking at me.

"That's okay. Don't worry about that," I said, shaking my head. "But do me a favor?"

Tom nodded.

I licked my dry lips. "Please tell Peter…," I sighed, biting my lower lip, "that I don't want to deal with him anymore."

My vision blurred as I tapped the hood above Peter a few times before looking up at Tom. "Bye, Tom. Please take care of him, okay?" I pointed to Peter with my chin, then turned away quickly to hide my tears.

"Drive safely, Rory."

I waved my hand over my shoulder and headed toward my car.

The sky was still dark, but I could tell the hue was becoming more of a dark blue. As I drove home, I began to realize how tired I was. The vomit smell was still there but not so strong anymore—just enough to make me keep my windows down.

Heaving a sigh, I turned on the radio to keep me company. I smiled bitterly as Alicia Keys sang "Fallin'." The coincidence brought all the feelings I'd been pushing down and denying myself rushing to the surface. My head said I should turn off the radio, but my heart said no, and my heart won. After the song was done, I turned off the radio and drove the rest of the way home in silence.

Around four-thirty, I sank into my couch and slept another four hours. I knew I would be late for work regardless because I couldn't drive the smelly car to my office. The detail shop near my apartment would open at eight. I'd decided to drive my car there and take an Uber to work.

I climbed up the stairs to my office around nine thirty. Arriving at my cubicle, I found a yellow sticky note taped on my monitor with Rowena's scribbles.

Bring my report to room 204 immediately!

I slapped my forehead because I had forgotten her report. I actually had texted her earlier that I would be late, but knowing her temperament, she wouldn't forgive me.

Yoo-Shi popped her head up over the cubicle. "What happened? Rowena has been pacing back and forth and looking way scarier than usual. Are you okay?"

I scratched my forehead and nodded. "Yeah, she needs the report for a morning meeting with Valerie and White Water team. I totally forgot about that."

"That witch! Well, after you are done, let's go down for coffee. You look like you need a strong, hot cup," Yoo-Shi said.

"Yes," I said, feeling thankful and relieved she was finally speaking to me again.

It took me five minutes to find the report and send it to the printer room, and then I sprinted to pick it up. On the way to the meeting room, I bumped into Phil and Vy.

"Whoa, take it easy, Rory," said Vy, grabbing my arm to keep me from hitting the floor.

"Thank you, and sorry. Rowena is waiting for me," I said, waving the papers in my hand.

The door to room 204 was ajar. All heads turned to look at me as I knocked before entering. Valerie signaled me to come in.

"Your report, Rowena," I said in a low voice as I extended the papers to her.

"Thank you, Rory," she said sweetly.

My eyebrows shot up to hear her speaking like that, and I recalled what Lena had told me about how she never showed her wicked temperament in front of people. I left quickly, glad to escape the stares.

After grabbing a coffee to get me through until lunch, I went back to my desk. The next few hours went by quickly without Rowena around to create tension. At lunchtime, I decided to walk to the youth park not far from the office. I didn't want to go to the lunchroom and endure the staring and whispering. Although the nasty email had only been sent to the finance and accounting departments, I'd bet the whole company had seen it by now.

I took an empty bench and watched the kids practice batting. Not feeling hungry, I didn't even get my sandwich out of my lunch box.

A buzz signaled an incoming text. I pulled my phone out and saw it was from Peter.

> **I'm sorry for troubling you earlier this morning. I really am. Please let me cover your auto detailing.**

I stared at the screen. I didn't want any help from him or Tom.

> **Don't worry about it,**

I replied.

Peter didn't respond.

I sighed, blocked his number, and put the phone back in my bag. With my right hand, I massaged my temple gently. I had a headache from lack of sleep since the speech a few days ago. I would need to keep drinking coffee to get through the day.

"Hi!" someone called out.

I looked up to see a bearded guy standing in front of me in sportswear but holding a couple tiny white flowers in his left hand.

"For you," he said, handing me a flower.

I was stunned but took the flower from him. "Thank you," I said puzzled.

"Don't be sad. Everything will be fine," the guy said, then continued walking. "Be happy, little girl!"

"Thank you," I said again.

The guy waved his hand over his head as he walked toward the other side of the youth park.

A warm feeling crept into my chest as I sniffed and stared at the flower. I didn't go to church often, but I believed in God. Was it possible that God had comforted me through the stranger?

My heart was lightened and warmed as I left the park. In the office, Rowena gave me the cold shoulder and pouted the rest of the day, but it didn't bother me. I didn't even notice the negative glances and sneers from people who still believed the nasty rumors.

From the office, I took another Uber to the detail shop to pick up my car. The cashier on duty was different than the one I met in the morning. A tall lady with a contagious smile, named Olivia, asked for the claim ticket for my car.

"Here is your key," she chirped. "The car smells much better now. Next time pull over, huh? Vomit odor is really hard to get out."

She must think I'm a drunk.

"It wasn't me, and that person won't have the opportunity to do it again. Thanks," I said with a nod.

"Have a good evening!"

My car smelled better, with no trace of barf, but the image of drunk Peter couldn't be erased easily. I'd never seen him drink like that while he lived with me. When I'd brought home a bottle of wine I'd gotten free from work, he didn't even touch it. I recalled Tom's remark about Peter being sober the last couple years. *Why did you relapse last night, Peter?*

As I pulled into my assigned parking spot, I noticed someone standing in front of my apartment. I frowned, recognizing the figure was Peter. What was he doing there? Peter gave a thin smile as I passed him.

I parked and saw Peter walking toward me as I got out of my car. I considered pretending to get a phone call, just to buy a few moments to think before I had to deal with him.

"Hi!" He greeted me with a bashful smile as I reached the sidewalk.

"Why are you here, Peter?" I frowned.

Peter swallowed and rubbed the back of his head. "Tom told me about your request, and I'll honor it. But I came here to thank you for helping me," he said, gazing at me ruefully. "Please let me pay for the cleaning."

"I'd told you not to worry about that," I said flatly.

Peter looked down, shifting his weight from foot to foot. He looked like a boy caught red-handed doing something terrible. There was no confidence or authority in his voice like I'd heard when he gave the speech on TV.

"Just… go home, please," I sighed, pointing at the entrance with my head.

He gave me a hurt look. "Fine, but do me a favor: don't go out with Jason anymore," he said.

I thumped my foot on the concrete. "You've crossed the line, Peter!" I shouted, pointing at him. "You have no right to tell me who I can go out with."

"But he is not who you think he is," he argued. His neck turned red. "At least let me protect you, as my ex-roommate. Please?"

"If you wanted to protect me, you shouldn't have posted all those nasty pictures!" I fumed, stomping my foot again before marching toward my apartment.

"Those *aren't* my pictures!"

Peter's voice sounded desperate, but I ignored him. As I neared the front door, I heard him slam his car door, and his tires squealed as he drove angrily out of the parking lot.

CHAPTER 35

Two days later, we had a town hall meeting to welcome Peter as the new CEO of White Water for the US and Canada. The meeting was held in the lunchroom, since it was the largest space and could fit everyone at one time. We had been instructed to stay in groups, which made it easier for him to who worked in which department. I sat next to Sylvia and Yoo-Shi with the rest of accounting staff in our designated corner, and our managers occupied the tables closest to the main walkway.

Peter entered the lunchroom with Mr. Hamilton and greeted everyone with exceptional calm and confidence. His demeanor was more mature than his age, and he looked incredibly comfortable talking to Dwayne, Valerie, and other members of upper management, people who usually made me nervous. Glancing at him, I found it hard to believe he was the same person who had lived with me the last four months. Peter must have had plenty of training to prepare him as one of the future leaders for his family business.

I looked at the floor while Peter gave a speech. Tom was nice enough and had informed me about the visit last night, but I still couldn't feel at ease. I noticed that most of the ladies, including Desiree and Rowena, had dressed up for Peter's visit. I found it weird that, when the gossip about him had been viral, they seemed hostile toward him, but when he was there in the flesh, they acted as though they adored him. All the single employes seemed to be wearing extra makeup and shorter dresses and giving him their sweetest smiles at every opportunity. Personally, I had my money on Jason in terms of handsomeness.

"How old is *Fred?*" Sylvia whispered to me, giggling at the new name being used for my former roommate.

Frederick Peter Alexander Ryder, aka Fred or Mr. Ryder, seemed worlds apart from the Peter I'd known. Earlier that morning, Sylvia and Yoo-Shi had taken me out to the parking lot and asked for clarification about the photos and rumors. I'd told them the truth and said that, for the sake of professionalism, we were no longer roommates. Yoo-Shi had given me a quick hug while Sylvia patted my shoulder gently, knowing how difficult it had been for me to find a roommate. They admitted they'd been confused and apologized for not talking with me sooner.

"He's twenty-three," I whispered back, secretly glancing up at him.

Sylvia chuckled. "My twenty-three-year-old cousin is still sleeping in my aunt's basement, while this guy is already running a seven-billion-dollar company."

"Euros," I corrected her, winking. "And without belittling Peter, don't forget that he is running his family's business. It's not like he had to start where everyone else would."

Sylvia grinned widely, then tugged my sleeve and whipped her head around to hide as she whispered, "Oh, shoot, they are coming! Desiree must want to introduce us to him," she said.

Desiree was walking beside Peter, wearing a big smile on her face, and she stopped in front of us. "This is Myriad Beverage, my group," said Desiree proudly. She proceeded to introduce her management team, starting with Christine, who was sitting closest. Her eyes seemed to expect something as she introduced me to him, but Peter's gaze and gestures were the same with me as with everyone else. I saw a hint of disappointment cross Desiree's face and thanked Peter silently that he had put our quarrel aside and treated me professionally.

During lunch, the office was quiet. Top management had invited Peter and the rest of his team to eat in the executive lunchroom with Mr. Hamilton. It was expected that the lunch would stretch two or three hours, so many employees took the chance to eat outside the office.

"Finally, we have time for lunch together again," I said, biting the roast beef sandwich I'd bought from the box lunch lady who always came to our office. I usually didn't buy from her, but today was an exception since I'd spent the night before packing to move and had been too lazy to make my lunch that morning.

Realizing Sylvia and Yoo-Shi were staring at me, I stopped eating and gazed back at them. "Are you guys waiting for my opinion about the meeting with Peter earlier?"

Their heads nodded almost in unison.

I rolled my eyes and wiped my mouth with a napkin. *If they only knew about our fight.* "Seeing him like that was weird. Even as we shook hands earlier, my mind couldn't process the fact that he had been my roommate. Still hard to believe," I said, folding my arms on the table and sighing. "We'll continue to act professionally, but I'm still upset with him."

"I understand your feelings, especially since the pictures are from his phone," Sylvia said, nodding her head.

"I don't think he made those nasty pictures, Rory." Yoo-Shi scratched her chin, pondering. "Look, he lived with you for four months. If he wanted to humiliate you, why now, when he is suddenly thrust into the spotlight? After being such a gentleman, as you'd been saying while you guys lived together. It doesn't make sense, don't you think?"

Sylvia blinked, then nodded slowly. "She is right. Anyone could have doctored those pictures to humiliate him, and you were just collateral damage."

For a moment, the three of us sat, lost in silence. The crunch of lettuce leaves in Yoo-Shi's mouth sounded louder in our ears.

"Ask him if he ever lost his phone," Sylvia said, breaking the silence.

"I don't want to speak to him, but I'll ask someone who knows him," I said hesitantly.

"You should," Sylvia said, and nodded to emphasize her meaning. "If those pictures were photoshopped, you should know who did it."

I nodded.

Still munching her salad, Yoo-Shi nudged my elbow. "Is he looking for a new roommate? I wouldn't mind applying." She grinned widely and down put her fork, clasping her hands against her chest. "He is…," her head tilted as she searched for the correct word, "an attractive person, though not an Adonis like Jason, but he seems thoughtful and kind with a hint of mischief in his eyes. God, I think I've started falling in love with him." Her face was comical with slightly pink cheeks.

Sylvia and I exchanged glances and covered our mouths to hide our giggling.

"Hey!" Yoo-Shi protested. "Stop laughing. I do like him now."

Sylvia shook her head.

I grinned widely. "If you do, I'm jealous." I was teasing her, but oddly, I did feel jealous.

"Ha, ha, ha! I like making you feel jealous!" Yoo-Shi made a face at me.

I chuckled and stretched to tickle her left side.

She tried to avoid it, but Sylvia tickled her on her right side. "You both are mean!" she screamed while laughing.

Sylvia and I stopped tickling her, and the three of us laughed as though we'd never been upset with each other. We talked about the girls getting all dressed up for Peter's presence in the office as we finished our lunches and giggled all the way back to our cubicles.

Rowena and Christine returned to their offices around three that afternoon, and the usual tension settled back over the room.

I rubbed my fatigued eyes from staring at the screen intensely. Lena's fuel analysis was confusing, and I didn't understand the notes she'd written in the file. Worrying about Rowena being upset at me if I didn't finish it quickly wasn't helping either.

My fear came true. Rowena called me to her office and asked about the report. Christine was there but excused herself to leave.

"I'm sorry, Rowena, but I need one more day to understand the report," I said.

Rowena's lips became thinner. "How long should it take to finish this report?" she asked sharply. "How about the aging report? I haven't received the updated one yet. You've known that report needs to be updated weekly."

From her expression, I could guess she wanted to say more but was wise enough to hold her tongue.

"I'll run the report before I leave today. I've been juggling Lena's tasks and my tasks. Sorry for the delay," I said.

Rowena frowned. "Didn't I tell you to submit your reports on time? Regardless of how many projects you have, you have to submit *all* your reports on time! I don't care if you have to cover Lena's tasks or not. I have a lot of *tasks,* too, plus you've been making a lot of mistakes lately. It's frustrating!" Rowena jerked her head. "At home, I have to manage my kids, and here, I have to manage you? So, why do I need you if you are going to make so many mistakes that I have to review all your work? Better I do your job myself, so I don't have to review it." Her cheeks were patchy red, and she was panting by the time she finished talking.

I lowered my eyebrows and squinted at her. The vein on my temple throbbed, and my jaw hurt from clenching my teeth tightly. *That's enough!* I screamed in my head. "Maybe you've forgotten that I always submitted my reports on time. Only after Lena left have I had a hard time, because you have me working two jobs in one shift. Don't you see that I've been cutting my lunches short and coming in earlier and leaving the office late? Sometimes not until seven in the evening," I said, trying to control my tone. "With all due respect, I don't think I always make mistakes. You just refuse to admit when I do my job right."

Rowena jerked her head back in surprise. "You never do the job correctly, or I wouldn't have to review all your work!"

Still staring at her, I rose slowly from my seat. "Good, then. As of today, you can do my job." I marched through the door and slammed it as hard as I could. My fingers clenched, and my chest tightened like a big balloon was being pumped and ready to blow up.

Sylvia and Yoo-Shi craned their necks from their cubicles as I stormed back to my cubicle. Sylvia rose from her chair, but Christine signaled from her office to stay and then walked over to me.

"Rory, come to my office, please," Christine said gently, motioning me to follow.

My chin trembled. Her gentle voice was like streams of water in my heart. I shook my head and said, "That's okay, Christine. Thank you. I just wish *you* had been my manager." I grabbed my bag, locked my computer, walked out of the office, and descended the stairs to the foyer.

My fingers tightened around the steering wheel as I hit a quiet freeway. My throat felt tight, and I could hardly breathe. I couldn't hold it in anymore.

"AAAAARRRRRGGGGGGGHHHH!!!!" I screamed. And I screamed again. The long screams released the tension on my chest, and hot tears ran down my cheeks for the rest of the drive.

When I arrived at home, without changing my work clothes, I turned on my notebook and sent a resignation letter to HR. Afterward, I threw myself on the bed and cried as hard as I could.

CHAPTER 36

When I woke up the next morning, I had a terrible headache from crying and thought to cancel my lunch appointment with Jason, but I changed my mind. It was still a good idea to be around friends. At least I would have someone to talk to.

At one o'clock, Jason arrived to pick me up. His eyes were red and his sandy hair was messy. I noticed some bruises with a slightly raw wound on his knuckles again; he looked worse than last time.

"Are you okay? You don't look so good today," I said carefully.

He gave a thin smile. "No, I'm good. Let's go," he said, and jerked his head to the car.

I sensed something wasn't right but couldn't pinpoint it. "If you don't feel like going out, let's do it next week," I suggested gently.

Jason kept walking to his car. "I already made a reservation. Come! I'm fine," he said over his shoulder.

Hesitantly, I followed and got into the passenger seat of his Acura RDX. Buckling the seat belt, I glimpsed the girl with the oval face and long brown hair standing behind a maple tree, peering at us—the same girl who had warned me about Jason.

"Hey, Jason, by any chance do you have any female friends with long brown hair?" I asked, my eyes still fixed on the girl.

"No," Jason said. His voice sounded like a grumble. Afterward, he pulled out to the road and drove faster than usual. He changed lanes often and honked at cars in front of us.

I shivered at the coldness in his eyes as he glanced at me. It was a similar feeling that I'd felt recently, but I didn't recall where and when. I coiled my fingers as the muscles in my body became tense. "Are you okay?" I asked again carefully, tilting my head to him.

"What is your relationship with Peter?" Jason snapped, his face tense and the veins on the side of his neck standing out.

"Roommates," I answered. "Former roommates, actually."

Jason scoffed, took his phone from his jacket, and tossed it at me. The movement made the car swerve slightly to the right. "Are these what roommates do now?" His face was crimson with fury.

My blood seemed to drain out of me as I scanned the pictures in his phone. "You got those pictures too," I said quietly, forgetting he also worked for Myriad.

I jumped in my seat as Jason slammed his fist against his side window, the muscles of his jaw bulging. The handsome and smiling Jason had suddenly disappeared.

"Yes, I saw those damn pictures!" he screamed at the top of his lungs, slamming his hand on the steering wheel.

I flinched. "Hey, calm down," I said, keeping my voice light. "Why are you upset? Those aren't real, and—"

"Oh, oh, oh, so sweet little Rory is defending herself," Jason jeered at me, grabbing my hand brusquely. "How many times did you sleep with him to keep your job, huh?"

"You'd better watch it, Jason," I warned, jerking my hand free.

"'You'd better watch it, Jason,'" he mimicked with a disgusted expression on his face. "You are a *slut!*" he screamed, which was quickly followed by a string of expletives.

I was speechless. I couldn't believe that behind his angelic face there was hidden aggression and uncontrollable anger.

He swung at my head a few times, but I dodged his arm by moving closer to the door. Jason's movements caused the car to swerve to the right, almost hitting the car next to us. When he tried to regain control, the car spun and rolled in the wrong direction. Two cars avoided us, but an F15 truck didn't have time. I grabbed the steering wheel and jerked it in a different direction, but it was too late.

Tires shrieking were followed by a loud bang and crunch. I was jolted to the front and to the right, but the seat belt slammed me back against my seat, knocking all the air out of my lungs. The car was pushed backward and banged from behind and the left, thrusting me back to the front and slammed me against the seat again.

Finally, I felt the car stop spinning, and everything went quiet for a second. I tasted blood in my mouth and felt a warm trickle down my cheek. Excruciating pain shot through my body as I attempted to lift my right hand. Breathing heavily, I saw two pairs of big eyes in an oval face, framed with long brown hair, looking down through my window, and everything went black.

I swam between unconsciousness and semiconsciousness. Cold air was pushed through my nostrils, and my ears caught incoherent voices. When I tried to move, the pain was unbearable, and I was slammed back into darkness. After some time, I heard someone crying softly, and I felt my hand being touched and kissed.

Auntie, is it you?

I wanted to see her, but I couldn't open my eyes because they were so heavy.

I'm sorry.

Then it was dark and tranquil again.

My throat was dry when I awoke. I tried to open my eyes. Everything appeared blurry, and a bright light floated in front of my face. When the light shrank, I could see two eyes looking at me.

"Rory, can you hear me?"

"Where am I?" I croaked, blinking and trying to push against the heavy pressure keeping my eyes closed.

Someone shouted, "She's awake!" and the face disappeared.

CHAPTER 37

My aunt was busy preparing homemade minestrone soup in a small bowl for me. Ever since I'd woken, after three days of unconsciousness, she hadn't wanted to do anything but nurse me back to health.

Aunt Amy had flown from Boston on the earliest flight she could get after she got the news about my accident. From the dark circles under her eyes, she mustn't have slept since she arrived.

"Here, your favorite soup," said Aunt Amy, smiling as she sat on the chair next to my bed. "I didn't add corn this time because I was afraid your stomach couldn't digest that yet." She held the bowl in one hand and spoon-fed me with the other.

I moved closer to her to make it easier. "You have to get some rest too, Auntie," I said. "I don't want you to be sick because of me."

My appetite wasn't back to normal, but I didn't want to make her worry, so I let her feed me a couple more spoonfuls. She'd endured enough anxiety from my accident. Although I had no significant injuries, my wrist was fractured, and I'd needed two inches of stitches on my forehead. Other than that, I was bruised and scratched.

"I'm getting old, but I'm strong." She winked at me, feeding me another spoonful of soup. Her eyes glistened each time I swallowed, and she nodded understanding when I signaled her that I was full.

After putting the bowl on the side table, she tucked a lock of my hair behind my ear gently. "I'm so glad to see you again. God must love me so much to allow me to still have you." Her tears started to spill over.

"Sorry I made you worry," I said, lowering my gaze.

Aunt Amy pulled up the corners of her lips. "Silly child. An accident could happen anytime," she said, adjusting my blanket. "I feel sorry for your friend. The doctor said he has a concussion and a broken leg."

I only nodded. I shuddered whenever Jason's face, twisting in rage, flashed in my mind. The memories were enough to harden my heart, leaving me no sympathy for his condition.

Slowly, I shifted my gaze to the big window on the left side of my bed. The sky was blue and cloudless. It was a beautiful day for sitting outside and enjoying the weather.

Peter had once remarked, "You are lucky, living in California, because the weather is good all the time."

"Too much sun will make you look old," I had said.

He'd laughed, shaking his head. "That's easy to say when you have tons of sunshine. You would miss it if you didn't see it so often."

Peter—how is he doing? Does he know about my accident? I wondered silently.

A gentle touch brought me back to the moment.

"Are you okay? Are you in pain?" asked my aunt.

I shook my head. "No, I'm good," I answered quickly.

My aunt's eyebrows furrowed, but she didn't press it. "Peter…He is no longer living with you, right?"

"Did he tell you?" I asked.

"No, but when I stopped by your apartment to take a shower, his room was empty," my aunt said casually, as if everything were normal. She took the half-empty bowl to the bathroom to wash it. A few minutes later, she came out wiping the bowl with a paper towel.

"A lot has happened since the last time you visited. Peter is—"

Aunt Amy touched her finger to my lips, silencing me. "You can tell me everything once you leave the hospital, okay?" she said gently. "Now, you'd better get some rest, and I'll be back this afternoon."

"Please be back," I said, almost begging. "I hate the hospital."

My aunt nodded. "Don't worry. With me beside you," she tapped her chest, "you will be better in no time."

I chuckled and nodded. "Love you."

"Love you back, pumpkin." And she headed toward the door.

A petite nurse came in after my aunt left, and she pushed a wheelchair. Abby was her name.

"Good morning, Rory. How's my patient today? No more headache or nausea or double vision?" she asked cheerfully as she parked the wheelchair near my bed. She took my hand to check my pulse and focused on her wristwatch.

"No double vision. Just a little headache and nausea," I answered.

Abby glanced at me and nodded. "Your pulse is great this morning," she said, releasing my hand. "Now, since you are getting better, the doctor ordered me to let you take some fresh air outside. Ready?"

I nodded, feeling excited to go outside for a while. While Abby removed my IV and hung it on the pole attached to the back of the wheelchair, I stepped down from my bed and sat on the chair. Once we were ready, Abby pushed the wheelchair toward the door.

The tightening in my chest lessened as we headed toward the garden behind the hospital. The grass, bushes, and flowers looked brighter. A finch perched on a magnolia tree, gazing at me with its little eyes. It flew away as my wheelchair was parked under the tree.

"I'll be back in fifteen minutes," said Abby, giving me a smile. "Enjoy the weather."

"Thanks, Abby!"

I was watching two squirrels running up and down the maple tree when someone called my name.

A girl with a ponytail in a long-sleeved, pale-yellow blouse and tight jeans walked toward me, and I recognized her as the same girl who had warned me about Jason.

"Hi," she greeted me. Her voice was soft, like a little girl's. "May I sit near you?" Without waiting for my reply, she took an outdoor chair and dragged it near my wheelchair.

I gazed at her as she sat down. "You've been around a lot lately. Aren't you afraid I'll call security because you're stalking me?" I asked calmly.

The girl gave a little smile and lowered her eyes for a second, then gazed back up at me. "I'm sorry. I should have introduced myself properly. I'm Cindy, Jason's ex-girlfriend." She leaned forward with her hand extended toward me.

"Rory. But you already know my name," I said, shaking her hand.

Cindy nodded slightly and leaned back.

"You've warned me three times about Jason. Why?" I gazed at her.

Solemnly, Cindy rolled her sleeve up, revealing a long, jagged scar on her arm. It was healed, but it wasn't an old wound. The hair on the back of my neck stood on end as I wondered about the cause of her scar.

"Jason is not who you think he is. He has suffered mental disorders and aggressive obsessions that affect his emotions and thinking. He is also bipolar. When I'd told him I wanted a break, he became violent and accused me of cheating on him. In his anger, he smashed a picture frame and took a big shard of glass to my arm. I was scared but able to run away. I'd never seen him like that before." Cindy's shoulders drooped as she let out a sigh and rolled down the sleeve. "Jason also likes to punch something to release his emotions if he is irritated."

The image of Jason's bruised knuckles came rushing back to my memory.

"I've felt pity for him," she said, fidgeting. "After we broke up, he begged me to come back to him a few times, and then he stopped. Later, I found out he was going out with you. I didn't want you to be his next victim, so I warned you. On the day you had the accident, I was following you and Jason. I'm sorry. If I'd explained it to you better ..." Cindy lowered her eyes.

"From the way you spoke about him, you still care about him," I said after awhile. "Do you still love him?"

Cindy looked up at me, blushing. "Tell me—am I stupid for loving a person like Jason?" she asked, her hands clenched together.

That was the same question I'd asked myself about my unrequited feelings for Peter. "Well," I cleared my throat, trying to find perfect words, "loving someone is good, but if you stay with Jason, you should know the consequences of loving him."

She nodded, her eyes glassy. "I've known, and yes, I love him very much," she said in a shaky voice.

I sighed and stretched to take her hand. "You seem like a nice person, Cindy. Many guys would love to have you as their girlfriend. Please don't return to him."

Cindy looked at me and smiled. I saw the determined look in her big eyes as she rose from her seat.

"Thanks for your concern, Rory. I think I'd better go now. Get well soon." Waving, she headed across the garden to the back entrance.

I watched until she disappeared through the door.

CHAPTER 38

The day before I left the hospital, my aunt asked if I would move back to Boston. I'd thought about it too. Since I'd realized she loved me as her own daughter, I wanted to know her more: her favorite food, favorite movie, favorite places. It had been years that I hadn't cared about such details, while she'd always understood what I liked and disliked. Boston was a charming city to live in, and I loved the architecture and the gardens there, especially the Boston Public Garden. The drawback of living in Boston was the cold winters and the muggy summers. But if I had a good job there, I could deal with the seasons.

After returning from the hospital, I started sorting my stuff to sell what I didn't need and pack up what I would take with me. During the sorting process, I found the pair of mugs Peter and I had bought together at the local street fair. The light-blue mug had ROOM printed across it, and the light-yellow one had MATE on it. How we'd laughed about finding such a set and snatched them up quickly for our morning coffee and tea routine.

Gazing down at them, I debated if I should throw them away. Then, I put the mugs in the "Keep" pile. Although our friendship had ended, these mugs were part of a good memory, anyway. I shifted and my gaze landed on the dog-shaped pillow. The pillow Peter had used to cover his underwear when he was playing his video game in the living room. His shocked expression when I walked in had been priceless.

I kept the pillow.

After several hours of sorting, I was finally done. The "Donate" piles were higher than the "Sell" pile. The "Keep" pile was the smallest but still required three large boxes to hold it all.

A week and a half later, it was time for us to say goodbye to Rick and Maggie. They drove us to the airport and helped us get our baggage out of the trunk at the curbside drop-off for Delta Airlines.

Maggie's eyes teared up as she hugged me. "Are you sure you won't return to California?" she asked.

"Maybe. Depends on if I have a job or not," I said. "But I'll make sure to stop by whenever I do visit California."

"Or we can visit you," said Rick, slinging an arm around his wife's shoulder. "Our daughter lives in New Jersey, so we could fly there and stop in Boston or vice versa."

"Yes, please visit us," said my aunt, giving them hugs.

As we headed toward the automatic doors, we couldn't help but keep looking back at them, waving several times. I'd miss them dearly.

Inside, the airport wasn't busy, maybe because it wasn't the weekend. It took us only five minutes to check our bags and get our boarding passes printed.

My phone had been buzzing inside my thin jacket ever since we got in line at the security checkpoint, but I'd ignored it. It was probably just texts from Sylvia or Yoo-Shi to say goodbye. I could check the messages later, once we got to our gate.

After I'd passed the security scanner and put my jacket back on, the phone buzzed again. I pulled it out and lifted my eyebrows. The screen read, "Tom calling."

"I think I should get this," I said to my aunt.

"Sure. See you at the gate," she said.

I nodded and pressed the green button.

"Rory?"

"Hi, Tom," I greeted, keeping my voice cheerful. "How are you?"

"I'm good. How's your wrist?"

"It's better now. One more week till the cast can be removed," I answered. "What's up? I haven't heard from you for a long time."

"It has been busy," said Tom. "Hey, Rory, there is something I need to tell you. Can I meet you today? Maybe for dinner?"

"I'm sorry, I can't," I said, tucking a lock of hair behind my ears.

An announcement came over the speakers for Southwest Airlines to San Francisco.

"Wait," Tom gasped. "Are you at the airport? Where are you going?" His voice rose as he spoke.

"I'm leaving California—for good, Tom." I sighed, gazing up at the ceiling. "I resigned from Myriad, and after the car crash, I thought it would be better if I lived closer to my aunt. She is the only family I have."

As I finished speaking, I heard incoherent sounds, and he exhaled loudly. "What time is your boarding? From which airport? LAX?" His voice sounded urgent.

I glanced at my wristwatch. "John Wayne. Our boarding time is 1:30, so it's about an hour from now," I answered. Something clicked in my mind, and my heart started pounding in my chest. "Why?"

"I have to talk to you. I'll get there as fast as I can," Tom insisted.

"You'll never make it," I said. "Better you tell me now, and save yourself a drive."

"I'm not in LA; I'm in Huntington Beach." He was panting as if he were running. "Please don't go past the last checkpoint. Wait for me. It's important! Be there in twenty minutes!"

"Tom…hey!" I shouted, but he had already hung up.

I stared at my phone, feeling bewildered. Shaking my head, I returned to the checkpoint and spoke to a TSA officer to see if I could go out and come back in again later. The officer nodded and told me I just had to go through the checkpoint again to re-enter.

Outside the checkpoint, I called my aunt and explained but promised I would be at the gate in time for boarding.

"Okay. Just don't be late," she reminded me.

Twenty minutes passed. The automatic glass door slid open as Tom rushed in. His face was red, and he was panting heavily.

"Hey!" he said as he stopped in front of me. "Thank you for waiting."

"Not a problem. Besides, I'm curious. Tell me what happened." I gestured toward a seat next to me.

He took a deep breath and sat down, then turned to me. "Rory, I owe you an apology." Solemnly, he studied my face.

I raised an eyebrow. "If this is about my quarrel with Peter, it has nothing to do with you."

Tom shook his head quickly. "No, it's about Phil." His eyes avoided mine as he sighed heavily.

"Um…you lost me," I said, perplexed.

Tom gazed at me. "About the pictures of you and Peter. Phil stole Peter's phone and exposed those pictures to the public." He placed his elbows on his knees, leaning toward me. "Peter and I figured out that someone had to have stolen his phone and fabricated the pictures. He said when he was in the rehab facility, his phone was missing for some time, but he didn't think anyone would steal it. We were sure it wasn't Marcus because he is practically a dad to Peter. But at that time, we couldn't figure out who would do such an awful thing.

"Then we suspected Kim Johnson, who is on one of the White Water teams. She has a crush on Peter. But we realized Kim would do anything to make Peter happy, so we crossed her off the suspect list. Later, our IT director found suspicious activity in Phil's office notebook and reported it to Peter." Tom sighed, rubbing his face with his hands.

I touched the base of my neck, glancing at him. "Why? Why would he do that? Why would he want to hurt Peter?" I asked.

Tom gnawed his lower lip. "Phil wants me to supplant Peter to inherit the Sandridge business. The board has always seen Peter as a wild, irresponsible person, so Phil thought if he could fabricate some pictures, he might manipulate the board to revoke Peter's appointment as CEO and choose me instead. But I'm not crazy about being in that position or being involved in the family business." He ran his hand over his hair.

"I'm baffled now. Why did Phil want *you* for the CEO position? And…if he is also the one who fabricated the pictures, why did *you* owe me an apology?"

Shifting in his seat, Tom studied my confused expression. "Rory, I'm Peter's half brother. Phil was my boyfriend. Your false assumption about my relationship with Peter and the difficulty over living with a male roommate gave Peter the crazy idea to continue the false assumption so he could stay in your place for the time being, until the project was done. He put me in the charade to convince you."

My jaw dropped. I was speechless.

Tom nodded his head. "Remember the fight in the rehab facility?" he asked, nudging my hand.

"Yes."

"I felt guilty for deceiving you." His cheeks turned pinkish. "I tried to convince him that lying to you would lead him to a difficult position, but Peter was stubborn. He refused, and I told him I didn't want to be part of his charade anymore."

I swallowed hard. "So, Peter isn't…?"

Tom nodded.

"He isn't, but I am," Tom said. "On the evening when you assumed Peter was confessing his *love*"—he made air quotes—"my dad was upset about my relationship with Phil, and Peter was trying to calm me and support me. My mom doesn't accept me either. Only Peter and Jane accepted me as who I am."

I blinked, trying to digest Tom's bizarre story. When I was about to open my mouth, the boarding call for Delta Airlines to Boston came over the PA system.

"I…I have to go," I said, rising from my seat.

Tom rose, too, and placed his hand on my elbow. "Rory, Peter never meant to hurt you because he likes—no, he is *in love* with you." His eyes fixed on me. "From the way you looked at him, I believed you felt the same thing. But he was too arrogant to stop his charade, and in the end, it hurt you both badly."

I stiffened. "What did you say?"

"He is in love with you, Rory."

Looking at him, I shook my head slowly. "No, I don't think so." I narrowed my eyes, feeling the tension in my neck. "He lies and uses me for selfish reasons. He cares about himself, Tom. Sorry to say that, but that's what I feel. He didn't tell the truth about many things. About you, about RTC being involved with my work. He needs a girl who is," I paused to take a breath and control my emotions, "easy to toy with. And I'm not that girl. I won't be fooled for a second time. Goodbye, Tom, and thanks for your explanation." I jerked my elbow free and stepped away.

Tom let me go but followed me.

From the corner of my eye, I caught a familiar figure rushing through the glass doors. My eyes widened. It was Peter. He was sprinting over to us, red-faced and glistening with sweat. Peter exchanged glances with Tom, who shrugged his shoulders and shook his head.

"Are you leaving?" Peter asked, panting, his eyes fixed on me.

I nodded.

Peter opened his mouth and closed it again. His shoulders drooped. "Well…
have a safe flight," he said, clearing his throat.

I nodded again while Tom nudged his arm, jerking his head toward me.

"I have to go," I said, glancing at Peter and Tom. "Bye, guys."

I turned and increased my pace to head toward the security line that was
now empty. As I got closer, I heard footsteps catching up behind me, and then
a hand grabbed my elbow to stop me. I whipped around to see Peter looking
at me. He pulled me into his arms and hugged me. I was stunned and tried to
wiggle free, but he tightened his arms around my shoulders.

"I…I love you, Rory. I *do* love you. And I'm sorry for everything," he whispered in my ear. His voice trembled. "I've many regrets in my life that I wish I
could turn the clock back on, and this is the biggest one." After a few seconds,
he pushed me away gently and gave me a weak smile. "Goodbye, Rory. Take
care of yourself." His lips trembled as he released me.

Speechless, I studied his eyes for the truth. In the background, the announcement for the final boarding call broke our silence. This time, my name was called
to the gate. I stole a glance at Peter as I scurried to the line and gave my boarding
pass and ID to be checked again. Holding the pass and the ID, the TSA officer
looked up and asked, "Aurorette Arrington? Your flight is ready to close the door.
Proceed to your gate immediately!"

I nodded and put my backpack and jacket into the screening conveyor. I could
feel Peter's eyes on me the whole time, but I didn't have time to look at him. Once
I was done, I took my belongings and ran to the assigned gate. I almost bumped
into a big guy coming out from a store.

"Damn you, girl!"

"Sorry, sorry!" I waved and kept running.

I felt my lungs burn from running so fast, and I literally skidded to a stop in front
of the flight attendant, who shook her head slightly as she marked my boarding pass.

When I entered the cabin, I heard murmuring, and a few people craned
their necks to see the late person who'd almost delayed the flight.

"What happened?" my aunt hissed as I sat next to her.

"I'm sorry. I didn't expect it would take this long, but I'll tell you later," I
said, catching my breath as I turned my phone to airplane mode.

My knees and legs were shaking from the sprint. What I needed now was
some quiet time to think. The nearly eight-hour flight would be enough for that.
As the plane slowly ascended, I noticed a distinct hollow feeling in my heart.

We arrived at my aunt's condo around midnight local time, which was still nine in California, but we were tired and ready to sleep. Since no stores or restaurants would be open that late, we ate a light dinner of leftover sandwiches and fruit we'd brought with us. After showering, we retired to bed.

I woke up at five. It was too early, but I couldn't sleep anymore. My mind had been busy rerunning everything from the last twenty-four hours. Sitting on the carpet in my room, I started unpacking my suitcases. One by one, I folded and stacked or hung my clothes in the closet. For almost two hours, I folded and stacked and arranged my wardrobe. It was good to keep my mind off Peter.

Standing in front of the closet with my hands on my hips, I felt more relaxed and happier to see the tidiness. A new beginning, a new life.

I flopped back down on the carpet after putting the suitcases in the corner of my room to take downstairs to storage later. I pulled my backpack closer and emptied its contents one by one on the carpet: a Kindle, a couple candy wrappers, a little notebook, a pen, ten one-dollar bills, a couple quarters and dimes, a lip gloss, a bottle of eye drops, and a white envelope folded in half.

A white envelope?

I took the envelope and flipped it over in my hand. No name was written on the surface, and it was sealed. I didn't recall ever putting that envelope in my backpack. Curious, I tore open the flap and took two pages out. Unfolding them, I could feel my eyes widen as I realized the letter was from Peter.

My heart pounded as I read. Peter knew me much better than I'd realized. Since I'd told him I didn't want to deal with him anymore, he knew I wouldn't accept any emails, texts, or phone calls from him. Every way to contact me had been blocked, so the only way he could explain everything was by writing a letter he had inserted in my backpack when he hugged me in the airport.

In his letter, he gave detailed explanations about everything, which mostly I'd already heard from Tom: about the pictures that were engineered by Phil; about his relationship with Tom, who was his half brother and not his lover; about Jason, who had a sadistic streak and had been stalking me, which Peter had learned about from through a private investigator; and, in the end, about his own feelings toward me that he had started realizing when he was in the ER. The more he resisted, the stronger his feelings had grown. He was overwhelmed because he was afraid to tell me the truth without making me upset. He also revealed his anxiety when I was in a coma after the car accident. It was his moment of truth about how important I was in his life.

At the end of his letter, Peter asked if I had the same feelings. If my mind changed, and I could ever accept his feelings, he begged me to contact him. If my mind didn't change, he wouldn't bother me anymore.

The words on the letter became tangled and blurry as a tear slid down my cheek. Wiping it with the back of my hand, I inhaled deeply, struggling to describe what I felt after reading his letter.

If he were in front of me, I might have yelled at him for lying to me, punched his shoulder for making me miserable, then hugged him for telling me the truth, then kissed him for loving me, and gone back to yelling again.

Suddenly, I heard my aunt call me for lunch.

"I'm coming," I said louder, shoving the letter under my pillow and glancing at the mirror to make sure no tears streaked my face before stepping out from my room.

"Are you okay?" asked Aunt Amy as we had lunch on the patio. "Your mind has been somewhere else since we got on the plane."

I put my fork down and wiped my lips with a napkin. I didn't know how to start or how to end. I also didn't fully understand how I really felt about Peter yet.

"Well, it started when I was looking for a roommate… ." Slowly I told my aunt almost everything, skipping anything I'd already told her.

My aunt listened intently and smiled at the goofy things Peter had done in the kitchen and offered a deep sigh and thoughtful gaze about the moment I misunderstood Peter and Tom's relationship. Her eyes widened at the part when Tom came to the airport to tell the truth and how Peter had given me his confession. I also told her about Peter's letter.

"So, how do you feel about Peter?" my aunt asked. "Do you love him?"

My fingers folded and unfolded the napkin in front of me.

My aunt took her cup and sipped her tea quietly while waiting for my answer.

"I'm not sure. Peter…he lives in a different world, a different lifestyle," I finally said. "I'm afraid one day I would grow tired of living in his world."

My aunt put her cup back and gazed at me gently. "Why are you afraid about the future?" she said, folding her hands on the table. "And there is no such thing as *his* world or *your* world. Now, listen to me. When your mom passed away and gave you to me, I was afraid of what would happen if I failed. Many times, I cried and asked God why I had to raise a kid when I'd never been married. But did you see what happened? You grew up to be a wonderful lady with a caring and gentle heart. You finished school and tackled many problems in your life. Did I see it when I brought you into my life? No. There was no way I could be confident that you would turn out as you have. But I never lost my faith." My aunt stretched her hand to lift my chin. Her eyes locked with mine. In a lower voice, she told me that Peter had arranged for her to get a first-class ticket so she could be with me after the accident as quickly as possible. He'd also arranged for the doctors to do extensive testing to make sure I was all right. However, Peter forbade her from telling me everything he'd done because he knew I didn't want any help from him.

"Peter cried at your bedside because you were unconscious longer than the doctors predicted. And I tell you this to give you a different perspective that he is a responsible person, despite all the news about him in the past." My aunt sighed, holding my hand. "If your heart loves him, you should tell him. If, in the end, you aren't meant to be, you can move on with your chin up because you tried."

Listening to her pragmatic advice, some concerns weighing on my chest lifted. I loved Peter, and yet I felt uncertain because he wasn't a typical twenty-three-year-old guy. On the other hand, my aunt was right—if I never tried, how did I know if everything would be fine in the end?

Rising from my seat, I leaned forward and hugged my aunt tightly.

She chuckled, patting my back.

"Thank you," I said, pulling away from her.

"Any time, dear," my aunt said, looking up at me with a smile. She pushed her seat back and stood up. "Now, please make this old lady happy by cleaning the table. Then accompany me to the store to buy some yarn. My fingers are itching for knitting again," she said, wiggling her fingers.

I chuckled weakly, dumbfounded, as she strode into the living room, leaving me alone with the dishes.

CHAPTER 39

I sat down on the bench under the maple tree, facing the statue of George Washington in the Boston Public Garden. After my conversation with my aunt, I'd texted Peter to say I'd read his letter and that if his feelings hadn't changed in two weeks, we could meet in this garden, but we were not supposed to contact each other until that day. He'd texted me back and demanded a reason. I'd told him that two weeks was enough time to think again about our feelings. If we didn't feel any love anymore, we wouldn't hurt each other and could just move on.

Sylvia had said I was stupid. I'd said I was wise because it was a fair game.

I glanced at my watch. It was 10:00 AM. I was an hour earlier than the time we'd agreed on, but I didn't care. I couldn't hold back my smile at the thought of seeing him again.

The trees had already started changing colors. It was early fall, and the weather had been hot yesterday, but it was a bit cooler today. In one more week, people would experience the beautiful foliage of the garden covered by a rich array of golds, yellows, and reds. Leaves would drop off following the absence of birdsongs, and the ground would become covered by colorful leaves.

I took out my Kindle to read, but the words swam in front of my eyes. Letting out a sigh, I closed it and put it back in my backpack, then glanced at my watch again. The clock seemed to be ticking slowly today.

I rose from my seat and started pacing back and forth. My fingers were tingling, and there was a fluttery feeling in my stomach.

It was ten minutes past our meeting time. No Peter.

I exhaled slowly and started chewing my nails, something I hadn't done for a long time, and paced around again. *Maybe I should wait another fifteen minutes, right? It would only be fair.*

Time didn't stop. It kept moving forward, and my heart sank as I glanced at my watch. Fifteen minutes passed, still no Peter.

Did he chicken out?

I swallowed the thought, staring down at my feet and the dried maple leaves coloring the ground around me.

A group of tourists led by a man holding up a small red flag was taking pictures in front of the statue. Kids screaming and giggling could be heard over the usual lunchtime crowd's chatter. Another thirty minutes had passed since the last time I'd checked my watch.

A painful lump rose in my throat. "This is pathetic!" I heaved a sigh as I stood up from my seat. "Go home, Rory," I said to myself.

Dragging my feet, I left the bench, feeling numb and hollow inside.

I was so stupid. Naïve. I'd deluded myself into believing Peter would come to me. Maybe he'd changed his mind in the final minutes. That was possible.

Exhaling loudly, I stopped and gazed up at the bright, baby-blue sky. When I blinked, a tear slipped out, and I wiped it away quickly. *No, I don't want to cry about this.* Then I pulled the corners of my lips up for a smile.

As I continued walking, I heard footsteps running toward me, and then my shoulder was bumped as a tall man jogged past me.

"Hey!" I cried.

The person tumbled to the ground a few yards in front of me, groaned, and rolled onto his back.

"Oh my God! Are you okay?" I cried, rushing to him.

My jaw dropped because that man was Peter.

Eyes closed, his face glistening with sweat, he stretched his arms and legs out and lay there panting. "Why…did…you…choose…this…park?" he asked, catching his breath. Gazing up at me through half-open eyes, he licked his pale, dry lips.

"I like this park," I answered, kneeling next to him. "And you're late."

Peter took several moments to catch his breath, then pushed up to a sitting position. "There was an overturned truck blocking the road ten miles from here," he said, swallowing. "I was stuck in the traffic. I was so excited to meet you again and forgot to bring my phone with me. So, I paid for my taxi and ran."

He fell back on the grass again. "I just ran ten miles for the girl I love," Peter groaned, drawing an invisible line as far as his arms would reach, "and you were leaving without me?"

My heart swelled as I looked down at him. It couldn't have been easy for him to find this place on foot.

"I thought you'd changed your mind," I said, sitting cross-legged. "I've been waiting for you for two hours."

"Can't be. Our appointment was at 11," Peter said, shaking his head and pushing up with his palms. The breeze played with his messy hair.

My heart ached, realizing how badly I'd missed him.

"Wait." He tilted his head to see me clearly. "You got here at ten?"

My cheeks warmed. "I was afraid I'd be late."

"I see," Peter said, sitting up and crossing his legs. Our knees touched. He took my hands and held them. "I'm sorry to make you wait for two hours," he said. "You shouldn't have had to. What would happen if I hadn't come?"

"*If* that happened, I would be sad—very sad—and would drown my sorrow with ice cream for weeks," I said, gazing up at him.

Peter chuckled and caressed my cheek gently. He shifted closer to me, his gaze locked with mine. For a moment, we sat face-to-face in silence.

"Hi," he said softly.

"Hi," I said back, my cheeks filled with warmth.

"You look thinner. Are you feeling okay?" he asked, stretching his hand to tuck a lock of hair behind my ears as he gazed at me with concern.

I looked down and nodded. "I'm fine. Just…so many things have happened in the last two months," I said, looking up at him.

Peter sighed. "I wish I could erase the bad memories and turn back the clock so everything would be perfect from our first meeting through today," he said, running his fingers along my jaw carefully, seeming afraid to hurt me. His look was tender as he gazed into my eyes.

Something in me quivered at the way he looked at me. I had to say something. "What would happen if you turned back the clock and made it right? What would you say to me on the day we meet for the first time?" I asked.

Taking my hand in his again, Peter narrowed his eyes and tilted his head to think about my question. "I know what I want to say." His eyes sparkled.

"What?"

"Hi, my name is Peter, and I'm going to love you for the rest of my life," he replied.

I chuckled. "You can't say that the first time you meet someone. Come on, be serious."

Solemnly, Peter leaned closer and kissed my forehead. His lips were warm and soft. "Maybe I would be totally speechless and captivated by you, like right now." He kissed the tip of my nose gently. Pulling away, he gazed at me and pulled my hand to his chest.

I could feel his heart hammering underneath his jacket.

His voice softened. "And I would be trying to calm my heart, because it would be thumping so hard my chest hurt, like right now." He kissed both of my cheeks, then met my gaze. "If everything were fine between us, I would tell you that you are the most beautiful girl I've ever met, and I would love you forever." Peter put his arm around my waist and pulled me closer.

Looking at his eyes, I could see clearly how much he cared about me.

Tilting his head, Peter pressed his lips to mine and kissed me gently.

My breath caught in my throat as our lips touched. Slowly, I wrapped my hand around his neck as I kissed him back. I could feel him smiling as we kissed there, in front of the Washington statue, with the beautiful foliage all around us, until a soft rumbling interrupted the moment.

Peter pulled away, wide-eyed. "What's that sound?" he said, scanning our surroundings.

Heat rushed to my cheeks. "I think my stomach knows it's past lunchtime," I said in a low voice.

Peter burst out laughing.

I bit my lower lip and gazed up at him.

"That's why I love you, Aurorette Arrington," he said, bringing both my hands to his lips and kissing them. Smiling, he rose to his feet and pulled me up. "Let's eat, my dear. Where would you like to go?"

I told him about an Italian restaurant not far from the garden. With our hands intertwined, we strolled toward the entrance where I'd parked my car.

Late in the afternoon, I took Peter to meet my aunt formally. Aunt Amy had taken a liking to him since the first meeting at my old apartment, and now it seemed she liked him even more. To my surprise, she asked him to stay with us for a night, sleeping on the couch in the living room with the promise that he would not sneak into my room.

Alone in the living room, we talked, kissed, and talked some more until it was late.

Peter playfully shooed me back to my room. "A promise is a promise," he said solemnly.

I couldn't help but giggle when he whispered that I should lock my door so he couldn't make any attempts to break in.

The next morning, he surprised my aunt and me, especially me, by making pancakes for breakfast without burning down the house. The pancakes were soft and melted in our mouths. Bashfully, Peter admitted that he'd hired someone to teach him how to make good pancakes so that one day he could make them for me. He'd just started his cooking lessons when I'd told him I didn't want to deal with him anymore, but he had kept practicing with the hope that I would forgive him one day.

EPILOGUE

Ahhh…love!

That crazy little thing had turned our lives upside down in the last six months. Peter and I had fallen in love the first time we met and simply hadn't realized it. We had laughed and cried, argued, then longed to see each other, and eventually been able to laugh at the whole thing because, in the end, everything fell into place.

Jason resigned from Myriad and agreed to get therapy for his mental health issue. Cindy took him back and became his emotional support. Love is strange. It is invisible, but its power can move mountains.

Lena won the case against Rowena and Desiree for unfair treatment in the workplace. I was happy for her but couldn't help but pity Rowena when I learned her husband divorced her after that. Working under her had taught me something: when you are responsible for managing people, you should have mercy and be kind to those working beneath you.

Sylvia was promoted to an accounting manager for the non-alcohol division, and she deserved it.

Christine's kindness and fairness led her to become a general manager, replacing Desiree, who got fired, and I believed the accounting department would be a better place to work under her leadership.

Yoo-Shi got promoted to replace Christine, and I knew she would continue to follow in Christine's wise footsteps.

I hadn't gone to Lizzy's and Terry's wedding because I was in the hospital. They became husband and wife in front of Lizzy's dying mom, who passed away two days later. I felt deep sadness for my dear friend, and Aunt Amy grieved over the loss of Lizzy's mom, who had been her friend. Although she was sad, Lizzy was happy to have been able to fulfill her mom's last request.

Peter and I had to build our relationship over a long distance because I got a job in Boston, and Peter had to work between LA and London. We figured it might be good for us to take our relationship at a slow pace; we were still young and full of ambitions and dreams. We called each other at least once a day, and Peter made sure his flights stopped in Boston each time he traveled back and forth between LA and London. Given my financial situation, there was no way I could afford to go to London. Besides, I was determined not to let Peter buy me the ticket; I wanted to maintain my independence.

We would take things as they came. As my aunt said, time would prove our love.

EXCERPT
NO SECRETS ALLOWED

CHAPTER 1

Acrisp, early winter morning greeted me as I left my aunt's house. Vapor rose in the air from my breath. Gazing up, I noticed the color of the sky matched the gray sidewalk, although the Weather Channel had predicted a bright, sunny day in Boston. Well, so much for expecting a warm day today.

As I turned onto the main street, the hustle and bustle of the city surrounded me. The sound of passing cars and the groaning and hissing of the city bus when it halted at the nearby bus stop overwhelmed the chatter and footsteps of people rushing to and fro. Twenty feet from me, a man yelled and waved his fist as a biker swirled past him on the sidewalk. It was against the law to ride a bike on the sidewalk, especially where it was prohibited by signs, but sometimes, people did it anyway. I chuckled and shook my head.

When I moved to this city four months ago, I hadn't liked its hustle and bustle. Too noisy. However, I was used to it now and felt something inside me come alive every time my ears picked up the familiar sounds.

I sped up a bit, speed-walking toward the O`ahu Café for my favorite winter drink, a mint-flavored mocha latte. Another nearby café had the same drink, but the one from the O`ahu was better and not too sweet. The best part was the location of the café near the bus stop, which allowed me to take shelter from the frigid weather while waiting for the bus.

My idea wasn't as brilliant as I'd thought because, looking through the big window, I saw a long line waiting inside the café. My favorite table near the window and facing the street was already occupied. When the café wasn't too crowded, I enjoyed sitting at that particular table while drinking my coffee, watching pedestrians pass by on the sidewalk.

Seven people stood in line, but thankfully, my bus wasn't scheduled to arrive anytime soon.

The bell above the café door made a soft ding as I pushed it open. A couple of customers near the door turned to see who had entered, as well as a young man in a beige apron behind the counter, whose brown skin made many people jealous of his natural tan. His long hair was tied up in a bun and hidden beneath his black beanie. I felt a twinge of envy over his long, shiny, black hair.

Standing next to a girl with a pixie haircut, who was currently taking the customers' orders, he waved to acknowledge me, and I waved back at him.

As I approached the counter, he signaled the cashier to change places with him so he could ring up my order.

"Good morning, Aurorette Arrington," he sang. "You look great this morning with your red nose like Rudolph." He tapped at his own nose.

"Good morning, Tyler Sheridan James Kahale," I teased him back. "You look great too, with your long hair that makes me jealous hidden under your beanie."

The wide grin on his face faded. Ty, as he wanted people to call him, had never liked his long name. He always said that he wanted to change his name to "Tyler James," making it short but cool. However, after his dad passed away, he decided to keep it.

"No more free espresso for you, since you called me by *that* name." He pouted, but his eyes twinkled with good humor. He rang up my usual order, a small mint mocha latte.

"I can deal with that." I smiled sweetly, tapping my card on the reader.

Ty scoffed and closed the register. He asked the girl with the pixie haircut to ring up the next order. The girl switched places with him, seemingly used to acting on the whim of the owner's son.

"Where have you been? You haven't come around lately," Ty said, pumping two shots of mint syrup into a cup. "My mom has been asking about you."

His mom, Dot, was my aunt's closest friend in Boston. After her husband had passed away, Dot had begun managing the café with Ty, her daughter, Brie, and three workers. My aunt came and helped out sometimes when the café was extra busy or if one of the workers couldn't come in.

"Busy, busy, busy." I sighed dramatically. "It's almost Christmas, and my office has been super hectic since October. I haven't had a chance to stop by because I've been exhausted by the time I get home. Please tell Dot that I'll stop by after work for her delicious chicken pesto panini tonight."

His mom's panini was one of the café's specialties. Made fresh, people loved the crunchy texture and delicious pesto sauce. Usually, I texted Dot to put aside one or two that I'd pick up later after work.

"Yeah, I'll tell her. By the way," Ty said as he poured an espresso shot into my cup, "I heard from her that your aunt got a new coffee machine for her birthday last month, but she doesn't drink coffee, does she? Now, tell me, why would someone give her a coffee machine? I'll bet the giver isn't a very thoughtful person. Just saying," he added, giving me a meaningful smile.

In return, my smile was sour. The giver was Peter Ryder, my long-distance, British-born boyfriend, who lived in California. He'd known that my aunt loved tea more than coffee and bought an English tea set for her birthday. He also bought a coffee machine for me from the same store. Somehow, the store had messed up the orders and sent the coffee machine in beautiful wrapping paper to my aunt instead of the tea set. My aunt was upset and thought Peter wasn't a thoughtful person. When I told him, Peter freaked out and complained to the store. My aunt felt better after he apologized and explained it to her. Later on, the store called for clarification and sent her another tea set by way of compensation.

"It wasn't his fault. The store messed up the order," I said quickly. "Besides, my aunt now has two beautiful new English tea sets while I got the coffee machine."

"Ha! I knew you'd defend that useless guy," Ty said, pointing at my nose. A proud smile plastered his face. "Aurorette, you should date me, not a guy who lives far away in California. Since I live close to you, I wouldn't make a blunder like that. Two years younger means nothing in this century. Besides, I think I'm more mature than him. And where does he work now?" Leaning toward me, he placed his hand behind his ear.

"Yeah, yeah, yeah. I've heard that before." I waved a hand. "And instead of dating *me*, you should find a girl your age. Besides," I leaned toward him and whispered in his ear, "you're working for your family business too." I gave him a wink.

His mouth opened slightly and then closed again. "But it's only temporary until I finish col—"

His words were cut off when a large, tall woman, her gray hair wrapped in a hairnet, came from the kitchen. "Ty! I'm busy, and the milk company will be here soon. I need you to receive the delivery." Her dark brown eyes widened as our eyes met. "Oh, hey, Rory. Sorry, I didn't notice you there. Where have you been, dear?"

"It's been crazy at work," I replied. "I'm glad I saw you today, Dot."

Dot smiled and nodded. "Well, enjoy the coffee. I have to get back to the kitchen again. Do you need some panini today? One or two?"

"Two would be great, and I'll pick them up after work. Have a good day, Dot."

"Thank you. I'll save you two panini."

Dot retreated to the kitchen, and Ty handed me my order. "Come again tomorrow. I'll give you a free shot of espresso," he said, his voice lowered so the other customers wouldn't hear.

"Okay, but I can't promise anything," I said.

He pouted.

I grinned widely before taking my drink to the condiment bar to retrieve additional chocolate powder and a lid.

As I turned, a young boy rushed toward the door and bumped my elbow, spilling the hot drink onto my hand. I shrieked and jumped sideways, losing my grip on the cup.

The next events seemed to happen in slow motion.

Mocha splashed onto the man waiting nearby for his order before the cup hit the ground, sending the rest of the hot liquid everywhere.

The man gave a tiny yelp and tried to shake the coffee from his light blue sweater. The brown stain was already spreading down his chest.

"Oh my God!" Ty screamed, grabbing a roll of paper towels from the counter before rushing toward us.

"I'm sorry," Ty and I said almost in unison.

"You should be careful next time, young lady," a voice said from behind me.

I turned and saw a bald guy standing near the condiment bar.

"He could have been scalded by the hot coffee," he continued.

"That's not my…" I glanced at the bald man before turning to my mocha victim. "The kid bumped my elbow and—"

"At the very least, you can take him to the doctor to treat his burns, and pay for his dry cleaning," the bald guy interrupted.

I took a breath. It was clear this guy loved making trouble. "Yes, that's what I'm going to—"

Before I finished, the mocha victim turned to the bald guy. "Hey, man," he said, "thanks for your concern. The coffee wasn't too hot, anyway, and I don't need a doctor. And this young lady"—he pointed to me—"didn't do it on purpose. That means she doesn't need to pay for my dry cleaning."

The bald guy mumbled and moved toward the door with his nose in the air. A few customers murmured and glanced at him as he left the café.

Sighing, the mocha victim turned to Ty. "Please show me where the restroom is, so I can clean my shirt." He pointed to me. "Would you mind watching my luggage while I change my clothes?" He indicated the luggage at his feet.

I nodded. "No problem at all."

"The restroom is this way." Ty ushered him down the narrow hallway. "I can give you our café sweater for free, too," I heard him say.

"Is your hand okay?" asked Dot, who had already come out from the kitchen. She must've heard the commotion.

I picked up a beige jacket from the floor, assuming it belonged to the mocha victim. One sleeve of the coat had a coffee stain on it.

"Yes, I'm fine, Dot," I said, searching for the young boy who had caused the ruckus. When I didn't see him, I assumed he must have run off.

"I've never seen that boy or the bald guy before," said Dot, following my gaze to the front door. "Let me replace your drink, dear."

Before I could decline her offer, she'd already walked behind the counter and apologized to the customers for the commotion.

Shortly after, Ty and the mocha victim came out of the restroom. The man now wore a bright pink sweater with the words "I need my coffee now!" printed above the cartoon picture of a sullen lady in pajamas with rollers in her hair. Ty had drawn the cartoon, and every time I saw it, I smiled.

But not this time.

As our eyes met, I mouthed to Ty, "Pink?"

Ty shrugged.

The mocha victim seemed relieved as I handed him his jacket. He put it on quickly, buttoning it up to conceal the sweater.

"I'm sorry we don't have any other color, sir," said Ty apologetically. "Our new order will be here in two days. If you don't mind waiting, I could go upstairs and lend you one of *my* sweaters."

The man shook his head. "That's okay. I have no time to waste as I have a plane to catch."

"How about me paying for the laundry service?" I offered, using the chance to look at him clearly.

He was a head taller than me, sturdy but slim. Behind his glasses, his eyes were blue with a hint of green. His light brown hair was neatly cut with clean edges, making him look like the classic gentleman. I guessed he couldn't be over the age of thirty-five.

"Don't worry about that. I was here for my business trip, hence I can charge my company for a new, expensive sweater," he said, half joking. "Thanks, but it's unnecessary. Besides, I got a free pink sweater." He grinned after saying the last sentence.

"But—"

"It's okay." He shook his head again. "Accidents can happen anywhere. And this wasn't your fault."

Before I could say more, Dot brought me a new mint mocha latte. After thanking her, I turned to the man, but he was already gone. I exhaled, waving at Ty, who was busy mopping the floor to prevent people from stepping on the spill. I tried to put the event behind me and walked to the bus stop.

All the way to work, I couldn't shake thoughts of what had happened earlier. That poor man was here for a business trip, and on the day he had to fly back home, his sweater and coat were ruined by a mint mocha latte. I bet he would buy a new sweater at the airport instead of wearing that bright pink one.

I pressed the red stop button as the bus rolled closer to my destination and waited until it came to a halt. Once the door opened, the fresh air rushed in, wrapping its cold fingers around me.

Walking slowly along the sidewalk toward my office, I pulled my beanie down to cover my ears and adjusted the scarf around my neck. The tip of my nose was growing numb from the frigid wind. I missed the mild winter season in Southern California. After living there for more than five years, I'd been spoiled by year-round warm and sunny weather.

Boston was beautiful, but I would have liked it more if the winter wasn't so harsh and the summer wasn't so humid.

No one had forced me to live in Boston. After I graduated from college, my aunt had suggested that I move in with her, but I loved California and was happy when I got a job as an accountant at Myriad Food and Beverage. I'd thought I was ready to settle down there. Many things had happened in August, including the horrible car accident after I resigned from Myriad. My aunt was my only kin, so after the accident, I decided to move and stay with her.

I entered my office building and took the elevator to the tenth floor, where I got off at Veles Capital, a financial holding company possessing a diversified line of community banking and commercial finance. I'd worked there as a senior analyst in the risk department for almost four months. My boss, Sally Kranda, was the nicest boss compared to my bitchy, bully boss at Myriad.

"Good morning, Marsha," I said, passing my coworker's cubicle.

"Hi, Rory. Good morning and happy Friday," Marsha Wilson said cheerfully over her shoulder.

"Happy Friday," I responded.

Sitting on my chair, I fitted my electronic notebook into its docking station and turned the power on.

"Too bad you didn't join our happy hour yesterday," Marsha said, sliding her chair to peek inside my cubicle while I logged into my computer.

"Why? Did something happen?" I glanced at her before turning my attention back to the computer.

Still sitting on her chair, Marsha slid into my cubicle. I probably should advise her to stop doing that, as her bulging, six-months-pregnant stomach made it seem rather amusing.

"Last night, Kelly was drunk and confessed her love to Ryan," she whispered.

I covered my mouth with my hand. "Really?"

She nodded. "Yup. Crazy, huh? I don't understand her. Did she think it was okay to get drunk during happy hour with her coworkers? If she'd wanted to get drunk, she should've just gone with her regular friends. We don't want to go out with people who can't control themselves. Besides, our happy hour is for relaxing and bonding, not for drinking excessively. That stupid girl doesn't know how to limit herself, and she confessed love to her senior while Leslie joined us for the happy hour." Marsha rolled her eyes when she mentioned

Sally's assistant manager. "It's a good thing Leslie doesn't care what people do outside the office. If she did, Kelly would be doomed."

"What did Ryan say?" I asked.

Marsha shrugged, tossing her bronze, shoulder-length hair behind her. "As you know, Ryan loves joking around. It surprised me how maturely he handled Kelly. Obviously, he isn't interested in her. Kelly knows he prefers you over her that's why she's always bitching about you."

It didn't take a genius to know that Ryan Harris had been crushing on me since I'd joined the company. He'd also been my classmate in university back in California.

I hadn't recognized him right away. Ryan had changed a lot, and the only things that had stayed the same were his sweet smile and his dimples. He was no longer a quiet, pale, lanky boy with long, dark brown hair, who wore black every single day. His lean and muscled body, along with his messy, medium-length hair made him look adorable. He'd also become a pleasant person to talk to, easy-going, and a reliable coworker. No wonder people, especially females, loved talking to him.

Meeting him again after years brought back the sweet memories in me. In college, we'd done everything together, starting from orientation, and some people mistook us for a couple. I didn't know what he'd felt toward me because he never said it. If he'd ever asked, I wouldn't have minded, because I liked him. Unfortunately, we'd grown apart after choosing our majors.

Since meeting again, Ryan had openly showed his attention toward me and looked unhappy upon learning that I had a boyfriend. I felt a familiar light flutter in my belly every time he looked at me, and I wished he had had the courage when we were in college.

I opened my mouth to respond when the general manager's office door opened. Sally emerged, her expression one of grave concern. She walked by us as though in a trance.

We exchanged glances, and Marsha slid her chair back to her cubicle while I focused on my monitor. We almost forgot to greet Ryan as he arrived and sat in his cubicle. When his head popped over the partition, he raised an eyebrow. I shrugged and jerked my head toward Sally's office. Without another word, he sat down and started working.

Twenty minutes passed, and Sally's urgent voice called out, "Rory, Marsha, Ryan, come to my office."

Right away, we all stood and hurried to join her.

"Please take a seat," she said, sitting in her chair.

I sat next to Marsha, and Ryan dragged an empty chair next to me.

Sally let out a heavy sigh before she laced her fingers together and gazed at us.

"Stone Dealership," she said, "our new automotive client in the California office, is in trouble. From their financial statements, I can tell they used the loan for personal expenses, because the million dollars we approved six months ago has quickly dwindled. This dealership is a subsidiary of Stone Transportation Services, one of our biggest clients. We can't share assumptions like that with them. Mr. Stone would be upset if we accused his younger brother of being incompetent." Sally stopped, taking another breath before continuing. "So, this project needs to be handled delicately, or Mr. Stone will move his businesses to another loan company."

My first day on the job, I'd been told that Stone Transportation Services had been one of the biggest clients at Veles Capital since its establishment two decades ago. The mutual relationship between the companies had been solid for years.

"And you know that, recently, Martin lost three of his field auditors and an accountant." She closed her eyes briefly before opening them again.

Martin Travers was the risk manager for the California office and Sally's counterpart. His team was smaller than Sally's, but I'd heard that he was losing some of his staff again this year because of his tough personality.

"I don't want to tell you why they quit simultaneously, but Martin needs our help. Also, the office doesn't have many clients in the automobile industry yet, and they don't have a person familiar with the business. So…" She turned to Ryan. "I want you to help the office."

The dimples in Ryan's cheeks became pronounced. I knew the business trip was a wonderful opportunity for him to expand his skill and experience, both of which would help him work toward a promotion. A willingness to go on business trips definitely improved the career outlook as well.

"And you, Rory," Sally turned to me, "your background in accounting would help Martin's team tremendously. You can give the dealership's employees basic accounting training. Martin also informed me that they've recorded everything incorrectly since the dealer joined us. The risk analysts are having a hard time analyzing Stone's financial report."

My heart leaped. California! I'd been thinking of it that whole morning, and suddenly, I'd been assigned there. What a coincidence. I couldn't wait to tell Peter. He would be dancing around like a crazy person.

I couldn't daydream about it for too long, though, because Sally's voice brought me back to the current conversation.

"And Marsha, I can't let you fly with them because of your condition, but I need your expertise to perform a deep analysis based on Rory and Ryan's findings. Leslie will take care of one of your clients, if necessary."

"How about you?" Marsha asked. "Are you going there too?"

She nodded. "I'll be there in two days, but I don't think you two will fly this week. You should be in California in a week's time. Belinda is already arranging our plane tickets and hotel."

Sally's eyes shifted to the picture on her desk of her husband hugging their daughter and son. Her finger trailed over it. Everybody in the office knew how much she loved her family. She didn't like to go on business trips, but she did what was needed. Her eyes remained on the picture another moment before she turned back to us.

"I know all of you have your own projects to do, but I need you to push them aside and focus on this one," she said solemnly. "And you two," her eyes shifted to Ryan and me, "I'm not your mom, but I do take care of my staff. Please act maturely and professionally, especially you, Ryan."

Ryan chuckled and spread his arms to each side. "Why me? How about her?" He pointed at me. "Her boyfriend is in California."

Sally rolled her eyes. "I was young once too."

"You're still young," Ryan said smoothly. "How old are you? Thirty-five?"

Sally chuckled. At fifty-three, she looked much younger than her age.

"Stop kissing my butt, Ryan," she said in her Boston accent, and laughed, waving her hand toward the door. "Get outta here!"

Grinning, Ryan walked out of the office, followed by Marsha and me.

We all loved Sally. She could be serious, but she could also be an easy-going person who loved to joke around.

When we returned to our cubicles, I checked the distance from the California office, which was located in a city called Irvine, to Peter's apartment and almost yelped. It was only twelve miles. Not far. My heart burst in anticipation of seeing his face in person, and I couldn't wait to tell him about my business trip to California.

CHAPTER 2

"I'm coming to California!" I almost shrieked during our video call that evening.

Peter's face broke into a wide smile. "Wow, that's awesome," he said in his British accent. "After that, can you take a week off?"

"I wish," I said, taking my phone to the kitchen so I could grab a glass of water. "This project will keep me busy starting next week until it's completed. I can't take any vacation until next year."

Aunt Amy, who was cutting fruit on the countertop, raised her eyes to me as I entered the kitchen and mouthed, "Peter? Say hi from me."

I nodded. "By the way, Aunt Amy says hi to you." I turned my phone toward her and let them wave before turning it back to me.

Peter rubbed at the back of his neck, and an expression of disappointment showed clearly on his face. "When will you fly here?"

"My boss said we're scheduled to fly next Sunday morning. I guess I could be there by Sunday midnight and rest before going to the office. Then I should fly back on Friday night," I said, taking a sip of my water.

"Could you fly out on Friday and stay at my house for the whole weekend?" he asked.

"Stay at what?" I asked, nearly choking on my drink.

"My house."

Across from me, Aunt Amy raised her eyebrows.

I shrugged. It was news to me, too.

"Don't you mean your apartment?" I asked.

Peter shook his head. "No, my house. I bought it two weeks ago."

What?

"You hadn't said anything." I glanced at my aunt before walking back to my room.

"Well…" Peter scratched his temple. "I wanted to surprise you, but since you mentioned you were going to fly here, I just blurted it out."

"Ouch, what a bummer," I teased, trying to imagine the kind of house he'd bought.

He grinned. "The house is small," he said as if he could read my mind. "Let me send you the link so you can see what it looks like."

I opened the link on my notebook and immediately thought the term "small" meant something far different for Peter than it meant for me. The 3,200-square-foot, two-story house on a 7,000-square-foot plot of land was huge compared to my aunt's 1,500-square-foot townhouse. My eyes nearly fell from their sockets to see the price of the place, but Peter's family could afford to pay that much.

Located in a beach town, Peter's new house was a combined design of modern and tropical, consisting of two-and-a-half bathrooms, four bedrooms, and a loft space. The backyard led to a sandy, white beach. The master bedroom included an en suite bathroom with a skylight above the bathtub, and its interior featured a palette of white, gray, and beige colors, giving it an elegant and cozy appeal.

"Have you checked the link? Do you like the house?" Peter asked when I'd gone quiet. "The picture doesn't do it justice. You need to come and see it for yourself."

"Yes, I'm looking at it now. It's awesome," I nodded. "I like the kitchen. It looks modern and roomy."

"Yes, I can imagine you sitting in there while I make pancakes for you." His smile broadened. "I *do* hope you can fly earlier on Friday."

I held my breath, imagining the possibility of spending time with him on the weekend. Besides, I was curious to see the house in person.

Chewing my lower lip, I said, "I hope so too. We'll see if my boss approves my flying on Friday morning."

Leaning forward, Peter looked at me. His light brown eyes widened and shone. "It would be fun to have you over for the weekend. I miss you, Rory. It took me a while to get used to living here without you. I miss living with you like we lived in your old apartment."

I smiled, remembering the good times we'd had as roommates.

"Yeah, I miss that time too," I admitted. "By the way, let's say I'm allowed to fly there earlier. I still can't stay at your house for the whole business trip. I may be needed for a late meeting or overtime."

"Yeah, I understand," Peter said. His shoulders drooped as he rubbed his eyebrows.

"At least we could have each other for the weekend. So, keep your hopes high and I'll let you know what happens tomorrow," I said, smiling.

He nodded.

"Hey, tell me about Tom. How's he doing?" I asked, curious about what his half brother had been doing.

Peter met my gaze and nodded, understanding that I didn't want to continue talking about staying in his house. "He's doing fine. But we haven't seen each other in ages because we've both been so busy. Just so you know, I think he still feels guilty about what Phil did to us last time, because he's avoiding me." He sighed. "I know my brother, so I'm giving him some space until he's ready to open up again. I hope he doesn't mind seeing you while you're here."

Phil, Tom's ex-boyfriend, worked as a finance manager for White Water, Incorporated, a prestigious wine distributor for US and Canada, where Peter was working as president of the company.

Born into the Sandridge family, Peter and Tom were part of Britain's old entrepreneurship families called Sandridge Group that had run many businesses in several countries for decades.

Their last name wasn't Sandridge but Ryder. It was from their grandpa's last name, the current chairman, who was born from the youngest daughter of Sandridge. Although their last name was different, Peter and Tom were in line to take over the businesses when the time was right.

Four months ago, when Peter had been assigned to replace his sister as president of White Water, Inc., Phil didn't like it. He didn't think Peter deserved to take the position, considering his wild youth of partying, drinking, causing trouble, and using drugs. Phil sabotaged the selection and spread rumors, fabricating photos of Peter. He hoped the elders of the Sandridge family would revoke the decision and choose Tom instead. However, Phil didn't know that Tom had zero interest in the family business, which was why he lived in California rather than London. Tom found out about the dirty trick his boyfriend had played and broke up with him after asking Peter to fire him immediately.

"Tom shouldn't feel that way," I said, feeling sad for the man. I liked him, and we'd been friends for a while. "This hasn't been easy for you either, has it?"

"No, it hasn't." Peter shook his head. "I already lost Jane, and I don't want to lose my brother too. I love him. He barely talks to me now, and of course I can't talk to Jane. I feel especially lonely when I want to share a burden that relates to our family."

He let out another sigh and stared into the distance, his face reflective.

I didn't have siblings, but I could understand his loneliness. "Let's hope he shakes those feelings of guilt sooner rather than later," I comforted him. "I miss him too."

A slight smile appeared on his lips. "Yes, let's hope so. Don't forget to let me know if you can fly in earlier, because I want to let him know you're coming."

I nodded. "Okay."

Although tired, Peter smiled. Nothing made him happier than seeing his girlfriend's smiling face, and she would be there next week. If he hadn't remembered he was in his office, he would have hollered with joy.

Since that morning, he'd been in back-to-back meetings. He wanted to rest on the couch in his office for at least an hour before teleconferencing with London, but he didn't want to miss a video call with Rory. Since he had another meeting soon, their call had been cut short, but it had been enough to make him happy.

"Rory," Peter whispered, caressing the picture sitting on his desk. She looked lovely in her pale-yellow dress. The light freckles on the bridge of her nose, that she always complained about, made her look adorable. He chuckled as he looked at her photograph, remembering how chaotic their first meeting had been.

He'd never wanted to work in his family's businesses. When Jane had asked him to help her with her project in California, he couldn't refuse. However, a week before Jane flew to the States with him, she'd had emergency surgery that forced her to stay in the hospital. Later, Jane instructed Peter to fly alone and stop at a rental place to cancel her stay, where she'd already signed a six-month lease.

Knowing her eccentric personality, Peter hadn't bothered to ask further. He'd assumed Rory was Jane's ex-boyfriend or male friend. Everyone in the Sandridge family, including his grandpa, let Jane do whatever she wanted because she was a brilliant businesswoman. If Jane didn't want to stay in a hotel, they would rent her a house. If she decided to rent a room in someone's home, they wouldn't argue with her.

When he'd stopped by to tell Jane's roommate about the cancelation, it had surprised him that Rory was a female name. In Britain, it was a male's name.

Jane's new roommate had seemed shocked about the cancelation, and Peter detected that Rory had some financial troubles. Seeing her distress, he'd offered to continue his sister's rental agreement.

To his surprise, she'd accepted.

It had never crossed his mind that living with Rory would change his life forever.

She taught him everything, including valuing money, something he'd never concerned himself with. He also learned to appreciate the money he earned.

Rory also taught him about honesty and acceptance. She wasn't shy to admit that she'd been born out of wedlock and raised by her old-fashioned aunt after her mom passed away. She told him the truth about not knowing her father. He also knew her aunt didn't approve of Rory having a male roommate, afraid Rory would make the same ill-timed decisions her mom had made.

Something had slowly changed inside him. Peter learned to be a good man, different from the spoiled and selfish person he'd been in his youth. He wanted to be better for Rory.

If Jane were alive, she would have been happy to see his transformation.

Thinking of Jane made his heart thud dully in his chest. She'd been gone for more than three months, but he couldn't seem to shake his sadness. Jane had been more than his sister, especially after his mom abandoned him as a child. Peter had attached himself to Jane. She'd been his confidant, his protector, and his "little mom." Whenever he had an issue, he'd always asked for his sister's advice.

Now, she was gone forever, and his brother wasn't talking to him. No one had been around for him through his anxiety over the new position as president of White Water.

Their father, Archibald "Archie" Ryder, had flown from London to California to give him some management training. Peter didn't have a close relationship with him. His presence didn't help because Archie was known for having an iron fist, and he never let Peter slack off. Nights, mornings, weekends, and weekdays, his father forced Peter to work better, harder, and faster. As a result, his body and mind were tired, and he wanted to take a break.

When people in the States were celebrating Thanksgiving, Peter had to fight to take some time off and spend his first American Thanksgiving with Rory and her aunt.

For the first time in a while, Peter felt brighter and happier, knowing Rory would be there soon.

ACKNOWLEDGEMENT

I t never crossed my mind that I could write a book in my second language. Growing up in Southeast Asia, I dreamed of writing a good book. My favorite authors—Enid Blyton, Robert Arthur Jr., Carolyn Keene, Frances Hodgson Burnett, Louisa May Alcott, and Agatha Christie—inspired me.

I began scribbling stories when I was nine and dared to send a few children's stories to local children's magazines when I was eleven. Unfortunately, all were rejected, and doubt was raised about the stories' authenticity. Maybe they didn't believe the eleven-year-old girl could have written the stories. That made me sad. In my late teens, I submitted a handful of movie reviews to local tabloids, which got published. The rewards were modest, just enough to buy lunch, but they increased my confidence.

After moving to the United States, I became busy with work and did not have time to write. One day, I started writing again, this time in English. It wasn't easy, but I kept writing. I kept most of the stories or articles to myself, sharing only a few with my husband so he could help with the grammar. Eventually, I entered a few writing contests for short stories.

In 2017, the idea for No Romance Allowed came to me, and I began writing it in early 2018. When I completed the draft, my husband encouraged me to seek a professional editor for feedback. I followed his advice. My editor was awesome! She taught me a lot about writing, corrected my grammar, and provided valuable input on the draft. The writing process has been a genuinely humbling experience.

While working on this book, I received tremendous support and encouragement. Now, I'd like to take a moment to acknowledge those who contributed to this project, both directly and indirectly.

As always, thanks to God for this valuable opportunity. Thank you for your encouragement and comfort.

Thanks to my dear husband, Steve, for letting me pursue my dream. I love you to the moon and back!

Thanks to my parents and siblings for your moral support and for believing in me.

Thanks to The Pro Book Editor for copyediting and line editing this story.

Thanks to Fine Fuse for proofreading this story.

Thank you, Leslie, for reading my first draft's seventeen chapters and asking me to write more stories.

Thanks to Rick, my neighbor in MV, who inspired me to create a father figure in 'Rick Perkin' for Rory. Rest in peace, Rick.

Thanks to my wonderful niece, Bernice, and my friends Nancy, Ralph, Asun, Ana, Fernando, Odie, Joy, Oline, Tepi, Dina, Jimmy, Angie, Irma, Ribkah, Icha, and my neighbors in MV for your support and enthusiasm when I told you guys that I wrote a book. I hope you enjoy this story!

Thanks to my readers for picking up this book and reading it. I hope you enjoyed the story as much as I enjoyed writing it. I hope you don't mind telling your friends and family about this novella and writing a short review on your favorite online retailer's website.

Happy reading,
Kana, September 2019

ABOUT THE AUTHOR

KANA WU is a bilingual author who writes her novels in English as her second language. She also enjoys traveling and incorporates the places she visits into her books.

Her debut novel, *No Romance Allowed*, won the Romance category for the 2020 TCK Publishing Readers' Choice Awards Contest.

Her second novel, *No Secrets Allowed*, earned a 1st Place Blue Ribbon for the Chatelaine Book Awards for Romantic Fiction, a division of the 2021 Chanticleer International Book Awards.

Currently, she resides in beautiful Southern California with her husband, surrounded by her books and the occasional hummingbird or wild bird visitors.

Keep up with Kana's latest news and updates by visiting her website or following her on social media.

 https://www.facebook.com/kanawuauthor
 https://www.instagram.com/kanawuauthor
 www.kanawuauthor.com